TAKING HER CHASE

DARE TO SURRENDER
BOOK TWO

DANIELLE PAYS

Edited by: Jen McDonnell, Bird's Eye Books
Cover by: Maria @ Steamy Designs

www.daniellepays.com

Chapter One

"Zach, can we get another round of birthday shots?" Harmony called out.

She was slurring, and if Chase Harvey didn't slow this down, he'd be holding her hair back while she puked.

"You might want to slow down, or you won't feel so good tomorrow," Chase said.

He glanced at their friends Nick and Lauren for support. They were sitting across from them in the booth at Brannigan's Pub, celebrating Harmony's birthday. He was happy he could call them friends now. When Nick first joined the Fisher Springs Police Department, Chase really didn't like him. Fortunately, it turned out Nick was a good guy.

Nick grinned and shook his head.

"You know better than to tell her what to do." Lauren laughed.

"Yes, Officer. You know better. Besides, I have tomorrow off, remember?" Harmony said.

Then her eyes scanned him up and down, and damn if his body didn't react. He tamped down those thoughts. Harmony had been his best friend since seventh grade. She had been there for him through a lot of shit, and he'd been there for her. Even when she talked about the douchebags she dated.

Yeah, he might be a bit biased. Thankfully, there was no douchebag in the picture tonight.

"Why are you so dressed up?" she asked.

"Because we're celebrating my best friend's birthday."

He wrapped his arm around her shoulder and gave her a squeeze. Nick arched a brow as he peered at the two of them over the rim of his nearly empty pint glass.

Chase made a mental note to dial it back. If Nick was picking up on his feelings, Harmony might too. Although it was hard not to touch her, as they were sitting next to each other in one side of a booth. And the more Harmony drank, the more handsy she was.

"I appreciate that," Harmony said. "And I appreciate all of you for being here tonight."

"Shots are ready!" Zach yelled.

"I'll get them." Chase quickly strode off in the direction of the bar. He needed a moment alone to get himself under control.

"Hey, stranger. You're looking sexy these days."

He spun on his heel to find a familiar, tall, blond

woman next to him.

"Haven't heard from you in a while," Bridgette said.

They'd had a friends-with-benefits relationship for a while, but he'd lost interest and ended it. He wasn't getting any younger and finding someone to settle down with was far more appealing. Well, finding someone else. The one person he wanted, he couldn't have.

"I've been busy," he lied, hoping she'd take the hint.

Nope. Next thing he knew, her hands snaked around his neck.

"Maybe you won't be too busy later."

Before he could pull away, Harmony was there. Bridgette dropped her arms, and Harmony looped hers through his. This was new. Harmony had never come between him and a woman. But then, he'd always been discreet.

"Thought I'd help you carry those shots." She turned to Bridgette. "Bridgette? I'm Harmony. We went to high school together."

"You're Harmony?" Bridgette smiled.

He squeezed his eyes shut. When he'd cut things off with Bridgette, she'd asked if it was because of Harmony. Apparently, he talked about her a lot. Now he just hoped Bridgette didn't say anything about it.

"Nice to meet you or see you again. I was just saying goodbye." She winked at him.

He shook his head.

Once Bridgette left, Harmony grabbed the shots and bolted back to their table. What the hell was that? He hadn't needed any help carrying the tray.

He started in the direction of his friends, but barely made it two steps before another woman was standing in his way.

"Officer Harvey? Is that you?" Her eyes roamed his body. "I thought you looked good in your uniform, but now you look damn delicious."

And this was why he didn't like to go out in this town. Too few single men. Normally, he could deal with the attention, but this was Harmony's birthday, and he just wanted to celebrate.

"Excuse me, but I'm here with someone."

Fortunately, the woman stepped aside, and he made his way back to the table. Harmony was glaring at him.

Wait, why was she glaring?

"I would have grabbed the drinks if you let me."

Her eyebrows quirked. "No big deal."

They each drank another shot, and whatever Harmony had been mad about seemed to fade away. Then he noticed that her skirt was riding high up on her thighs as she sat next to him. He was about to pry his eyes away when a drop of her drink fell right onto her bare skin.

"Oops." Harmony smiled at him.

What happened next, he could only blame on a combination of the shots and sitting too close to her. He reached down and wiped the drop away with his finger, then brought it to his mouth. When his gaze met hers, her eyes had darkened.

Shit. What was he doing?

"Didn't want to waste any," he said as he averted his gaze.

What the fuck? That was the best he could come up with?

Zach turned on some music, and Harmony asked Chase to stand up so she could get out of the booth. At this point, he'd do anything to get her focus away from what he'd just done. Once she was up, he sat back down. Mistake. Her hips were following the rhythm. Right in front of his face. He tried not to watch, but it was impossible.

"Let's dance!" Harmony grabbed his hand and led him out to the dance floor.

Her body moved in ways he wasn't used to seeing. When she turned away from him and shimmied closer, he backed up a step. The smile on her face as she glanced back at him was full of mischief. "This isn't middle school, Harvey. You can touch me."

Harvey. The name never sounded right coming from her. After entering the police academy, he'd asked everyone to call him by his last name. Even Harmony had finally obliged.

She inched back again and placed his hands on her hips. When her backside grazed against his crotch, his fingers dug deeper into her flesh. He needed to think about something else before his friend discovered she was making him hard as hell.

Swamps, alligators, baseball.

It was working. Then she spun, tossed her arms around his neck, and pressed her body up against his.

Shit.

Her hand squeezed his pec. "You've been working out more."

All he could do was nod.

"Why? You trying to impress Bridgette?"

Was that a tinge of jealousy in her voice?

"No, it keeps me out of trouble." *And away from women like Bridgette.*

Certain she could feel his heart beating fast, he stepped back as a faster song came on.

They continued dancing for several songs, her hips entrancing him the entire time. By the end, he'd run through the entire Seattle Mariners lineup and their stats.

It was a blessing when the music finally shut off.

"Hey, guys, I'm sorry, but it's time to close up." Zach frowned. "Harmony, I hope you had a great birthday."

"I did. Thank you."

They returned to the table a little out of breath.

"Nice dancing." Lauren eyed her friend. "Do you guys need a ride?"

"No, we're going to walk to my place. I told her she could crash there."

Nick raised a brow.

Chase pulled Nick to the side so Harmony wouldn't hear. "I'll be sleeping on the couch, Dad."

Well, that wasn't really true. He had a king-sized bed, and they had slept in it together many times after nights out at the bar. But they always stayed on their side. Although, fuck, after how riled up he was tonight, maybe he *should* sleep on the couch.

"Ready?" he asked Harmony.

"Ready."

The cold air whipped at them the moment they stepped outside. It was a typical windy and frigid January night. Even with her coat, Harmony was already shivering.

"Want to make a run for it?" He grinned at her.

"Sure. Here, hold my hand in case I fall."

He reached for her hand and cursed how good it felt in his.

"Ready, set, go!" she yelled.

Once inside his house, they brushed their teeth and got ready for bed. She was over so often that she even had some of her things there. She made it into bed first while he grabbed a couple glasses of water.

"Here. Drink some water. You'll be happy you did in the morning."

"Thank you."

He set his cup down, stripped down to a T-shirt and boxer briefs, then crawled into bed, careful to stay on his side.

"Goodnight, Harmony."

When she didn't respond, he turned. She was sitting up, holding her glass of water.

"Are you going to puke?"

She chuckled. "No. I'm fine."

She lay down then turned to face him. Moonlight lit up the room and cast rays across her face.

"Did you have fun tonight?" he asked.

She nodded even as her eyes welled with tears.

"What's wrong?"

"My mom never called."

Dammit. He instinctively reached out and pulled her into his arms. Every year, the same thing. "I'm sorry."

Her hand traced circles on his chest, and he instantly became aware of how close they were. "Chase?"

His heart rate picked up. She never called him by his first name anymore.

"Yeah?"

"Have you ever wondered what it would be like if we kissed? I mean, would it be like a brother and sister gross? Or would it be something else?"

His heart thundered within his chest.

He knew damn well it would be something else. Why was she bringing this up now?

"Why do you ask?"

He felt her shrug.

"Have you thought about it?"

"Yes," she whispered.

"Do you think it would be like kissing a family member?"

The room was so silent, he swore he heard a frog croak outside.

He swallowed. How drunk was she right now? How drunk was he?

She met his gaze, resolve hardening in her clear eyes. "No."

Then she uttered the words he couldn't fight.

"Kiss me, Chase." With her face mere inches from his, she nearly begged the last part. "Please."

All control gone, he crushed his lips to hers.

It was more than he ever dreamed about. That one kiss had his body molten in seconds, but when her hand reached for the top of his boxer briefs, reality set in, and he jumped up.

Shit, what was he doing? This was his best friend. He couldn't risk everything on some drunk kiss. He had to be sure this was what she wanted.

"What's wrong?" She was now propped up on her elbows in his bed.

Damn, he wanted her.

"I just need more water."

He practically ran out of the room.

Great, he'd kissed her and then run scared. No, he was going to go back in there and tell her the truth. He wanted her, but not drunk. She'd understand.

But when he went back into the room, he heard her soft snores. She'd fallen asleep.

Shit, she was probably drunker than he'd realized.

He carefully crawled into bed, making sure not to disturb her. He ached to pull her into his arms, but that would probably wake her. No, they needed to wait until they were both sober, then they could see if they felt the same way.

The room was bright. Too bright. He pried one eye open and discovered he'd forgotten to close the curtains last night. His eyes caught the rest of his bed, and he also discovered he was alone.

Shuffling out to the kitchen, he needed caffeine for his headache. Damn, he couldn't remember the last time he was hungover. Normally, he was careful not to drink too much, in case the chief called him in for an incident report.

He stopped short when he saw Harmony sitting at the kitchen table, drinking a cup of coffee.

"How did you sleep?" she asked.

"All right." He walked into the kitchen slowly, trying to get a read on her. "How do you feel?" he asked as he poured himself a cup of coffee.

"Really hungover. I guess I got crazy. Tell me I didn't do anything stupid."

He nearly choked on his coffee. "You don't remember last night?"

"Bits and pieces."

He turned away to hide his disappointment.

Well, at least he had an answer to his question. Thank God he'd put the brakes on last night. She had been too drunk to even remember their kiss. What kind of monster was he to even agree to it? Should he tell her about it?

No, she'd hate him.

"No, you didn't do anything stupid. I watched out for you."

"Thank you."

She rose from the table and put her coffee cup in the sink.

"I should go. Thanks again."

"You need a ride?"

"No. Lauren is coming to pick me up."

He watched as she shuffled to the front door.

"See you later, Harvey."

Then, with that gut punch, she left.

Harvey. After calling him by his first name last night.

Dammit!

He wanted to punch something. Why the hell did he let her leave? Oh yeah, because she'd think he was an asshole if she knew the truth that he almost took advantage of his drunk best friend.

Chapter Two

Ten months later

"I'm gonna do it," Chase said as he perched on the edge of Nick's desk. The edge was the only spot not covered in paperwork.

That reason right there was why he preferred working patrol, and not being a detective. Of course, it wasn't Nick's fault. His predecessor left a lot of undone paperwork that Nick had been trying to catch up on for the past year. Not an easy feat.

Nick lifted his gaze from the papers in his hand. "Do what?"

"I'm taking your advice."

A smirk donned Nick's face as he turned back to what they called their perp wall. It contained photos from the FBI's most wanted list. The odds of any of those guys visiting Fisher Springs were almost zero, but Chief

Dunin made it clear he wanted that wall kept up to date.

Nick yanked down two photos. "I've given you a lot of advice. You need to be more specific." Then he tugged the mug shot of Carl Marucam off the wall.

"Wait, why are you removing Carl's photo? We have good reason to keep that up there."

Carl Marucam came into their purview last year, when Nick was working on a case to find out who was threatening Lauren. Carl was part of a syndicate in Portland, but they believed he came north looking for Lauren's stepbrother. Once he found out her stepbrother was dead, he left. Or so they all hoped. Nick tracked down a mug shot at the time and posted it to the wall to keep everyone aware of who he was and warn them that he was dangerous.

"I got a call from the officer in Portland. Carl's been sent to prison for two years. Turns out this arrest—" he pointed to the photo, "was one he couldn't get out of."

"Huh." That charge had bothered Chase from the moment he heard about it. Carl was a lot of things, but he wasn't stupid. He never did the dirty work. Yet he'd been caught dealing heroin. "The officer is certain Carl's doing time?"

"Sounded pretty certain to me. But you changed the subject. I want to get back to me being right."

"I didn't say you were right. I said I was going to take your advice."

Nick spun around and faced him. "And that advice would be?" He crossed his arms and stared at

Chase.

"The kiss. I'm going to ask her if she remembers it."

"Thank fuck." Nick's mouth fell open. "Oh, I meant to say, you mean your lady friend you will not name? The one you kissed last year?"

"That's the one. Why did you say 'thank fuck'?"

Nick's brows pulled into a frown. "Why tonight?"

He was avoiding the question.

"Why not tonight?"

"Have you talked or texted with her recently?"

"What the fuck does that matter? I don't understand. I thought you said I should do this. I finally have the courage to do it, and now you're, what, trying to talk me out of it? What gives?"

Damn, he was already a ball of nerves just thinking about doing it. The last thing he needed was for his motives to be questioned. The time felt right. What more did he need?

Nick scratched the back of his neck. "You're right. I didn't mean it that way. You two should definitely talk about it."

Chase stared at Nick, who was now avoiding eye contact.

Shit, he knew who the friend was.

Harmony would only be at the diner for another fifteen minutes, so there wasn't time to grill Nick about what he did or didn't know. Although, now he wondered if Harmony had said something to Lauren.

Maybe she hadn't forgotten after all. But if she remembered and didn't bring it up, what did that mean?

He needed to get out of his head.

"I'll see you later."

He grabbed his jacket and pushed his hands through the sleeves as he exited the Fisher Springs Police Department. Snow had fallen, but thankfully, it hadn't stuck to the roads. Maybe tonight would be a quiet night with no calls. He'd love to take Harmony back to his place to talk about everything.

Over the last couple of months, he swore he'd caught her staring at his chest and arms a few times. His body had changed since Nick came to town. Now that they were friends, Nick was sharing tips at the gym, and it showed.

While she was staring more, he was finding more and more excuses to touch her. She never pulled away, and she hadn't said anything.

But damn, what if he was wrong? Harmony had been his best friend since the seventh grade.

The memory of the day they met made him chuckle every time. Being the new kid at a school sucked. But he'd made fast friends with Larry Longmire, and Larry had dared him to shoot spitballs at a girl. Any girl. That's when Chase had seen her long, red hair, and he couldn't look away.

Before class started, he ripped off the small bits of paper and put them in his mouth. Then he lined them up in the straw and *pow, pow, pow*, all three spitballs landed in her hair. The class started to laugh. She jerked around, and her hand went to her hair. She found those spitballs, then immediately glared at him. He was still holding the straw, so there was no point in denying what he'd done.

What sealed their friendship was what she did after class. After the bell rang, she remained in her seat. He got up, planning to apologize to her, but just when he reached her, she turned around and spat several spitballs at his face. Where the hell she had gotten a straw, he'd always wondered. She never got up. But as those spitballs hit his face, he was stunned. No one stood up to him.

Once he was certain she was done, he opened his eyes. She was grinning up at him.

"I'm Harmony Brose, and no one messes with me."

He stuck out his hand. "Hi, Harmony. I'm Chase. I like you."

From that moment forward, they were best friends.

So tonight, he could bring up the kiss as a 'haha, funny, do you remember' type of event. Then he could gauge her reaction before he spilled all his feelings. Because once he went down that path, there was no going back.

A quick check of his phone. Her shift ended in five minutes. Chase pushed open the door of Lucky's Diner. Harmony had worked there for the past several years because it allowed her the flexibility to photograph weddings on the weekends. Scanning past the bright red booths to the stools at the counter — this place was a replica of a fifties diner — he spotted Harmony.

She was wearing the usual uniform of the hot pink Lucky's Diner T-shirt, which she hated, but he enjoyed. It was form-fitting, and her jeans were tight too. With her long, red hair flowing down her back, she was the sexiest woman he knew.

But then he noticed the man she was next to was undressing her with his eyes.

Who the fuck was this? He'd never seen the guy before. Based on his suit and shiny loafers, it was some rich guy, passing through town.

Wait, why was she smiling and twirling her hair at this douchebag? Yes, twirling her fucking hair with her fingers while staring at some rich prick he'd never seen before.

He grabbed Kate as she walked by. "Who is that guy?" He nodded toward Harmony.

Kate's eyes lit up. "That's Mr. Rodney's grandson. He's moving to town to take care of Mr. Rodney."

Chase narrowed his eyes at the man. "Why? Mr. Rodney has a caretaker."

Kate ignored him. "That man is hot, but unfortunately for me, he only has eyes for Harmony. From the moment he walked in, they were staring each other down."

Well, damn. This asshole had to go.

Chase slowly approached Harmony, catching

the end of her conversation.

"It's a date then." The asshole winked at Harmony.

Chase was now standing next to them. He cleared his throat to pull them out of their sappy starefest.

"Oh, Harvey, I didn't see you there."

No, she didn't.

"This is Rance Rodney. He's Mr. Rodney's grandson."

"Rance, this is Officer Harvey."

The man stretched his hand out, and Chase took it, making sure to grip it firmly.

Rance chuckled. "I didn't expect a police welcome. Do you greet all the new townsfolk?"

"No." He eyed the man who was wearing cufflinks with his suit. No one around this town would wear cufflinks and shined loafers.

"Just me then? Better be careful, you're making me paranoid." The man laughed.

Chase's gaze met Rance's. "Do you have something to be paranoid about?"

"Harvey!" Harmony took hold of the man's arm. "I'm sorry for that. He's a bit cranky sometimes." She tossed him a look over her shoulder as she led her new friend to the door.

Once Rance finally left, Harmony stood in front of Chase with her hands on her hips.

"What the hell? Why were you so rude?"

"I don't like him."

She threw her arms up. "Why not? You just met him. What could you possibly not like?"

"Gut feeling." He left off that his gut was churning because he'd had to watch her flirt with the douche.

Harmony sighed. "You are the most frustrating man I know. There's nothing wrong with Rance. You need to stop being so judgmental anytime someone new comes to town."

"Wait, I'm not—"

"Yes, you are. Remember when Nick moved here? You hated him from the moment you first saw him."

"Well, that was different."

"Yeah? How so?"

Shit. He couldn't tell her the truth. For the last ten months, anytime Harmony talked to a new man in town, he went a little berserk.

Running his hands through his hair, he tugged a little to calm his heart. It surprised him she couldn't see it beating through his shirt.

"What's going on?" Her voice was softer now. "You look stressed."

Stressed. Yep. That about covered it.

"When Nick came to town, he took over Joey's job. Joey was my friend, and I thought he only needed time. Then Nick walked around like he was better than everyone else. I wasn't the only one who didn't like him," Chase snapped.

"But now you're best friends."

"He changed." He was still an arrogant fuck, but he'd softened since he'd gotten together with Lauren.

"I'm so jealous of you," Kate said as she joined them.

"You should be." Harmony chuckled. "He was hot."

Chase worked hard to contain his growl.

"He asked me out. On a date! Can you believe it? Do you have any idea how long it has been since I've been on a date? Since I've had sex? Hell, since I've been kissed?" Upon delivery of that last line, she stared right at him.

Those eyes now did funny things to him. Had he been wrong, and she did remember their kiss? Did she want him to bring it up? Or maybe not bring it up?

One thing he knew, if he stayed there another minute, he was going to lose his shit. After waiting ten months, he ended up being a few minutes too late.

"I've gotta go."

Before Harmony could stop him, he was out on the sidewalk, walking away from the diner as fast as he could.

Chapter Three

"No, he did not just storm out of here having a hissy fit!" Harmony threw a stack of napkins toward the door.

It was not at all cathartic.

"You know, if I didn't know better, I'd say he was jealous," Kate said as she bent down to pick up the napkins.

Harmony laughed. "Jealous? No, that was Harvey being his usual, overprotective big brother self."

"You're probably right. He does give off a big brother vibe."

Although she knew better, she couldn't get the idea out of her head. Could Harvey be jealous?

The thought made her heart race. But it was only wishful thinking. She'd been naive to think one kiss would change their relationship. The moment he'd jumped out of the bed, mid-kiss, to 'get water,' she realized she'd made a mistake. Then the next morning, he walked into the kitchen and acted like nothing had happened. That had crushed her. Unfortunately, she hadn't been able to think of anyone but Harvey since.

But that was in the past. He'd made his position clear by ignoring the kiss. Now, Rance was here; this was her fresh start.

The door whipped open, and with the burst of cold air came Tabitha. Harmony had been good friends with her since high school. She was known as the town gossip, and always seemed to know everyone's business. For that reason, Harmony kept her personal life to herself when she was around.

"Did you meet the new man?" Tabitha asked.

Kate pushed off the counter. "Not only did we meet him, but Harmony has already staked her claim."

Harmony rolled her eyes. *Thank you, Kate. Now this will be all over town within the hour.*

"The man came in and only had eyes for Harmony. He asked her out."

Tabitha squealed as she jumped up and down. "I'm so happy for you! I know how hard it has been to find a man."

Harmony's single status had been a regular topic for Tabitha. Even though Tabitha was now divorced, the fact she had been married for five years somehow elevated her above the 'singles' in her mind.

"When is the date?" Tabitha asked.

"I don't know. He's going to call me to set it up."

"Oh." Her friend's smile turned to a frown.

"I have to get back to work." Harmony knew she

was being rude, but she'd had enough.

"That's fine. I need to go see Ms. Finkle anyway."

Harmony snorted, but quickly covered it by coughing when Kate and Tabitha looked her way.

Ms. Finkle was the other town gossip, and the fact she and Tabitha were good friends made her laugh. She couldn't ever be mad at Ms. Finkle, though, because she was the nicest woman. She wouldn't be surprised if it turned out Ms. Finkle was Tabitha's long-lost grandmother.

The moment Tabitha was out the door, Harmony turned to Kate. "All right. I'm out of here. It's been slow, so you should be fine."

"No worries. But, hey—" Kate grabbed onto Harmony's arm, slowing her passage toward the back. "I really want to hear about any date you have with Rance. I need to live vicariously through someone."

"We should go to the city sometime soon for a night out," Harmony said.

"I'd like that."

After tossing her apron in her locker and retrieving her purse, she shot a text to Lauren.

Harmony: *Up for happy hour?*

The response was immediate.

Lauren: *I'm at Zach's waiting for Nick. Join us!*

She didn't need any more invitation than that, and frankly she didn't care if she would be a third wheel. What she needed was some girl talk to figure out what to do about Harvey. Not that there was much she could do.

The cold wind whipped her hair into her face as she stepped outside. While she loved Fisher Springs for its breathtaking views of the snowcapped mountains, she could do without the bone-chilling wind gusts.

Fortunately, Brannigan's Pub, or 'Zach's place,' as they affectionately called it, was only a couple doors down from the diner.

"Over here!" Lauren called from a booth in the back.

Harmony shivered as she shuffled past the other patrons, scanning the crowd as she went. She had no idea where Harvey had stormed off to, but she let out a sigh of relief when she discovered it wasn't here.

When she approached the table, she saw two glasses of red wine and a bowl of tortilla chips sitting there.

"Is Nick here?"

"No, he just texted me. He's running late. Something came up with Harvey. I got you a glass of wine."

Just hearing his name sent tingles down her spine. Tingles! What the hell was that about? He was her best friend. Nothing should be tingling.

Actually, she should be used to this by now. Things had felt strange since their kiss. Ten months of pretending she didn't feel anything other than friendship for the man. It didn't help that he'd started going to the gym with Nick. Each week, she'd watched as his body grew sexier and sexier.

Nope. Her mind could not go there.

"Thank you. I needed this today." She peeled off her coat then sat across from her friend.

"Why? What happened?"

"Harvey." She spat his name out almost like a curse.

Lauren's lips curved up. "What did he do this time?"

"I'm upset, and you're smiling?"

She shrugged. "I like how you two spar."

The door opened, bringing in a couple and a cold breeze.

"We don't spar."

"You do. Do you think it's your way of working out your sexual chemistry?"

Her gaze jerked to her friend, who was wearing a smile.

"What are you talking about?"

Before Lauren could answer, Nick plopped down in the seat next to her.

"I heard you have a date with the new guy in town," he said as he reached for a chip.

"New guy?" Lauren asked.

"Mr. Rodney's grandson is moving to town to take care of him," Nick explained.

"Wait, I thought he had a caretaker? She looks like she's just out of college." Lauren's eyes went from Nick to Harmony.

"Not anymore."

"There's a new guy in town, and you already

have a date with him?"

"Rance Rodney. He came into the diner and asked me out. With the shortage of men in town, who was I to say no? Besides, he's hot."

"Be careful. Don't go anywhere alone with this guy. We don't really know anything about him." Nick reached for another chip.

"You sound just like—Wait. Nick, how did you hear I had a date?"

He slowly looked up from the chip bowl. "Uh, excuse me. I need to see what's delaying my beer." He shot up and was at the bar in a few strides.

Harmony crossed her arms. "Unbelievable!"

"What's going on?" Lauren took another sip of her wine as she stared off toward Nick.

She filled Lauren in on what went down at the diner, including Harvey storming off to have a tantrum.

"Then it looks like he went and complained about it all to Nick," she finished. "The guy is new in town; he isn't a criminal. And if I want to date him, I will!"

That smile from earlier returned to Lauren's lips.

"Stop smiling. There's no sexual chemistry between me and Harvey."

Lauren leaned forward. "I beg to differ. Do you remember the night of your birthday party?"

Harmony swallowed. She remembered it all right. It was the night that started all of her problems. "What about it?"

Lauren shrugged a shoulder. "After that dirty

27

dancing you two did, we were certain you would be a couple by the next morning. You were pretty drunk, though. I guess you guys just passed out. Then lately, I've barely seen you two together."

She felt the heat rising to her cheeks.

Damn her pale skin. A hint of embarrassment, and she turned pink.

"I need to use the bathroom." Harmony stood up.

"Sit down," Lauren ordered, pointing at her face. "Spill it."

Harmony sat back down and drained her wine for fortitude. "There's not much to spill. We went back to his place that night. We kissed, then I fell asleep. The next morning, he acted like nothing happened."

"Wait." Her friend leaned across the table. "What do you mean by kiss? Like a peck on the lips, or..."

"I mean the 'or' version. We were lying down, and I swear, when he pulled me close, I felt his... you know. He was hard. But then he jumped up like it was a mistake, and the next day, he didn't say anything. He must have regretted it, so I didn't say anything either. I didn't want to ruin our friendship by telling him I wanted to do it again."

"Is that why you two don't hang out anymore?" Lauren asked.

"We hang out. Just not nearly as much as we used to."

The door opened, and another burst of cold air

came with it.

"You should ask him about the kiss. It's obviously put a strain on your friendship."

"I can't."

"Harmony. We meet again." Rance was standing at the edge of the booth. He flashed a smile toward Lauren. "I'm Rance. I'm new in town."

"I'm Lauren. I've already heard about you. News travels fast."

He laughed. "It does. I'll have to get used to that, I guess."

Harmony scooted over. "Do you want to join us?"

"That would be lovely, yes."

Nick returned with his beer. "You must be the new guy."

"Yes, I'm Rance." He stuck his hand out.

Nick shook it. "Detective Nick Moore. Nice to meet you."

"Wow, another officer. How many are there in this small town?"

Lauren wrapped her hands around Nick's bicep. "There's Nick, Harvey, and Chief Dunin."

"Well, look at that. My first day here, and I've already met two thirds of the police department."

"We like to keep an eye on newcomers." Nick glared at Rance while he took a pull of his beer.

"I'll keep that in mind." Rance stretched his arm across the back of the booth behind Harmony, and his fingers brushed her shoulder.

No tingles. Rance was a good-looking man, no doubt, with those piercing blue eyes and that blond hair. But there were no tingles.

The squeak of the door opening caught her attention. Her head jerked up just in time to meet Harvey's eyes. His stare was intense, and she felt tingles everywhere. But then he noticed who she was sitting with.

As quickly as he'd entered, he left.

Chapter Four

Anger seeped through his veins at the sight of that man sitting with Harmony. He'd been in town, what, all of a few minutes, and he seemed to be glued to her hip. And what the hell did she see in that guy? Sure, he was a good-looking man. Even Harvey could see that. But there was something just below the surface that didn't sit right with him.

Don't fool yourself. Any man Harmony looks at like that won't sit right with you.

Before he knew what he was doing, he found himself pulling up in front of Mr. Rodney's house.

The house was one of the nicest in Fisher Springs, excluding the Chanler Mansion, of course. All of the bushes flanking the walkway had been trimmed back, and the yard looked well-tended to. Whoever was taking care of Mr. Rodney certainly had been taking care of the house. The old man himself was a bit of a mystery.

Chase had seen him around years ago, but he'd always kept to himself. He'd overheard from Ms. Finkle that the old man had hired a caretaker. Or, more likely, his son had hired one.

"Dementia," Ms. Finkle had whispered. "Such a shame. After he lost his wife, it didn't seem like he wanted to be here anymore but at least he had his memories of her. Now he's losing those too."

Chase ascended the steps of the front porch and hoped that Rodney's original caretaker might still be around. He needed to learn a little more about Rance.

After knocking on the door, Chase paced the porch. The door swung open, and there stood Mr. Rodney.

"Officer Harvey! How wonderful to see you!"

He had to swallow back his surprise. Based on the rumors he'd heard; the odds were good that Mr. Rodney wouldn't remember him.

"Mr. Rodney? I'm hoping to ask you a few questions."

"Sure! I'd love to have someone to talk with. You can call me Donald. Why don't you have a seat there. I was just coming out to get some fresh air. It gets so stuffy inside."

Chase turned to the two chairs Donald had motioned to. He sat in the one farthest away.

"Such a beautiful day we're having," the old man said amiably. "I like to get outside whenever the sun pops out. Such a rarity these days."

This man was as coherent as he was. Why was

everyone saying he had dementia?

"I met your grandson Rance this afternoon," Chase offered.

"You did? He's in town? I'd love to see him."

Ah, perhaps this is why. "Your grandson says he's staying here with you, taking care of you."

"Bullshit," the old man said as he slowly sat down in the chair next to him. "Rance moved to the other side of the country as soon as he turned eighteen. He didn't even come home for his mother's funeral."

He'd heard dementia took away memories, but he hadn't heard it replaced them with false ones. Or maybe Rance felt bad and was trying to make amends before it was too late.

"You haven't seen him?"

"Not in years."

"Well, maybe I'm confused then. The man I'm talking about is about six feet tall, blond hair, blue eyes."

Donald crossed his arms. "Officer Harvey, are you yanking my chain?"

He studied the old man. Donald was serious.

"No, why would you think that?" Chase asked, confused.

Donald laughed. "Blond hair and blue eyes? No, my grandson has brown hair and brown eyes. There isn't a blond anywhere in my family. Not on my wife's side, either."

The hair on the back of Harvey's neck stood up. Something wasn't right.

"Then who is the man staying with you?"

Donald narrowed his eyes, and his hand jerked out to point at Harvey. "You're a police officer."

He glanced down at his uniform and chuckled. "Yes, you know this."

"I'm glad you're here. I have a crime I'd like to report."

Chase took a deep breath. *Here it comes.* At least maybe he'd get to be the one to arrest the arrogant prick who'd been sniffing around Harmony.

"The neighbor boy has been stealing the apples off my tree." Donald pointed to a tree in the yard that was currently sitting not only appleless, but also barren of all leaves, as one would expect in the winter.

Chase ran his hand over his face. "How old is your neighbor?"

"He goes to high school with my son. Same grade. Fourteen."

Well, there went his hopes of arresting Rance.

"Donald, a man named James lives next door. He inherited that house when his parents died. James is fifty-five."

The old man's eyes widened. "No, that's not right. Where did the leaves go?" Donald shook his head and Chase knew he now saw the same lifeless tree.

Tears welled in the old man's eyes. "I miss her. I miss my Marcia."

Chase nodded. He'd never known love like that, but from what he'd heard around town, Donald and Marcia had truly been in love.

Donald wiped his eyes. "I want to go inside now.

Can we talk later?" he asked softly.

"Sure thing." Chase hopped up and reached out to help Donald out of the chair.

Once he was sure Mr. Rodney was inside and warm, Chase walked over to visit James. James might know what color hair Mr. Rodney's grandson had.

He rang the doorbell. The sound of a dog barking made him jump.

After a few minutes, no one came to the door, and the dog sound died off.

He rang the doorbell again. The barking dog returned, and then went quiet.

"He went out of town."

Chase spun around. Across the street, a girl of no more than thirteen sat on her own steps, watching him. He made his way over to her.

"What was that?" he asked as he drew closer.

"James went out of town. He's paying me to pick up his mail and water his plants."

"Do you know when he'll be back?"

The girl shrugged. "My mom said it could be a few months."

Well, shit. That's a dead end.

"And he left his dog?"

"He doesn't have a dog. His doorbell is hooked up to some app of a dog barking. He said it's for security."

Huh. That was a pretty convincing bark.

"Thanks for telling me." Chase gave her a final nod, then made his way back to his car.

Maybe he should go back to Zach's and confront Rance? No, he couldn't do that. He had no proof, and he would look like a jealous fool in front of Harmony. Really, what evidence was there that this man wasn't Rodney's grandson? None. Just wishful thinking on his part because the man had the balls to do the one thing Chase hadn't. Ask Harmony out on a date.

He punched his steering wheel. He saw the way she looked at Rance. He might have missed his chance. And why? Because he was a big fucking coward.

He needed a drink. But damn, the only bar in town worth going to was Zach's, and he couldn't go there.

Maybe they aren't there anymore.

He whipped out his phone and shot off a text to Nick.

Chase: *Are all four of you still at Zach's?*

Before he could pocket his phone, Nick answered.

Nick: *Three of us are here. Wait, how did you know there were four of us?*

Chase: *I stopped in earlier and saw the new guy there.*

Nick: *And now you are checking to see if he's gone?*

Asshole was going to make him admit it.

Chase: *I don't like him. Thought it was better to avoid him.*

He stared at his phone. Bubbles appeared, then disappeared. Finally, Nick's message came through, and Chase lost his breath.

Nick: *I know Harmony is the friend you're crushing on. If you let that dipshit swoop in without telling her how you feel, you're a pussy.*

Well, shit. Nick had a point.

Chase: *On my way.*

★ ★ ★

Chase took a deep breath before opening the door to Brannigan's Pub.

Immediately, his eyes locked with Harmony's. She was sitting in the same booth, but thankfully, Rance was gone. After ordering a beer from the bar, he plopped down in the booth.

"What, you decided to stay this time?" Harmony bit out.

Shit, was he being obvious? He'd held it together for ten months, he needed to keep it together now. Wait, did she slur?

"You drunk?"

She shook her head. "Nope."

Ignoring her original question, he leaned over the table toward Nick. "Hey, there's something I want to talk to you about when we get a chance. A possible police matter."

Nick glowered at him as he took a pull from his beer. Then he pointed the bottle in Chase's direction.

"This better not be about who I think it's about."

He let out a sigh and leaned back. "What if it is?"

Nick shook his head. "No good will come from it."

"When is your date?" Lauren was grinning when she asked Harmony.

"I don't know yet. But I think he'll call soon." Harmony was peeling the label off Nick's empty beer bottle.

"Well, after the way he was looking at you in that booth, I'd say he'll call."

Chase couldn't stand another minute of this. "Don't go out with him."

That caught their attention. Both Lauren's and Harmony's gazes whipped to his.

Harmony crossed her arms over her chest. "Not this again. I know you don't like newcomers, but that is no reason for me to turn down a date. A date, Harvey. Do you have any idea how long it has been since I've had a real date?"

Ten months, five days.

He knew exactly how long. Thank God that guy had been a loser. He never saw date number two.

"I don't trust the guy." He took a long pull from his beer.

"Is that really all it is?" Nick asked arching a brow at him.

He glared at his friend. "My gut feelings are usually right."

There, he'd answered and avoided.

"Hmm." Nick leaned back, gearing up to start some sort of shit-show. He could feel it. "Gut feeling? Is that the only feeling involved?"

What the actual fuck?

He kicked Nick.

"Ouch," the detective yelped.

"All of Mr. Rodney's grandkids have brown hair," he blurted. "Not blond like Rance."

"How the hell would you know that?" Nick asked while rubbing his shin.

"I talked to Mr. Rodney."

"You mean the older man with dementia?" Harmony asked. "I shouldn't go out with Rance because you don't think he is really Mr. Rodney's grandson? I can see why you would think that. It is common, after all, to pretend to be related to someone with dementia so you can take over their full-time care."

She was practically yelling.

Chase finished his beer and set it on the table.

"Look." He turned to her.

The fire in her eyes turned him on. She was so beautiful. Shit. He was getting hard just staring at her.

Rance. We're talking about Rance.

Yep. That worked.

"I know Mr. Rodney has dementia, but my gut is telling me it's not a good idea for you to date this new guy."

"Because of his hair. I see. And what if his hair is dyed or sun-bleached? Did you consider that?" Harmony glared at him.

He stood. "I should go."

"Harvey, wait."

Yep, she had returned to calling him Harvey.

"I'm going to go out on a date with Rance unless you can give me a better reason not to."

She was challenging him. Of course she was. He'd never tried to get between her and some guy before. And as far as she knew, he had no reason to do so now.

Despite Nick trying to push him into saying something to Harmony, he couldn't. Since that night ten months ago, she had given no signs that she had any interest in him. The flirting the night of her birthday was surely the result of alcohol, and he needed to remember that.

So, instead of telling her the truth, he nodded at her and walked away, cursing himself every step.

His phone buzzed in his pocket once he hit the sidewalk. Hoping it was Harmony, he checked the message.

Nick: *Pussy.*

Yes, he was.

Chapter Five

Despite it being a small town, Main Street was lined with cars tonight. Harmony parked two blocks from the restaurant. Normally that wouldn't be a problem, but then, normally she didn't wear four-inch heels. Why the hell did she wear these shoes anyway?

After checking her phone, she realized she was early for her date with Rance. She was happy he'd agreed to meet her at the restaurant. While he seemed like a nice enough guy, she'd rather not have him know where she lived just yet.

A knock on the passenger window scared her. When she turned, Chase's face grinned at her.

Leaning over, she unlocked the door. He slid his long frame inside, scrunching down as he did.

"You need a bigger car," he said as he searched for the lever to push the seat back.

"Fits me just fine."

"This is why we always take my truck if we go anywhere."

When he tried to push the seat back, he discovered it was already as far back as it would go.

"Fine with me. It means you're always driving."

He stopped messing with the seat and stared at her. "You like me to always drive?"

"I do."

He reclined the seat but held her gaze. "You like me in control, don't you?" He winked.

She swallowed.

Were they still talking about driving?

"Depends." Her voice came out a little breathier than she meant it to.

He stretched his arms over his head, dangling them above the back seat, causing his shirt to come up and expose his abs.

She wanted to lick every last one. Her eyes slowly traveled up his body to his eyes.

He was watching her as she ogled him.

What the hell was she doing?

Her hands went to her face to hide her embarrassment. "I'm sorry," she blurted as she peeked at him through her fingers.

A slow grin spread across his face. "You can stare at me anytime you want."

She lowered her hands. "No, I don't mean to." She let out a sigh. "It's just you've been working out so much this past year, and you're looking good. Really good. I should've probably said that sooner."

Okay, how was she going to play this off as a friend simply complimenting another one when she felt her ears and cheeks burning? She must look like a tomato at this point. If she could change anything about herself, it would be that tell.

She turned to stare out the driver's window to avoid what she would assume was his shit-eating grin.

"You think I look really good?" Now his voice was the one sounding husky.

Before she answered, she spotted Rance crossing the street ahead of them.

She turned to Chase, who had clearly also spotted the man, based on the scowl on his face. She undid her seatbelt. Her movement caused her coat to open a little, and his eyes swept over her. She immediately warmed even more.

Then he blinked in surprise. "You're dressed up. You have a date?"

Suddenly feeling defensive, she glared at him. "I do."

He nodded and turned to stare out the passenger window.

She was just about to tell him she needed to go, when he spoke.

"What do you want in a man?" he asked softly.

You. I want you.

"What do you mean?"

He turned and pinned her with his gaze. "What kind of man are you looking for?"

"A nice guy."

He shook his head. "A nice guy?"

"Yeah, what's wrong with that?"

He grew serious. "Are you telling me you would be happy with a nice guy who bought you flowers and had vanilla sex with you once a week for the rest of your life?"

"Where the hell is this coming from? Why would a nice guy only have vanilla sex once a week? Maybe he's wild in the bedroom and it's anything but vanilla, and it's daily."

She could see Chase's chest rising and falling. His eyes were dark as they watched her. Then his lips quirked up.

"You want wild in the bedroom?" he teased.

She swallowed hard. She knew what she wanted in the bedroom, but she wasn't comfortable talking to Chase about it. Not when he was looking at her like he was ready to pounce.

But why the hell not? Over the years, she'd heard rumors about Chase. Rumors that she hadn't been able to get out of her head.

"I want a man who is kind and treats me with respect. But in the bedroom, I want a man who takes charge, talks dirty, and knows what the hell he's doing. Is that too much to ask?"

Chase stared, his nose flaring like a wild beast, ready to attack his prey. Then his gaze moved to her mouth, and she was certain he was going to lean over and kiss her, hard.

His intense stare had her so turned on, hoping

this would be it. All these months, she'd sworn he wasn't into her, but right now, this was something.

He grabbed her thigh, just above the knee, and goosebumps broke out all over her skin. Out of nerves, she licked her lips, and his eyes zeroed in and darkened further.

Would this be better than the first time? What if it wasn't?

He was so close, but then a loud knock on her window made them both jump back.

The windows had steamed up a bit, so she rolled hers down. Rance stood on the other side in a very nice suit.

"Hi, I thought this was your car. Ready to walk to the restaurant?" he asked.

Chase growled.

Rance bent down. "Oh, hi, Officer Harvey. I didn't see you there."

"Give me just a minute. Okay?" Harmony asked him.

"Sure thing. I'll wait at the corner."

Once the window was rolled back up, she turned to Chase. He was grinding his teeth and staring straight ahead.

"You're still going on a date with him?" His voice was calm.

Too calm.

"I said I would, and he's here."

At this point, she really didn't want to. As much as she wanted to like Rance, she couldn't stop fantasizing about Chase.

Crap. She could have sworn he'd been about to kiss her, but then he didn't. Did he want her, or didn't he?

"Is there any reason I shouldn't go on this date?" she asked. *There, here is his chance to stop me.*

He continued to stare through the windshield.

"Chase, what is going on here?"

She held her breath, hoping he would admit he felt something. She was certain he had been going to kiss her.

Rance was staring at them in the car, probably wondering what was taking so long. He took a few steps back in their direction.

Their time was up.

"I told you what I thought of him. This is a bad idea, but if he's what you want, I'm not going to stop you," he snapped.

Chase opened the door and got out.

She rushed to get out and head off a confrontation between the two men, but when she made it to the sidewalk, she realized Chase had gone in the opposite direction. She watched him walk away, his shoulders slumped forward.

Maybe his issue was simply distrust of Rance. Because if he'd actually wanted her, she had pretty much told him he needed to take charge. But he didn't. He'd walked away.

"I've heard great things about this place," Rance said as he came up behind her. Then he reached out and took her hand, intertwining their fingers.

Harmony stared at their joined hands as they walked and felt nothing. Absolutely no chemistry of any kind. But as the man talked, she got the feeling he was a nice guy. Maybe the more she got to know him, the more chemistry she would feel.

At least, she could hope.

Chapter Six

After checking his phone for the tenth time in the hour, Chase shoved it back in his pocket. He was so close to kissing her in the car, and he chickened out again. Well, it wasn't so much chickening out as realizing that the woman he wanted was about to go on a date with another man. Talk about pouring cold water on his libido.

"I told you that you should have said something sooner," Nick said as he popped a chip into his mouth.

"Said something about what?" Zach asked as he grabbed three beers from his refrigerator. He popped the top on each one, then handed them off to Chase and Nick.

Normally, Chase enjoyed these nights hanging out with Nick and Zach. Especially when they hung at Zach's. The man had an endless supply of beer and chips. He claimed he liked to try out beers before selling them in his bar. Chase didn't care what his reasons were, he usually appreciated it. But tonight, he was in a foul mood.

Harmony was three hours into her date, and he hoped like fucking hell she would text him tonight. But why would she? That wasn't the norm. And for all he knew, maybe she planned to make it an overnight date.

No. He couldn't handle that.

Nick turned his shit eating grin to Chase. "You want to tell him, or should I?"

"Tell me what?" Zach bellowed.

Zach owned Brannigan's Pub, the only real bar in town, which usually put him in the center of all the gossip. The idea of not knowing something drove him into a tizzy faster than anything else.

As much as Chase didn't want to share his business with everyone, Zach was great with women. Maybe he'd have some decent advice. Plus, with the three of them sitting around Zach's kitchen table, Chase wasn't going to be able to divert their attention off him.

"All right, you want me to tell him, then?" Nick leaned forward in his chair, getting ready to start in on his diatribe.

"No. I'll tell him."

Both sets of eyes shifted to Chase, and all of a sudden, he felt like he was back on the stage at his high school, trying out for the talent show. Why the hell his friends hadn't told him he really couldn't sing wasn't clear to him back then. Now he understood. They got a kick out of it.

"A while back, after a party and much drinking, I kissed someone who is just a friend."

Zach's eyes went from Chase to Nick, back and forth. "You kissed Nick?" He puckered his lips.

"A female friend."

"Aye, so Harmony?"

What the hell? Out of nowhere, Zach had some sort of accent.

"Why do you have an accent all of a sudden?" Nick asked.

Zach smiled. "Sometimes it comes oot when I get excited."

"I thought you were born and raised in Seattle?"

"Aye, but my mom is from Ireland. It rubbed off on me a little."

"That can happen?" Chase asked.

"Yeah, it can. Now stop tryin' to change the subject, Harvey. You kissed Harmony, didn't you?"

Chase closed his eyes. Well, he couldn't stop now.

"Yes, Harmony. Then the next morning, she made coffee and acted like nothing happened."

"Whoa! Wait a minute. You said you kissed her, then you jump to 'the next mornin', she made coffee'? I think you left a hell of a lot oot." Zach crossed his arms.

"No, that's what happened. We were drunk, and we walked to my place. We've done that many times over the years. We both fell into my bed, but instead of passing out, she started asking me these questions."

"What kind of questions?" Nick asked as he

shoved chips into his mouth.

Damn, that should be gross, the way he was shoveling chips into his mouth, but Nick was blessed in the looks department, so everything he did looked cool. Except he was eating the barbecue chips.

Chase grabbed the bag. "Slow down. You know those are my favorite. Eat what you brought."

Zach went to his cupboard and pulled out a matching bag of barbecue chips.

"Here, now you each have a bag. Get on with your story."

Nick laughed. "You must be really excited to hear this."

"You," Zach pointed at Nick. "Shut the hell up. You," he pointed at Chase. "Go."

Chase let out a breath. *Here goes nothing.* "She asked if I had ever wondered what it would be like if we kissed. Then she asked me to kiss her."

"Oh, she likes you. That helps." Zach nodded. "You kissed her?"

"I did. And it wasn't just a peck. But I stopped it before it went too far." Chase leapt up out of his chair and paced the room.

Zach's hand stopped midair, a chip dangling from his fingers. "What do you mean you stopped it?"

"I said I needed water and jumped out of the bed. When I returned, she was already asleep. Then the next morning, when I discovered she wasn't in bed, I searched for her. She was in the kitchen and acted like nothing had happened."

"What did she say when you brought it up?" Zach asked.

"He didn't bring it up," Nick interjected.

Zach's head whipped from Nick to Chase. "You didn't say anythin'?"

"No. I thought maybe she was too drunk and didn't remember. What was I going to say? 'Oh, remember when you were drunk last night? I took advantage and kissed you.'"

Zach frowned. "No, but I'm guessin' she was worried she'd gotten drunk and pushed herself on you, considerin' you jumped and ran with no explanation. Then the next morning, you didn't say anythin'? That's cold."

"How the hell are you so insightful when it comes to women?" He was frustrated at Zach for throwing out accusations, even if they did sound like they could be right.

"I have five sisters."

All right, maybe Zach did know what he was talking about.

"You said the kiss happened a while ago? How long?"

"Ten months. It was the night we were celebrating her birthday at your pub."

Zach's eyebrows shot up. "Ten months? Please tell me you've brought it up since then."

Chase shook his head.

Zach set his bag of chips on the table. "And she hasn't said anythin'?"

"Nope," Nick interjected before crunching another chip.

Zach stared at Chase. "And now she's datin' someone, and you're jealous?"

"In his defense, he was going to bring it up, but that just happened to be the day Harmony met the new guy, Rance," Nick pointed out.

"Why the fuck would you wait so long?" Zach asked.

"That's what I want to know too," Nick chimed in.

Chase fell back onto his chair. "We've been friends for fifteen years and never once has Harmony indicated she had any interest beyond friendship. Never once. Then the one time she does, she was so drunk she doesn't remember. I was afraid if I brought it up, it would ruin our friendship. Her parents practically abandoned her in high school. She used to tell me I was the only person in the word she trusted. Then I kissed her when she was drunk."

He let out a heavy sigh. "I'm afraid if I tell her about it, she'll think I took advantage and the trust will be gone."

Zach grunted and grabbed a handful of chips. Silence filled the room except for Zach's crunching.

"You keep sayin' she doesn't remember. Why are you so convinced of that?" Zach asked.

"Because like I said, she didn't say anything."

"Neither did you!" Nick barked.

"Here's how I see it. She wanted you and finally

got up the courage to do somethin' about it. But then the way you reacted, well you fucked up. Big time. Now you need to fix it," Zach said.

"Since you're so wise, tell me how do I do that?" Chase asked.

Zach chuckled. "Easy. Talk to her."

Fuck.

"I tried earlier today."

"What happened?" Nick asked.

"Rance showed up. Turns out they had a date planned. She left with him."

"Ouch," Nick said.

"Does Lauren know how you feel? Any chance your girl Harmony knows and is ignorin' it?" Zach asked.

"Lauren suspected something that night, but not anymore, since he and Harmony barely hang out now," Nick said.

Zach leaned back and rubbed his chin. "Okay, since you obviously can't be direct, you need a plan."

"I can be direct," Chase said defensively.

Nick and Zach laughed.

Chase sighed. "Okay. I need a plan."

"First of all, you need to stop goin' by 'Harvey'. See if you can get her to call you by your first name." Zach set his beer down, then smacked Chase's arm. "What the hell *is* your first name, anyway?"

"Chase. And what is this plan of yours? Don't I just need to woo her or some shit?"

Zach stared at him for a moment, then burst out

laughing. "How did I not know that? Chase?"

"I don't tell everyone. It's really not that funny."

"Chase… and you're a patrolman? Oh, man, you must have endured a lot of chase jokes durin' the academy."

"I'm an officer, but yeah, it wasn't cool."

Zach continued to laugh. Nick held his beer bottle up to his mouth to hide his grin.

"That's right, you motherfuckers. Enjoy my pain." Chase shook his head.

"Sorry." Zach composed himself. "But I'm serious. You need to get Harmony to see you as Chase, the sexy police officer who will protect her and maybe even put her in cuffs."

"I don't know. It sounds like she saw him that way the night of her birthday." Nick was still grinning.

"Yeah, he said she was drunk. But in the harsh light of day, either she realized her mistake, and pretended nothin' happened or she thinks he rejected her. That's not good fer my boy here." Zach put his hand on Chase's shoulder, giving it a squeeze. "Right now, she probably sees you as Harvey, the safe sidekick after you ran scared from her kiss."

"What do you think he should do?" Nick winked at Chase as he egged Zach on.

Chase rolled his eyes. There was nothing these two could come up with that would help him. He was on his own.

"Wait, did you say her birthday? That night you guys dirty danced at my pub?"

"That's the one," Nick said.

"If I recall, there was a hot blond hittin' on you, but the next moment, Harmony pulled you onto the dance floor fer some dirty dancin'."

The memories of the night were coming back to him. "I'd forgotten about that."

"She marked you."

"Shit, dude, she pissed on you?" Nick laughed. "Kinky."

Chase threw a chip at Nick. "Asshole."

"No, what I mean is that she saw someone hittin' on him, so she pulled him onto the dance floor, and let all the women know he was with her." Zach raised an eyebrow and finished his beer.

"No, she just wanted to dance. It was her birthday, so I went with it."

"You two ever dance like that before, or since?"

Now that he thought about it... "No."

"Has she seen you flirt with another woman? Get hit on? Anything like that?" Nick asked this time.

Since that kiss, he hadn't had any interest in any other woman. There hadn't been flirting on his part. Nothing. He'd tried, but his mind always drifted back to Harmony.

"No."

Zach whacked him in the chest. "There you go, then."

Chase's head fell back. "There I go what? What are you saying?"

If Zach suggested he have some woman hit on

him just to make Harmony jealous, well, he wasn't going to play games. He was getting too old for that shit.

"Wednesday is ladies' night at the pub. Come in after work and have a beer. I'm sure there will be some ladies who will want to dance with you."

"That can't be right," Nick said. "Ladies' nights usually draw the guys."

"Yeah, but not that many," Zach said.

Chase was thinking about Zach's suggestion. "You're suggesting I move on?"

How the hell would that fix his problem? If he could have moved on, he would have done so ten months ago, or anytime since.

"No, Nick here needs to get Harmony into the pub on Wednesday too. How you do it doesn't matter."

"You want me to dance with a woman and make her jealous? Zach, I'm not interested in playing juvenile games."

"All right. But let's say you're there, and some woman hits on you, and Harmony doesn't react? Doesn't care?"

To know she really didn't want him at all? That would suck. He took a pull from his beer to hide his frown.

"At least then you would know to stop pinin' fer her, and you could go home with the new woman. Win-win," Zach declared.

"You know, it couldn't hurt. Harmony is dating that douchebag," Nick added.

"You don't like him either?" Chase hoped his

friend had some dirt on the guy.

"No, he's dating your woman."

Nope, no dirt.

"Yeah, but I'm still not sure about playing games."

Nick shook his head. "I agree with you there. Don't play games. But I will say, if you are in the pub on ladies' night, you'll get hit on. Just a fact. You're an attractive guy in a town full of single women. And I'll find a way to get Harmony there to witness it. Just be ready if she goes into a jealous rage."

Reaching for Nick's chips, Zach grabbed a handful. "We need to seal up our plan fer Wednesday," he said to Chase. "Shall we all start callin' you Chase now?" He held a straight face for all of five seconds before he bent over, laughing hard.

Nick held up his beer bottle and spoke into it like a walkie-talkie. "High-speed pursuit. Chase, I need you to chase them down. Over and out." Then he started giggling.

Yes, giggling. This grown-ass man.

"Sorry, couldn't resist!"

Nick and Zach were now laughing much harder than the joke called for.

And this is who I'm taking advice from.

"I'm so fucked."

Chapter Seven

The door to the Fisher Springs Police Department swung open, bringing with it a cold winter breeze. Chase glanced up from the game he was playing on his phone to see an older man walking toward him, wringing his hands.

After setting his phone down, he stood. "Can I help you?"

The man shoved his hands in his pockets. "I hope so. My daughter is missing."

A missing person? He hadn't ever had one in his career in Fisher Springs. But then, this was a small, sleepy town where his usual calls involved goats escaping onto the town highway.

"Please, have a seat." He motioned to the chair across from his desk. "Why do you believe your daughter is missing?"

The man sat down, and immediately, his foot

was tapping. "My daughter has been working for Mr. Rodney."

"Mr. Rodney?" The hairs on the back of Chase's neck stood up.

"Yes, she's been his caretaker for about seven months. Mr. Rodney is such a nice man. Anyway, she calls us every Friday, and then comes over for family dinner on Sundays. She always brings her laundry. You know how it is, you being young yourself. She never could find an apartment around here with a washer and dryer. We were happy about that, though, because it meant she came home once a week at least. Truth be told, my wife would do most of her laundry. I always told Barbara not to because our Bella needed to learn to take care of herself. But Barbara wouldn't hear of it, she's always babied Bella. Bella is our youngest."

The man stopped to take a breath. Chase needed to redirect him, or he would end up hearing the man's life story.

"First, can you tell me your name?"

"Oh yes, of course. I'm sorry. My name is Edwin Daniel. My daughter is Bella Daniel."

Chase opened a missing person file on his computer and started to fill it in.

"Did she miss one of these Sunday dinners?" He perched his fingers above his keyboard.

"Yes, she never called Friday, nor did she come over Sunday. We've been calling her since Monday morning, but this morning, instead of going to voicemail, there was a recording that the number is no longer in service. But Bella never went anywhere without her phone. None of this makes sense. Something has happened to her, we know it."

Chase noted that the man looked like a genuinely worried father. There was nothing suspicious about his demeanor.

"All right. I need to get some basic information first, then we'll go from there."

The man nodded.

Chase spent the next hour getting the man's name, his wife's name, and all the information he could about Bella. He made a note to run a trace on her cellphone. He also wanted to obtain a search warrant for Mr. Rodney's place. Rance was looking guiltier by the moment, as far as he was concerned. But the odds that Judge Milton would sign a search order based on the little evidence he had were slim. He needed more.

"Has Bella ever taken off or disappeared like this before?"

Her father shook his head. "No, never."

"And it's possible she's been gone up to a week and a half?"

"Yes."

"Does she get along with Mr. Rodney?"

Mr. Daniel frowned. "Well of course. Everyone gets along with Mr. Rodney. He's such a nice man."

"What about his grandson?" Chase's gaze shot to the man. "Does she get along with him?"

The man shifted in his seat, appearing uncomfortable.

Interesting.

"Grandson? I believe so. What does he have to do with this?"

Chase nodded. "I understand Mr. Rodney's grandson took over his care."

Mr. Daniel shook his head. "No, that doesn't make sense. If Bella were let go, she would have told us."

"Who pays your daughter, Mr. Daniel?"

"I don't know. I haven't seen any of her pay stubs."

Chase leaned back and shoved his hand in his hair. "Maybe she quit and was too embarrassed to tell you."

"Look, I know my daughter. She wouldn't quit and leave town without telling her parents. No. Bella is a good girl, she wouldn't do that."

As much as his gut told him something was up with Rance, he also knew how often parents didn't really know all there was to know about their children.

"How old is Bella?"

"She's twenty-two."

Chase sighed and pushed back from the desk. Yep, at that age, he would guess there was a lot her parents didn't know.

"Do you have a photo of her?"

Mr. Daniel pulled out his wallet and drew a photo from it. "This is a few years old but she hasn't changed too much. There are better photos of her with us in her apartment. I have a spare key. We can go there today."

When he saw the young woman in the photograph, the hair on the back of his neck stood up.

"This is Bella?"

"Yes, my beautiful Bella." Mr. Daniel had tears in his eyes. "I'm so scared for her. It isn't like her to not tell us where she's going."

I'm scared for her too.

Chase kept that thought to himself as he stared at the woman in the photo. She had long, red hair and fair skin. His mind immediately went to Harmony.

Rance comes to town, and Bella goes missing. Then the man pursues another redhead. Coincidence?

It could be. Maybe this young woman is enjoying some freedom away from her parents — if they went to her apartment, they could find a layoff notice or something similar.

On the other hand, if Rance wasn't the nice guy he was pretending to be, they could be walking into a crime scene, or at the very least a place that held evidence. But without a warrant, the evidence would be inadmissible.

His desire to prove to Harmony that Rance was a schmuck was strong. But if something had really happened to Bella, he needed to do this by the book.

The chief walked into the station. "Harvey, everything all right here?"

"Yes, sir. Mr. Daniel is here to report his daughter is missing. I'm gathering information now."

"Missing person?" Dunin asked. "That's

unusual for Fisher Springs. Any chance she left town of her own accord?"

"That's what we were discussing," Chase said.

Turning to Mr. Daniel, Dunin asked, "Have you been to her apartment?"

"Yes, when she didn't return our calls, I went there. I thought maybe she was sick and needed help. But she wasn't there."

"Did you see her keys, wallet, cellphone?"

"No."

This sounded more and more like a young woman just trying to avoid her parents.

"But her medication was on the counter," Mr. Daniel added. "She wouldn't leave without it."

"What medication?"

"Insulin. She's diabetic."

Maybe he was wrong in thinking she was simply dodging her parents. A known diabetic wouldn't leave their insulin at home, would they? Hell if he knew.

"It will take some time to get a search warrant to get into her apartment."

"I'm on the lease, too. Can't I give you permission to go in?"

"You're on the lease?"

"Yeah, she asked me to cosign so she could get the apartment. She didn't have any credit."

Chase stood. "If you're on the lease, you can definitely give permission to enter the unit. The chief here will likely send out our detective, Nick Moore, to investigate. Is that what you want?"

"Yes, please."

"Actually, Harvey," Dunin said, "why don't you take care of this one? Moore's caught up with Ms. Finkle again."

"Seriously, again?" Chase let out a sigh.

Ms. Finkle lost her cat nearly daily. When Nick had first started, they forgot to fill him in, and next thing they knew, he'd gone out to help her. He felt so bad, he'd given the woman his private cell number. Needless to say, Nick was with Ms. Finkle almost daily now, looking for her cat.

"Yeah. I'd intervene, but honestly, it's too funny." Dunin laughed as he walked toward his office. "Keep me up to date on this one, Harvey." He turned to face them. "Mr. Daniel, we will do everything we can to find your daughter."

Then he went into his office and closed the door.

"All right, then. Let's go."

* * *

On the drive over to Bella's apartment, Chase yawned several times. He was tired. Ever since Rance came to town a few days ago, he hadn't been sleeping for shit. The idea of Harmony falling for a guy like that had been eating at him. But now he needed to wake the hell up and focus on this case.

He reached for the coffee he'd brought with him, and gulped it half down. Then he parked his cruiser beside Mr. Daniel's car. They'd pulled up to one of the two apartment buildings in Fisher Springs.

He followed Mr. Daniel into Bella's unit. Once inside, he noticed a dining table, two chairs, a couch, and a table that held a television. Against the wall were several boxes.

"She move in recently?" Chase asked, staring at the boxes.

"No, but I know she's hoping to find something better. She said there was no point in unpacking when she would be moving again soon."

Chase nodded. Then he spotted a photo on the kitchen counter, it was Bella with her parents.

"You can use that one if you'd like," Mr. Daniel said.

Chase picked up the photo. Bella could pass for Harmony's sister.

"Are any of her clothes missing? Like maybe she packed a suitcase and left?"

They entered her bedroom, and her dad opened her closet.

Chase sighed. It was full of clothing. If anything was missing, he'd never know.

They weren't going to get any answers fast unfortunately. He ran his hand through his hair and pulled. He hoped like hell nothing happened to this girl. Otherwise, Harmony could be in danger too.

"The next step will be to see if her credit cards have been used. Then I'll question those who last saw her. Do you have any idea who that would be?"

"Yes. I'll make a list of names and phone numbers."

"Thank you, Mr. Daniel. I'll be in touch soon."

★ ★ ★

After Chase wrapped up at the apartment, he went back to the station to finish filling out the missing person report.

Despite his lack of sleep, he knew in his bones that Rance was behind her disappearance. He needed to prove it as soon as possible. Harmony had gone on at least one date with the asshole, maybe more. He didn't know. She certainly wasn't confiding in him.

He hoped she wasn't sleeping with him. The idea of her alone with him at his home made his blood burn.

Wait, he was supposedly living with his grandfather. No, he would likely try to get Harmony to invite him to her place. And she'd complained several times how it had been too long since she'd had sex.

Did she see this guy as a good time, for sex only? Or was she falling for him?

Maybe he should go to the diner, like old times, and see if she wanted to talk. He could push his own feelings down for her, right? He needed more information on this guy.

Checking his watch, he noted that her usual shift would be ending soon. He grabbed his jacket and walked the short distance to the diner. Despite the fact he'd known Harmony most of his life, and used to feel comfortable around her, now his stomach was a knot of nerves. What if she saw through his questions? What if he looked like a jealous asshole? Well, hell, maybe he should just come clean before she gets too serious with Rance. But his nervousness turned to disappointment the moment he saw Kate working the dining room alone.

"If you're looking for Harmony, she's not here," she said by way of greeting.

"Where is she?"

Kate smiled. "She might be on a date with the new guy."

Chase slumped onto a stool at the counter. "Again?"

"He seems nice enough. She'll probably keep dating him unless you do something about it."

Chase wasn't one to get embarrassed, but he hadn't expected that comment.

Turning away, he avoided her intense gaze. "Why would I do something about it?"

Kate laughed. "We both know the answer to that."

Well, shit. How was it that everyone in town seemed to know how he felt except Harmony?

His phone buzzed in his pocket.

Nick: *When will you be at Zach's?*

Chase: *Why would I go to Zach's?*

Nick: *His pub. Ladies' night, remember? Lauren is*

picking Harmony up in an hour.

Shit. How had he forgotten?

Chase: *Guess I'll show up in an hour.*

At least she wasn't out with Rance. But now he had to hope Zach's plan didn't backfire on him. If he had to watch Harmony take another man home, he'd lose his mind.

Chapter Eight

Lauren and Tabitha practically dragged her to Brannigan's Pub. It wasn't that Harmony didn't like Zach's bar. It's that she didn't want to go on ladies' night. Men from Davenport often showed up looking for one night of fun, but she wasn't in the mood. After her one so-so date with Rance, and Chase's juvenile attitude, she was tired of men.

"Why can't we just hang out at your place, Lauren?"

Lauren looped her arm in hers as they walked into the pub. "I've never been here for a ladies' night, and I want to check it out. Now grab us a booth while I order drinks."

Harmony followed Tabitha to a booth being vacated by four women.

"Wow, this is the busiest I've seen this place," Tabitha said as she scanned the crowd. "Hey, isn't that

Harvey at the bar?"

Harmony's head jerked that direction. She made immediate eye contact with Chase, who was standing next to Lauren. He smiled and gave her a nod.

That crooked smile of his was so sexy. Damn.

Realizing that Lauren might have trouble carrying three drinks, she excused herself from the booth to help her friend. She came up behind Lauren and overheard the end of their conversation.

"You think flirting is a good idea?" her friend was asking Chase.

His eyes widened when he spotted her. "Harmony, good to see you." Chase leaned in and gave her a hug.

Those arms wrapped around her, and it sent off such a zinging sensation that she had to take a breath to keep from jumping up and wrapping her legs around him. When had her attraction to him become so strong?

She knew. It was after she'd discovered what a good kisser he was. The memory of their kiss was seared on her brain forever.

She pulled back, despite the fact she wanted to melt into his arms and enjoy the feel of her hands on his muscular back, and breath in his scent. She'd always loved how he smelled.

"You too," she said. "I came to help with the drinks," she told Lauren.

"Sounds good."

As she reached for her drink, the universe sent her a message loud and clear. Some half-dressed brunette snuggled right up next to Chase. She could tell from his expression he didn't know her.

"Hey, handsome. Can you buy me a drink?" the woman asked.

Sure as shit, he grinned then turned and summoned Zach over to take their drink order.

Lauren stepped in front of her, carrying Tabitha's drink as well as her own. Harmony gave one last glance at Chase and wished she hadn't. The brunette was feeling up his bicep.

Once she and Lauren got back to the table, she wiped away a tear before her friends noticed. It was one thing to know Chase didn't think of her that way, but it was entirely another to have to watch his mating ritual with another woman. To distract herself, she scanned the room, and saw only a couple of men.

"Where are the men? I thought there would be single men here."

"Why do you care? You snagged the best looking one in town." Tabitha took a sip of her drink.

"No, I'm afraid I snagged that one," Lauren said holding up her left hand to flash her engagement ring. "But how are things with Rance?"

Harmony shrugged. "It's okay."

She'd only gone out on the one date with him so far. He'd asked her out again for Saturday, but she wasn't sure she should go.

"Just okay? Is he bad at sex? Maybe you can train him," Tabitha said.

Harmony shook her head. "We haven't had sex.

We had one date, and he kissed me on the cheek."

She glanced up to see her friends staring at her like they'd sucked on a lemon.

"What? He was being a gentleman," she said defensively.

"Is there any chemistry?" Lauren asked.

Harmony shook her head. "Maybe it will come."

"Good evening, ladies." Nick leaned over and kissed Lauren.

Nick and Lauren were perfect for each other. There was a time when Harmony didn't think they'd figure that out. But now here they were. Perfect.

"I want what you two have," she said. "Is that so much to ask?"

Lauren leaned across the table and took Harmony's hands in hers. "No, it's not too much to ask. I want it for you too. But remember, I didn't like this guy when I first met him. You have to keep an open mind. You never know when someone you already know might surprise you."

Harmony let her gaze drift back to the bar. The brunette was writing something on a napkin. She handed it to Chase before leaning in and giving him a hug.

Even though it was just a hug, the thought of someone else's arms holding him was too much.

A few minutes later, Nick asked, "Who wants another round? I'm heading to the bar."

"I'll take one," Harmony said, not looking up from her project.

She'd been slowly peeling the label off Tabitha's beer bottle to distract herself from looking over at Chase.

"Hey there," someone whispered in her ear.

She jumped.

Chase. The brunette was missing.

He placed his hands on her shoulders. "Sorry, I didn't mean to scare you."

"I'm fine."

"Actually, she's probably frustrated, based on the information we just got," Tabitha offered.

Harmony shot her a look. Tabitha was used to them airing all of their personal business in front of each other. She didn't know that Chase was the last person she wanted to share with right now.

Chase kept his right hand on her right shoulder, rubbing gently as he leaned in. "What has you so frustrated?"

His lips touched her ear, and she thought she might combust. His fingers continued to rub her shoulder, and she shivered.

He leaned down again. "Cold?"

"I'm fine."

"Harvey!"

They both turned to see Bridgette, the blond from her birthday, smiling as she pulled Chase into her arms. Her hand quickly made its way down, giving his ass a pat.

Harmony looked away. She hadn't wanted to admit it, but the evidence was plain as day in front of her. Chase was a player. She couldn't sit here and watch this.

Grabbing her phone from her purse, she clicked on the text message from Rance.

"Why don't you come over, and I'll make you feel good?" Bridgette's voice somehow carried over the music to her ears. If this was the type of woman he pursued, then she never had a chance. She could see that now.

Typing her reply, she accepted Rance's offer of a second date. Something to look forward to.

Although, as she sat there, she realized she wasn't looking forward to it.

When she glanced back up, she saw Bridgette storming off with a pout. That didn't mean Chase wasn't a player, but at least he might be smart enough to avoid someone like Bridgette.

Chase returned his attention to Harmony, putting his hand back on her shoulder.

"I'm going on a second date with Rance," she told the group. "This weekend." She plastered a smile on her face and tried to look happy.

Rance was a very nice-looking man. Even though she had yet to feel the chemistry she felt with Chase, she was determined to give Rance another shot.

Chase's hand froze on her shoulder, then dropped as he took a step away. "You're still dating him?"

After taking a large sip of her wine, she turned to him. "Sure am. He's nice enough."

"Nice enough?" Chase's eyebrows shot up to his hairline.

"Yeah, nice enough. If you haven't noticed, there aren't a lot of options in this town. At least Rance is a gentleman and not a player."

"Shit," Nick muttered into his beer bottle before taking a pull.

Lauren's eyes were large as they shot from Harmony to Chase.

Chase stepped back.

"It was good seeing you all, but I'm going to call it an early night," Chase bit out.

He walked away without a glance to her.

"You really think Rance is your best choice?" Nick asked.

"Yeah." Her eyes stayed on Chase as he made his way to the door.

Just before he reached the door, he pulled something white from his pocket and threw it in the trash. Was that the brunette's number?

"Then why do you keep watching Harvey like you hope he comes back?"

Her gaze snapped to Nick. Did he know? She glanced at Lauren, who was avoiding her eyes. Damn, her friend had shared her secret.

"What? Harvey? Why would I—"

"Stop. I see how you look at him. Maybe you should tell him." Nick finished his beer and set it on the table.

"Tell him?" Harmony laughed. "He's probably

meeting that brunette back at his place." She knew in her gut that wasn't true, but she kept up with it anyway. "He's a player. No, I need someone who wants the same things I want."

Nick laughed. "You think Harvey's a player? I would bet my salary he's going back to his place right now, alone."

"Well, regardless, I let him know once how I felt. It didn't go so well. I'm not going down that road again."

"I think you should try again," Nick said.

Wait, why was Nick saying this? Hope bloomed inside as the wine was starting to do somersaults in her stomach. Maybe she'd been wrong to never bring up the kiss. She promised herself she would talk it out with Chase soon.

Chapter Nine

"I can't believe he signed that. And before 10 a.m.," Chief Dunin said as they walked out of the courthouse.

Fortunately, Judge Milton understood that a woman's life could be at stake. Mr. Daniel's statement was likely what swayed him. But the fact Bella's cellphone had been canceled the same day Rance showed up in town helped as well.

Chase was as surprised as the chief that the judge had signed the search warrant to search Mr. Rodney's house. The judge was known for denying such requests. But of course, having the chief with him likely helped. Everyone knew that Dunin usually went by the book. He wouldn't have made this request if it weren't urgent.

"I'm calling in Moore, and then we can all head over." The chief stepped away, holding his phone to his ear.

Chase couldn't wait to see the look in Rance's eye when they walked into his so-called grandfather's house armed with a warrant. Finally, he could prove to Harmony this guy was lying to everyone about who he was and why he was here. He just knew he was hiding something. He could feel it in his bones.

The sooner he could get Harmony away from him, the better. The idea that she was dating a man who could be a murderer made him sick. The fact that the woman was last seen, and her cellphone was canceled, the same day Rance came to town was too suspicious.

"Let's go. Moore will meet us there."

Chase drove them to Mr. Rodney's house. To be safe, he parked a few houses down. No point in tipping the guy off. But then Nick drove past them and parked in front of Mr. Rodney's house. Chase shook his head. So much for surprise.

With the search warrant in hand, Chase marched up the porch steps, not even bothering to wait for the other two. He pounded on the door, then took a step back, bouncing back and forth on his feet. The adrenaline was running through his veins. Finally, he had his chance to catch this guy.

The door slowly opened, and Mr. Rodney stood wrapped in a robe and nothing else.

"Mr. Rodney, I have a warrant to search your home." He held up the document.

Mr. Rodney stared at him for a moment. "Who are you?"

Chase swallowed. Their conversation the other

day had clearly been forgotten. "I'm Officer Harvey. I have a warrant to search the premises."

The man frowned. "Search for what?"

"Anything related to the disappearance of Bella Daniel."

"Bella?" The man's vacant expression disappeared, and in its place was a smile. "Such a lovely girl. I haven't seen her in a while. Where did she go?"

"That is what we are here to find out, Mr. Rodney. We need to come in."

The old man looked down, finally realizing his robe was open. He quickly tied it shut and stepped out from the doorway. "Yes, of course. Please come in."

Chase, Nick, and the chief entered the home. The entryway was large, with a staircase just ahead of them that curved as it went upstairs. To his left was a sitting room, to his right an office. Straight ahead was a hallway that presumably opened up to the rest of the house.

"I'll take these two rooms," Nick said, pointing to the sitting room and office.

"I'll go upstairs," Dunin said, already ascending the staircase.

Chase made his way down the hallway to start on the back part of the lower floor. The hallway led to a family room complete with two lazy boy chairs and a television. One wall was comprised of several bookcases that held numerous books and board games. The room looked very lived in, but one thing struck Chase as odd. There were no photographs. He didn't know much about dementia, but he would have thought it would help to have photographs of the man's family around.

"What's going on?"

Chase spun around to find Rance standing behind the couch with Harmony at his side. Harmony was here. It was still early morning. Why was she here? His eyes moved from her legs up her body. Were her clothes rumpled? Had she stayed the night here? The image of her and Rance together infiltrated his mind, and he ground his teeth together to keep from punching the man.

"I said, what's going on?" Rance was louder this time.

Chase pulled the warrant out of his pocket and handed it to him.

"We have a warrant to search the premises. It would be best if you waited outside."

And there was the look he was waiting for. "A warrant? Why?"

Chase stared him down for a moment. The man was literally holding a piece of paper that stated why he was there, but he couldn't be bothered to read it.

Harmony grabbed the paper and quickly scanned it. "They are looking for any information or evidence related to the disappearance of Bella Daniel."

"She was Mr. Rodney's caretaker. She was last seen the day after Rance showed up. Her dad filed a missing person report."

"The young woman with the red hair kind of like mine?" Harmony asked.

"That's the one," Chase said.

"Bella said she was going to take a cruise with her best friend. I'm sure that's where she is," Rance interjected.

Now this was interesting. Rance admitted to talking to her.

"A cruise?"

"Yes, when I arrived, I told her I didn't need her services anymore, and I gave her two weeks' pay to make up for the fact I was letting her go. She was quite excited and said she finally had enough to take a cruise."

Chase crossed his arms. "You expect me to believe this woman just left on a cruise without telling anyone? She left without telling her parents where she was going? She left her insulin at home. There is no indication any of her clothes were missing."

Rance shrugged. "I really don't care what you believe, Officer." His eyes were practically radiating fire.

"Harvey, can I talk to you for a minute?" Harmony stood, mimicking his crossed-arm stance.

"No, I have a job to do. Please wait outside." Without giving them a chance to respond, he turned his back and began searching for anything that would help them find Bella.

"Asshole," he heard Rance say under his breath. Then he listened as they shuffled out of the room and through the front door.

"You okay?" Nick was leaning against the wall.

"Fine."

"You two find anything?" Dunin stood in the doorway, hands on his hips.

"Nothing in the office or sitting room," Nick said.

"I'm still searching." Chase picked up his pace. The conversation with Rance had derailed him.

"There's a closet full of guns in what appears to be the room the grandson is staying in. I saw him head outside with Harmony. I'm going to question him now," Dunin said.

Chase nodded but kept searching.

"Harvey."

He looked up to see the stern look on his chief's face.

"I know we don't have anything on Rance yet, but my gut says something's wrong with this guy. You need to tell Harmony to stay away from him."

Something between a chuckle and a cough came out of Chase's throat. "I've told her. Many times. You see what good that is doing."

"Hmmm." The chief kept staring at him. Then he turned his attention to Nick. "How about you? You're engaged to her best friend. Maybe she'd listen to you."

Nick shook his head. "Believe me, I've tried."

"That's too bad." The chief stepped back. "I'll be out talking to Rance while you two finish up here."

Once the chief was gone, Chase turned back to the shelves.

"I don't know whether she really finds this guy charming, or if she is with him as a fuck you to you,"

Nick said.

Chase dropped the papers he was holding and stood tall. "Why do you think she'd date some guy just to get to me?"

"Maybe because you've been gunning for the guy since she met him," Nick said. "She doesn't like to be told what to do."

"You think I'm pushing them together?" He moved books around, looking for any clues. Several volumes fell to the floor. Maybe he was yanking them off the shelf harder than was necessary.

"You still haven't talked to her, have you?"

"No. I can't. Not now that she's dating some guy." He shoved the books back on the shelf, hard. "Dammit!"

"I'll take the kitchen," Nick said, shaking his head as he walked away.

It didn't take long to finish their search. There was no evidence downstairs.

Nick led the way outside. As he followed, Chase spotted the chief still talking to Rance, over by the cruiser, and hoped he had been able to get some information out of him.

He'd barely gotten down the porch steps before Harmony was in his face, her hands on her hips.

"I know you are only harassing him because I'm dating him. Stop it," she hissed.

Now *that* pissed him off.

He took a step back and sucked in a deep breath. "Is that really what you think of me? That I get my kicks off harassing innocent people?" he bit out.

She opened her mouth, but no words came out.

"Do you think so low of me as a police officer that you believe I'd make up some warrant just to sniff around the man you're sleeping with?"

She blinked several times. "I'm not sleeping with him," she said quietly. "Not that it's any of your business."

"Bullshit. You're here early in the morning. I'm not blind." He pushed past her.

He needed to get away from her before he said something he'd really regret.

"Harvey, stop right there."

He spun around, grinding his teeth to keep from speaking.

"Early morning? It is after 10 a.m. That is hardly early. And not that it is any of your business either, but I came by to deliver a pie from the diner. Mr. Rodney loves apple pie, so I brought him one."

She stepped up into his space. "Why are you so aggravated about me dating? I don't recall it bothering you before. What changed?"

Those chocolate brown eyes of hers bored into him, trying to extract the truth.

He couldn't lie to her. He never could.

Staring at the ground, he wondered how he was going to get out of this.

"Just say it, Chase." Her voice was so quiet, he almost missed it.

His eyes shot to hers. She never called him

Chase. Well, except for that night.

"You remember, don't you?" he whispered.

Her eyes welled with tears. "Of course I do. And if you thought it was a mistake, you should have just said so instead of pretending it didn't happen. It was like being ghosted. It hurt."

So many emotions rolled through him. She'd gone all this time thinking he regretted what happened?

"No. When I woke up, you weren't in bed. Then in the kitchen, you didn't say anything. You went on like it was any normal day. I knew you had been drunk. I thought you'd been too drunk, and I'd taken advantage of you. I'm so sorry. I wanted to talk about it. It's all I've been able to think about all these months."

"Yeah?"

He nodded and slipped his hands onto her shoulders.

"What would you have said? That morning, in the kitchen." she asked.

Tears slipped down her cheek. He wiped them away. This was his chance to get it all out there.

Chase took a deep breath and started. "I would have told you that I value our friendship more than anything else."

"Harvey!" the chief yelled from the patrol car interrupting them. "Let's go."

Rance stalked toward them. "I'll tell you what I told Dunin. There's nothing illegal about a closet full of guns. I'm an avid hunter."

Before he could finish what he wanted to tell

Harmony, Rance had his arm around her. "Let's go have some of that pie. I need something to soothe my nerves after the morning I've had."

Harmony went with him but looked back over her shoulder. "I'll talk to you later."

His heart broke as he watched her go back into the house with that man. After finally getting the kiss out in the open, how could she go off with Rance?

He kicked some rocks off the walkway.

Fuck.

At least now he knew where she stood. And it wasn't with him.

Chapter Ten

"He said what?" Lauren stood next to the counter at Lucky's Diner with a look of sheer disgust on her face.

"He said he valued our friendship. Thankfully, Rance came up to us so I could get away before I did something stupid." Harmony wiped down the counter a little harder than necessary.

She wasn't going to hide it. She was pissed. And she felt like such a fool. All that chemistry she felt with Chase had clearly only been in her head. He must have felt like he was kissing his sister.

"Wait. That's all he said? Then what did you say?" Lauren asked.

"I didn't get a chance. Dunin interrupted us."

Lauren grabbed Harmony's arm stopping her assault on the counter.

"Interrupted? So maybe he had more to say?" Lauren asked.

Nick stormed in during the lull in customers between the lunch and dinner rushes.

"What is going on between you and Harvey? He keeps throwing one hissy fit after another since your confrontation on Mr. Rodney's front lawn."

"I'm sorry you have to deal with his tantrums, but I'm sure it has nothing to do with me."

"That's what you think?" Nick crossed his arms, and she couldn't avoid staring a little.

The man was built. His arms were the size of her thighs.

If I had to guess, I'd say he was upset that your search this morning didn't find anything to charge Rance with."

Lauren popped out from the back, holding her purse. "I'm ready to go."

Nick nodded to her then turned back to Harmony. "For the record, just because we didn't find anything doesn't mean Rance is innocent. There was enough evidence for the judge to sign off on that warrant. Keep that in mind as you're dating Rance. If anyone is exploiting their power, it's you."

Harmony threw down her towel. "What the hell does that mean?"

"Tell me you aren't dating Rance only to get to Harvey. He asked you not to date him, and you don't like being told what to do."

Harmony moved past Nick to wipe down a table. The last thing she needed was for him to read her lie. "He's never been bothered by someone I've dated before. Why would he be now?"

Nick sighed. "Why don't you ask him? Come on, Lauren, let's go."

Ask him? What if Lauren was right and he had been interrupted. What else would he have said?

In all the years she'd known him, he'd only had one serious relationship. In high school. After that ended, he'd sworn off relationships, and for the last ten years, he'd kept his word.

Unlike Harmony, who'd been in one serious relationship after another, until a couple of years ago.

She'd finally seen the pattern. Always choosing men who needed to be saved but didn't want saving. Of course, she was drawn to that because it justified keeping her emotions to herself. She'd never loved any of those men.

After taking some time to herself, she'd put herself back out there and discovered that all the single men had coupled up. The problem with life in a small town. But then Rance came along, with his good looks and manners.

It turned out he was too much of a gentleman. They were two dates in, and all he'd done was kiss her cheek. Though if she were being honest, she didn't want more. Not with him. Whenever she closed her eyes, it was Chase she imagined kissing her.

Why was it so hard to find a man who could kiss her like he meant it? Was that really so impossible to find? But Chase had kissed like he meant it. And lately he has been acting like a jealous boyfriend. That had to mean something. She knew what she had to do. After she closed the diner tonight, she'd find him and hash this out. Her stomach churned as she imagined that conversation.

The bell over the door jingled, and Harmony glanced up.

"Good afternoon, Ms. Finkle. Late lunch today?" she asked.

The woman shuffled past the tables.

Ms. Finkle was the oldest town resident. She knew everyone and everything. What she didn't know, she tended to make up. Harmony had grown closer to the old woman since hearing Nick's nearly daily stories of rescuing her cat. She'd made a point to bring her a pie now and again. Their conversations had become a highlight she looked forward to.

"No lunch. I'm here for a pie. I've been craving your apple pie, so I decided I'd just come and get me one."

How long had it been since she'd brought her a pie? Guilt gnawed at her.

"I'm so sorry. I meant to come by before now."

Ms. Finkle placed her hand on Harmony's arm. "Now, don't apologize. It isn't your responsibility to keep my pie cravings satisfied. Besides, I know exactly why you've been busy, and I must say I approve. Mr. Rodney's grandson has grown into one fine specimen. I recall him being a bit of a string bean. Looks like college was good for him."

"Well, a lot of boys do fill out in college."

"I'm surprised how light his hair has gotten, but I know some men these days change their hair color. Normally, I'd find that off-putting in a man, but that body more than makes up for it." Ms. Finkle winked. "With a body like that, he must know what he's doing in the bedroom, right?"

Holy shit. Did Ms. Finkle just ask how Rance was in the bedroom? Harmony could feel the tell-tale warmth spreading up her neck to her face. Wait, his hair had gotten light?

"Sorry to embarrass you, dear. I'm just trying to live vicariously and all that. I'm too old to participate in those kinds of shenanigans anymore."

"Well, there's nothing to share. We haven't even kissed. I mean he kisses me on the check after each date. What do you mean you are surprised by how light his hair is?"

"When he was a boy, his hair was nearly black, just like his mother's. But you know, things change as you get older. Now what is this about him kissing you on the cheek? How many dates?"

"Two."

"Oh, honey. That's not good."

"Tell me about it," Harmony said under her breath.

Ms. Finkle shook her head. "No. You're young. You shouldn't settle for anything less than tear-your-clothes-off attraction."

Harmony made her way behind the counter and pulled an apple pie out of the cooler. "I would love that, but there aren't many single men in this town. I'm lucky if I feel any chemistry.

She set the pie next to the register and rang it up.

"Oh dear. You are way too young to be so cynical."

Harmony slumped back and leaned against the back counter. "I'm not cynical, just realistic."

Ms. Finkle paid for the pie and was almost to the door when she turned back. "You owe it to yourself to make sure you're not missing out on something with the right man. Don't settle, Harmony."

The bell jingled above the door as she left.

Harmony stood there, staring at the empty diner, with the old woman's words playing in her head.

Don't settle.

Maybe after tonight she wouldn't have to.

The bell jingled, and Harmony continued to set utensils and napkins on the table in front of her. "You can have a seat anywhere. I'll be right with you."

She'd been working at the diner for so long, everything felt mechanical. Nothing like when she was taking photos. Just thinking about the Jameson wedding last weekend made her giddy. It was probably a combination of doing what she loved and the ability to get out of town.

Then her mind drifted back to Chase. He used to go with her on shoots, if his schedule allowed. Until about ten months ago when, all of a sudden, he was always busy on the weekends.

Having him there to help and share in the

festivities had always been her favorite part of it all. They had a running joke about what they would want, or not want, at their wedding.

Yes, they'd joked about getting married. They agreed if they were still single when they turned forty, they would get married. It would be a small wedding, in a barn decorated with lights and white flowers. She would walk down the aisle to the *Ghostbusters* song, because he used to sing it to her in the seventh grade when he was bragging about something or other.

She had memories of a scrawny Chase jumping in front of her in the halls of their middle school, busting out, "Who you gonna call? Chase Harvey!" and he would point his thumbs at himself as if that made it cooler. He was such a dork.

He wasn't that scrawny kid anymore. No, since he'd befriended Nick, he'd been working out, and it was noticeable. She had such a hard time not staring at his arms whenever he took off his jacket.

"Hi, can I get a soda? Lemon lime flavor, please?" a woman's voice asked.

Harmony jumped. She'd already forgotten that someone had come in. She really needed to learn to be more aware of her surroundings.

"Sure thing."

She filled up a glass with ice and soda, then spun around to face a young woman who looked familiar. The woman had long, red hair.

Another redhead in town? Wait.

"Bella Daniel?"

"Yes, that's right."

The soda fell out of Harmony's hands and crashed to the ground, sending glass skittering everywhere.

What the hell? Harvey had said this woman was missing, but she was here now and looked fine.

"I'm sorry. Let me clean that up," Harmony said as she gritted her teeth. Bella was never missing.

"How did you know my name?" Bella asked.

Harmony stood up. "You're Mr. Rodney's caretaker, right? You were reported missing to the police."

Harvey wouldn't lie about that, would he? No, he'd had a search warrant. And Nick said there was evidence.

"No, I *was* his caretaker. But not anymore. And obviously, I'm not missing. I went on vacation. Now I'm back. Why would someone think I'm missing? Oh my God, was it Mr. Rodney? He gets so confused."

Harmony collapsed into the chair next to Bella. The woman shifted in her seat to face Harmony, and she caught the faint smell of cigarettes and vanilla. Harmony's eyes were drawn to her purse, then her shoes. Both were from a high-end designer. Maybe she should consider getting into caretaking, if it paid that well.

"Your parents filed a missing person report. You've been gone nearly two weeks."

Bella's hands went to her mouth. "My parents filed a report? Shit. I had no idea they would do that."

Harmony nodded, still trying to wrap her head around this. "They said you normally spoke to them, and you hadn't."

Bella rolled her eyes. "Ugh. No, they called me every week and insisted I come over every Sunday. When I would tell them I needed space, they'd show up at my apartment anyway. They're suffocating. That's one of the main reasons I got a new cell phone and number."

Harmony couldn't help but feel a pang of jealousy. Her parents had made it clear as soon as she turned eighteen, they planned to resume the life of traveling they used to have. But once she was sixteen, they'd decided she was adult enough to be on her own and had taken off to Europe for months at a time.

That's when she became popular at high school. Once word spread her parents were never around, there was a party at her house every weekend. To be honest, she spread the word. The rest of the week she had to live in that house by herself. But on the weekends, she was surrounded by friends. She would have traded all of that if her parents had wanted to spend time with her.

It was Chase who'd gotten her through those times. He had stayed by her side no matter what.

Harmony tried to sympathize with Bella. She needed to learn why she left. "It sounds like they're controlling."

"They are. That's why, when Mr. Rodney's grandson gave me all that severance pay, I flew to Florida with my friend, and we got on the next available cruise to the Caribbean. It was so much fun!"

"Severance pay?"

"Yes, Rance said he was going to take care of his grandfather now and gave me a generous severance payment."

"And you just left without telling anyone?"

"Well, I told my friend, since he went with me. But I didn't tell my parents. They would have tried to stop me and given me a guilt trip about spending money when I don't have a job. They're a buzzkill."

Well, they would have had a point. But Harmony didn't say that out loud.

"I should go. It sounds like my parents are worried about me." Bella stood and left.

It wasn't until she was gone that Harmony realized she'd never gotten the woman another soda.

Nick entered the diner.

"You just missed Bella Daniel." Harmony stood and carefully walked around the broken glass.

His head whipped toward the door. "What?"

"Bella Daniel, the missing caretaker. She just got back from vacation with her friend. You know, the one who was never missing?"

Nick gave her that same half-angry look Chase had. "I've got to go find her."

Then he threw the diner door open hard, making it bang against the back of a booth as he left.

Chapter Eleven

"Can you believe that, after that, she followed the douchebag back into his house?" Chase slurred his words while waving his beer bottle around. "She remembers the damn kiss, but still wants that dickhead. Fuck." He slammed the bottle onto the bar, surprised it didn't break.

Zach put a mug of something in front of him. "Drink that."

He tried to focus on it but struggled. "What is it?"

"Coffee. You're drunk. Now sober up." Zach walked away, staring at his phone.

Before he could respond, he heard Zach talking on the phone.

"Yeah, he's drunk. Can you come by? Thanks." Zach pocketed the device.

"Who was that? You didn't call Harmony, did

you?" he demanded.

"Nick."

A gush of cold air pulled his attention to the front door. Scott Fisher walked in with Marjorie on his arm.

Scott fucking Fisher. The guy snapped his fingers and got whatever he wanted.

The guy had dated Marjorie in high school, but then dumped her when he went off to college. She pined for him for years, even while he was dating Lauren. Finally, last year, he took her back.

She hadn't been the only one trying to get with Scott. The man always had a string of women after him. For the life of him, Chase didn't know why. Scott was an asshole.

Their feelings for each other were mutual.

"Hey, Harvey," Scott called from the other end of the bar. "I can't say I'm surprised to see you in here drinking alone."

"Scott, leave him alone," Zach ordered.

"Oh, no worries, Zach. I saw Harmony out with that new guy. I know exactly why Harvey is in here, drinking. He can't even begin to compete with a guy like that."

"Get out," Zach shouted.

"*What?* I'm an upstanding member of this town. You can't throw me out!"

"I can and I just did. Now go." Zach came around the bar.

"Throwing a Fisher out? That's not going to be good for business, Zach. Why don't you rethink this? My family made this goddamn town." Scott was puffed up like a damn parrot.

Marjorie wrapped her hands around Zach's arm, and pouted as she looked up into his eyes. "Let us stay, Zach."

"It's okay, Marj," Scott soothed with false bravado. "Harvey needs privacy to cry into his beer. His woman left him for some man who looks like he just walked off a movie set. Real nice guy, too."

Something broke inside Chase, and before he had time to think, he shoved Scott up against the wall.

Zach pulled him off before he could land a punch.

"Leave now," Zach commanded. "Or Nick will deal with you."

Scott's nose flared.

The mention of Nick's name was always enough to get him to leave. This time was no different.

"Marj, let's go."

Chase made his way back to the bar. Wrapping his hands around the mug of coffee, he let the warmth soothe him.

"Scott's right, you know," he said.

Zach scoffed. "Scott's not right about anything."

"No, he is. Rance does look like a damn movie star. And even though I know in my gut something isn't right with the guy, his record is clean. Everyone loves him."

"If something isn't right, you'll figure it out."

Chase drank his coffee, pondering his friend's words.

"Hey, where'd your accent go?"

Zach laughed. "I told you, it only comes out when I'm excited."

"What happened?" Nick asked as he slid onto the barstool next to him.

Without even asking, Zach filled a glass from the tap, and set the beer in front of Nick. "Harmony told him she wanted distance. He's been in here drinking for two hours."

After finishing off the coffee, Chase shoved the mug down the bar. "Scott was here, and he said some things to me."

"Scott's an asshole. Don't listen to him."

"No, he was right."

"Scott was trying to rile you up. It worked." Zach arched an eyebrow as he stared Chase down. "I had to break the two of them up," he explained to Nick.

"Shit, Harvey, you're a police officer. You can't get involved in barfights. You'll lose your job. What if Scott reports you?"

"He won't," Zach said.

"How are you so sure?" Nick snapped.

Zach chuckled. "I said your name. That boy almost pissed himself. What the hell did you do to him, anyway?"

Nick shook his head and took a drink of his beer. "Nothing."

Zach grinned "Liar. Remind me to never piss you off."

Chase was finally starting to see straight again. He scanned the pub, making note of a few patrons filling the booths near the back.

"I overheard something you might be interested in." Nick took another drink. "But you have to swear to keep it to yourself."

Chase snorted. There wasn't anything he was interested in tonight except forgetting his feelings for Harmony.

Nick forged ahead anyway. "Harmony stopped by, and I don't think she realized I was home. Lauren asked her how it was going with Rance."

"Stop. I don't want to hear this." The idea of that man touching Harmony was too much. He didn't need those images in his mind.

"Yes, you do. Harmony said she was ready to scream. All the man has done is kiss her cheek and ask about Lauren and Lauren's step family, the Chanlers. Well, when he isn't talking about himself."

"They haven't even kissed?"

"Nope."

They must have been on at least three dates by now, if his calculations were accurate. How could a man date Harmony, and *not* touch her? Damn, she was sexy as hell, and she didn't hide the fact she loved sex.

"Why is he dating her?"

Zach laughed. "You know some men aren't as into sex. Or maybe he's old-fashioned."

Both Nick and Chase turned to him.

"You're not into sex, Zach?" Chase teased.

His friend's hands went up. "Hey now, I'm just saying some guys. If it were me, I would've done a lot more than kiss her by now."

"Yeah, you would have held her hand too?" Nick taunted through his grin.

"Fuck off." Zach walked out from behind the bar and headed to the booths to check on his customers.

"What I'm wondering is why this guy is asking about Lauren. I don't like it." Nick leaned in and whispered. "William owed a lot of money. What if this guy is here to collect?"

William, Lauren's stepbrother, had died the year before, after taking a large loan from Carl Marucam. After Carl's visit, they'd hoped any dealings with him were over.

"You think he works for Carl?" Chase slurred. Shit, he needed the coffee to kick in.

Nick arched a brow. "Not sure. You feeling okay?"

"Getting there. Back to Rance, I thought he was some big businessman from New York. It's unlikely he's associated with Carl. As much as I want to find something wrong with the guy, I can't."

"I requested a background check on him just to be safe."

"The chief was okay with that?"

Nick shook his head. "I didn't ask the chief. I went through my friend with the county again."

Danielle Pays

Chase reached out and patted Nick on the shoulder. "Well, thank you for this. I've felt something wasn't right since he got here. Zach's convinced the only thing wrong is that he's dating Harmony. But if your gut tells you something is off too, then maybe I'm not going crazy."

Nick finished his beer. "No, you are, but that's a separate issue." His lips quirked in a small grin before he turned serious again. "There's more. I wasn't going to tell you, but seeing the condition you're in..."

"What?"

"Lauren asked Harmony if she really wanted to sleep with Rance."

Chase waved his hand in the air. "Stop. I can't hear this."

"Harmony said no."

His gaze jerked to Nick's. "She said *no*? Then why the hell is she dating him?"

Nick shrugged again. "I dunno. But let's go."

"Where?"

"I'm going to walk you home."

Turning, Nick shouted, "Bye, Zach. Thanks for the beer!"

Zach turned and waved. He was leaning against a booth, talking to two brunettes. One had her hand on his arm, touching his tattoos.

"I wonder how many women he gets just because of those tattoos," Chase said.

Nick laughed. "We can tease him about that tomorrow."

Once outside, the wind whipped up, and damn it was chilly. They made it down the block, but just before they turned, Rance came out of the hardware store.

Shit. Not who Chase wanted to see.

"Officers. Good evening."

"Good evening to you too," Nick was pouring on his charm. "What are you getting at the hardware store?"

Rance smiled. "Duct tape, garbage bags, bleach. You know, for all those girls who have gone missing. Oh wait, Bella wasn't missing, was she? Yeah, I saw her coming out of the diner earlier. That was some great police work there, Harvey."

Nick stepped between him and Rance. "That's uncalled for. I was hoping we could put that behind us and move on."

"Hard to put it behind you when the town police are looking to frame you for crimes that didn't even occur."

"That's not what happened."

Rance crossed his arms and stared at Chase. "I get it. Your life sucks. I won your girl. But from what I hear, you had years, and didn't do jack-shit. Lucky for me, she was primed and ready to go, if you know what I mean." Rance winked at Chase.

No one talked about Harmony like that.

Before Nick could stop him, Chase stepped around the detective and punched Rance as hard as he could.

Rance hadn't been expecting it and didn't do anything to block the punch. The man went down, and his bag fell to the side, spilling its contents.

"Shit, Harvey." Nick shook his head. "How are we going to explain this?"

"I'll tell the chief what he said about Harmony. Dunin sees her like a daughter. He'll know I was justified."

"You *punched* me? What the hell?" Rance was rolling on the ground, rubbing his temple.

Nick bent down and retrieved Rance's items and put them back in the bag. "Look at this. He really did buy duct tape. But he also bought a box of latex gloves. What project is this for?"

"None of your business." Rance ripped the bag out of Nick's hands. "And thank you, Harvey. I can't wait to tell Harmony you punched me with no provocation. I bet she will feel really sympathetic when she finds out her crazy ex-friend went ballistic." He leaned in. "I bet she will do *anything* to make me feel better."

Chase raised his fist again, but this time, Nick was there to stop him.

"Leave. Now," Nick ordered.

"Have a pleasant night, Officers. I know I will." Rance winked at Harvey before turning the corner and leaving.

Chapter Twelve

Harmony stared at her phone. Her plans to talk to Chase last night were ruined when she couldn't get an older couple to leave the diner so she could close up. By the time she'd gotten home, it was too late to call him.

Before she chickened out, she sent him a text.

Can we talk tonight?

His response was immediate.

Chase: *Yes.*

Good. She couldn't wait any longer. But first she had to deal with Rance. Her jaw clenched at the knock on her door. Not exactly the reaction she should have when her date was there to pick her up. Which was exactly why she was ending it with Rance tonight. It wasn't right to string him along.

Last night, it had hit her. Nick was right. She was only dating Rance to get to Chase. It wasn't something she wanted to admit, but there it was. There were no sparks with Rance. He had to know it too. Hell, he hadn't even tried to kiss her.

Plus, if he asked any more questions about Lauren, she was going to cause the man harm. Yes, Lauren was blond and beautiful. But she was taken, and dating Harmony wasn't going to get him any closer to her.

When he'd suggested again they double date with Nick and Lauren, and play cards at Lauren's place, she knew he was more interested in Lauren than her. And now she knew, even if Chase didn't feel the same, there was no place for Rance in her life.

Taking a deep breath, she reached for the doorknob, and swung open the door.

"Harmony, I'm glad you want to talk. I was on my way here because I have to tell you. It's important."

Chase stood on her doorstep, looking like he hadn't slept in days.

"What happened to you?" she reached out and stroked his cheek.

His eyes were red-rimmed; his hair looked like he hadn't combed it.

"Aren't those the clothes you wore yesterday?"

Then she noticed his hand. His knuckles were cut up and bruised.

Instinctively, she reached for it. "Come with me."

He followed her inside, kicking the door closed behind him. She led him to her bathroom and instructed him to rinse his hand under the faucet.

"No, that will hurt."

She quirked her brow. "Officer, you can't handle a little water on your cut?"

He rolled his eyes and rinsed his knuckles. "Shit, that stings."

"Sit." She pointed to the toilet.

He obeyed, and she got to work on his hand. First, she dried it off, then she found some antibiotic cream, and put in on before putting a Band-Aid on each knuckle.

"Fluorescent Band-Aids?" He inspected her handiwork, and even she had to admit, it looked bad. But at least he wouldn't get infected.

"Yep." She put her supplies away in one of the drawers under the sink.

"Thank you," he said.

"What did you punch? And why do you look like you were up all night?"

"I was up all night drinking 'cause the woman I want doesn't want me. I punched Rance."

She swore her heart stopped beating. He wanted her?

"The woman you want?"

That's not what he'd said at Mr. Rodney's house. But maybe Lauren was right, there had been more.

Using his non-injured hand, he pushed some of her hair behind her ear. "Yeah, I tried to tell her, but she walked away with another guy."

"Chase, what are you saying?"

There was another knock at the door.

"Are you expecting someone?" he asked.

"That's Rance. Um, he's here to pick me up for a date."

Chase swallowed, and his gaze dropped to the floor.

She'd never seen him like this.

"Why did you punch him?" she asked softly.

He lifted his head, and those beautiful brown eyes bored into hers. "He said things about you. Things he shouldn't have said. No one talks about you like that."

Her Chase, always protecting her. Even when she told him to stay away. But what could Rance have said? He'd been nothing but a gentleman.

"What did he say?"

The knocking on the door grew louder.

"Ask Nick, he was there too. Thanks for the Band-Aids. I'll let myself out so you can have that date." He stood and moved past her.

"Chase, wait, there's something I need to tell you."

He kept moving toward the door. "Doesn't matter. You have a date to get to."

By the time she caught up to him, he'd already opened the door. Standing on the other side and wearing a stunned look was Rance. His right eye was black and blue, which somehow only magnified how blue his eyes really were.

He took in Chase's rumpled clothes, messed hair, and bandaged hand. Harmony could practically see the steam coming out of Rance's ears. He was pissed.

"It's not what it looks like," Chase said.

"No?" he asked through clenched teeth.

"No, asshole." Chase balled his fists. "I just came by to tell her I punched you, and *why*."

Rance visibly flinched.

Chase turned to Harmony, "Do you want me to stay? He looks angry."

She quickly grabbed her keys from the table by the door. "We are all leaving."

After Chase stepped out, she followed and locked up the door to her apartment. Then she pushed past them and walked to the courtyard area that all the apartments faced.

It had a few benches and a water fountain. The sound of the fountain was peaceful, and on sunny days, she liked to read on the benches. And on nights like these, she appreciated the bright outdoor lighting. It was a small apartment building, and usually had a unit or two available. Fisher Springs was a small town, after all.

She sat down on a bench, then looked up to see Rance standing next to her, and Chase walking away.

"Chase."

He turned but continued to walk backward. "Enjoy your date." Then he strode off.

Rance wore a smug smile as he watched. Harmony was so tired of feeling like a pawn in the middle of their pissing match.

"We need to talk," she said to Rance.

He sat next to her and took her hands in his. "Look, I don't know what Chase told you about last night, but you have to know he was drunk. Nick had to intervene once he hit me. He was out of his mind."

Chase was a lot of things, but she knew he would never hit someone without provocation.

"What did you say to him?"

"Baby, I didn't say anything. The man just went off."

Pulling her hands from his, she scooted a few inches away. "If I ask Nick, he'll say the same thing?"

Rance laughed. "I doubt it. They're best friends. Of course Nick would lie for him."

She could see that Rance was lying. He had a tell, for crying out loud. Why hadn't she seen it before? Time to test it.

"You didn't say anything bad about me?"

"Baby, no, of course not."

If she wasn't looking closely, she would have missed it. But the corner of his mouth ticked up, just a little.

"Do you want to sleep with Lauren?"

His eyes widened. "No."

No tick. Interesting. Then why did he ask so many questions about her? And why did he want to go on that double date?

It didn't matter. She had to end this.

"We need to stop seeing each other. You're a nice guy, but there's no chemistry between us."

Without warning, Rance pulled her as close to

him as he could and kissed her.

The entire act took her by surprise. She stared at him with her lips tightly pressed together. His eyes were closed, and his tongue licked her bottom lip.

Instead of chemistry, she felt gross. This was wrong. This wasn't anything like her kiss with Chase.

His tongue pushed at her lips.

No. She had to stop this.

She turned her face, which resulted in him licking her cheek.

He huffed in disgust and let her go. "We can have chemistry. You just have to try."

Try? What the hell? Now it was her fault they didn't have chemistry? Who the hell was this guy? Clearly, his nice guy act was just that, an act.

"It's over. Please leave." She stood and walked back to her apartment. She didn't hear footsteps behind her, which was a good thing.

By the time she made it to her door, she turned around, and he was gone.

Locking all the locks on her door, she peeked out the peephole. She was sure he was gone, but she felt uneasy.

She grabbed her phone off the table and sent Chase a text.

Harmony: *The thing I needed to tell you was I was ending it with Rance. We're done. Can we talk?*

Chase: *I'm on my way back.*

For the second time in her life, she was nervous to see Chase. But unlike the time in his kitchen, they couldn't ignore what was going on between them.

After waiting several minutes, she paced her living room. Chase had just left. How far could he have gotten? He should have been here by now.

Impatient, she walked out into the courtyard.

"Harmony?"

She turned around at the familiar voice. *Chase.*

Before she could say a word, he was right there, his hand around her waist. She wrapped her arms around his neck and took comfort from his embrace.

"I'm sorry I didn't say anything the morning after our kiss," she stared into his eyes. "After you jumped out of bed in the middle of it, I thought you thought it was a mistake. I waited for you to bring it up, and when you didn't, I was crushed. I wouldn't have asked you to kiss me if I hadn't wanted it. I've wanted you for a long time, but I was afraid to ruin our friendship."

Chase's grip tightened. Heat emanated from his eyes. Before she said another word, his lips collided with hers.

There was nothing sweet about this kiss, and she felt the months of pent-up emotions as he kissed her deeper. She wanted to pull him into her apartment and tell him to never stop. But he must have realized where they were, because he leaned back and smiled at her.

"I want to do this right. Let me take you on a date. I'll pick you up, and we'll go to dinner."

"I get to see the suave Chase?"

His head fell back as he laughed. "No, you get to

see the smitten Chase."

The sincerity in his eyes cracked her heart open a little more.

.

Chapter Thirteen

"You and Harvey are really dating now?" Kate asked as she passed by in the kitchen.

"Yep. He insists we take it slow. I pointed out to him that we've known each other since middle school, but he said he wants to take me out on proper dates."

As much as Harmony was ready to jump his bones, she understood why he was insisting they wait.

"He said he wants us both to be sure before we cross a line we can't uncross."

Kate frowned at her. "If this doesn't work out, and next month, he's dating that new blond woman who just moved to town, you'll be all right with that?"

The 'new blond woman' Kate was referring to was a masseuse who'd moved to Davenport and started working at Mindy's salon with Bridgette.

She squeezed her eyes shut. Now she was imagining Bridgette's hands on Chase's ass the other night. Would he have taken her home if Harmony hadn't been sitting right there?

"Hey, take it easy on the napkins, would you?"

She glanced up to find Kate grinning at her, and a bunch of ruffled napkins angrily stuffed inside the container.

"No, I wouldn't be all right."

"I can see that. You two need to admit that you are both in too deep already."

"Tell *him* that. Honestly, between that and Rance not so much as kissing me, I'm starting to get a complex!"

Male laughter came from behind her. Harmony froze. They'd been alone in the diner…

She swiveled around, wondering what humiliation she might have to endure now. *Please don't be Chase.*

Standing in the doorway was a man she'd never seen before. Likely an out-of-towner who was only stopping through. His dark hair curled down to his shoulders from the beanie he was wearing, and his eyes were dark as they stared her down. His jeans were ripped in a designer way, and his button-up shirt stretched over his broad chest and looked like his biceps might rip through the fabric à la The Hulk style. Near his hands, part of a tattoo poked out of his shirt sleeve. She wondered if his entire arm was covered. What was it with hot men coming to town lately?

"I'm not surprised Rance couldn't deliver. My cousin wouldn't know what to do with a woman even if he had a diagram. Now, I, on the other hand..." The man walked closer until he was inches from Harmony, "I wouldn't hesitate to give you multiple mind-blowing orgasms."

The man oozed sex, and last week, Harmony would have been wet with need from such a come-on. But after the way Chase had been teasing and torturing her with his holdout methods, he was all she wanted.

"Damn," Kate said. "If she's not interested, I am."

While her friend was standing there with a puddle of drool pouring out of her mouth, Harmony caught the important part of that sentence.

"Your cousin?"

"Yep, but don't tell him I'm here. I was just coming in to get a pie to surprise him and my granddad."

Kate stepped between them and placed her hands on his chest. "Oh." Harmony swore she saw her friend squeeze just a little. "I can get that for you. What kind of pie did you want? Oh, is that a tattoo on your chest?"

When Harmony glanced over, the man unbuttoned a couple of buttons, further revealing what appeared to be a large dragon splaying over his pec.

"Yes. You like?"

"I do. Now the pie..."

The man's gaze moved to Kate's as he smiled. "I'd like your cherry pie."

Oh no he didn't.

Kate staggered a little as she moved to the counter, but Harmony wondered if she really would have fallen for this a few weeks ago. The man knew he was hot, and he was using it. Right now, not only did she not find that sexy, but it annoyed the hell out of her.

"Okay, you can stop with the cheesy lines."

"Harmony!" Kate hissed at her. She handed him the pie, and he handed her a twenty-dollar bill.

"Keep the change," he purred. Then, turning to Harmony, "No wonder my cousin didn't do it for you. All he has for game are his lines. You look like you need more mental stimulation, Harmony."

She almost forgot she was wearing a name tag on her uniform.

"And your name is?"

The bell over the door jingled as Ms. Finkle walked in.

"I'm Jace Callahan." He held out his hand to shake hers.

Before Harmony could even consider shaking the man's hand, Ms. Finkle had her hands on his arm.

"Little Jace, is that you? I haven't seen you since you were a tiny thing. Wow, you are all grown up. And you have so many tattoos." Ms. Finkle frowned.

Harmony coughed to hide her laugh. Ms. Finkle was not hiding her distaste.

The man turned and stared down at Ms. Finkle.

"You probably don't remember me," the woman said. "I was good friends with your grandmother, Maria. What is your mom's name?"

The man's gaze met Harmony's.

"This is Ms. Finkle," she told him. "She's harmless."

He nodded. "My mother is Laura. Now, if you ladies will excuse me, I need to go find that good for nothing cousin of mine."

Jace flashed them all a smile, showing off a dimple on his right cheek, and Harmony swore the light twinkled off his too white teeth like in a toothpaste commercial. Then he patted Ms. Finkle's hands as he slowly pried them off his arm and made his way out the door.

Ms. Finkle's eyebrows shot up. "Did he say Laura?"

"Yes, he did," Kate said as she resumed stocking the napkin holders.

"That's odd. I don't recall anyone named Laura in that family."

"Maybe someone married a Laura," Harmony offered.

"No, I got to know the family quite well. Maria was one of my best friends, and my son was good friends with their oldest son David. I've been to all the weddings. There's no Laura."

The hair on Harmony's neck stood up. Damn, Chase had her suspicious of everything.

"Do you think he's lying?" Harmony asked.

Kate snort laughed.

"What?" Harmony asked.

"Having an officer for a best friend has really

warped your mind," Kate said as she placed the full napkin holders on each table. "Did you guys ever think perhaps Jace came from an affair?"

Harmony fell into a chair. "That's possible, I guess."

They both watched as Ms. Finkle shook her head.

"No, I remember little Jace. I swear he was Susan's boy." When she glanced up and saw Harmony and Kate staring at her, she waved her hands. "Let's not talk about that. Maybe I remembered wrong. I have been having some memory troubles lately. That's actually why I'm here. I'd like a piece of your blueberry pie, please."

"Pie helps your memory?" Kate asked. "That's enough reason for me to eat it."

"Honey, not just any pie. I read blueberries are good for the brain. But you're young. You shouldn't need help there yet."

Harmony laughed. "She needs help remembering not to go after the bad boys."

Kate threw a towel at Harmony. She ducked, and it landed in a chair.

"You should try it sometime, Harmony. The bad boys are fun."

"You know what?" Ms. Finkle went on, seemingly oblivious to the girls' fun. "I'll consult my yearbooks when I get home. Otherwise the names will just drive me crazy." She took a seat at a table. "I wouldn't want anyone trying to con Mr. Rodney."

"Why would anyone con that nice old man?" Kate asked.

"Well, for his money of course. Harmony, dear, could I have a glass of milk too?"

Mr. Rodney had money? His house was in decent condition, but nothing else about his life indicated he was rich. Maybe Ms. Finkle was just talking. She liked to do that. But it wouldn't hurt to find out more.

She grabbed a plate and pulled the blueberry pie from the cooler. After plating a piece and pouring a glass of milk, she brought it to Ms. Finkle and sat down next to her.

"I'll be right back," Kate said as she stared out the window. When she glanced at Harmony to make sure it was all right, she grinned. "You know I have a weakness for bad boys."

"Go. It's fine."

Kate practically ran out of the diner.

"I wonder what has the girl in such a rush," Ms. Finkle said.

Harmony leaned to the left and found Kate standing in front of the store across the street, talking to Jace. He towered over her, and with his long hair and leather jacket, he screamed bad boy.

"A man." No point in telling Ms. Finkle which man, because that would take her off topic. Keeping the woman focused was hard enough.

Ms. Finkle took a bite and smiled. "You make the best pies. You really should open a bakery."

"Thank you. I enjoy making them. It's relaxing."

Baking was relaxing, but it wasn't her passion. Now maybe *photographing* pies...

"Now tell me, why do you think Mr. Rodney has money?" she prodded.

Ms. Finkle wiped her mouth on a napkin. "Mr. Rodney inherited his dad's fortune about forty years ago. That's how he paid for his kids to go to the best schools. He just keeps it tied up in investments, but he told me he gave each child a lump sum to give them a head start in life, and when he dies, the rest will go to some charity."

A fortune going to charity. Well, that would be motive right there.

Kate walked back into the diner with the biggest grin. Harmony arched her brow, but her coworker just shrugged.

Kate went through men faster than Harmony went through chocolate. And that was fast.

"How much do I owe you, dear?" Ms. Finkle was holding a five-dollar bill and digging in her purse for more.

"Nothing. This was my treat."

"You can't keep doing that. You need to save up for that bakery you're going to open."

"Actually, I'm working on my photography business. I've done a few weddings."

Ms. Finkle's eyes lit up. "Weddings? How lovely. Do you photograph pets?"

She knew where this was going, and she needed

to shut it down fast. One photo session with the Finkle cat, and she'd be known only as a pet photographer.

"No, sorry. I have allergies. Only weddings."

"Darn. Well, if you hear of anyone who photographs cats, let me know."

The woman was up and at the door faster than you'd expect for her age. "Good luck with your officer friend, dear."

"How'd you know?" Harmony asked.

"Hush. I know everything in this town." The woman grinned at her. "Actually, I just happened to be driving past a certain apartment building at the right time. You two look good together. I'll see you soon."

"See you soon," Harmony said.

The familiar heat crept up her neck to her cheeks. The idea that Ms. Finkle saw that kiss with Chase felt wrong. It was like kissing in front of her mother.

Once Ms. Finkle left, Kate sat down with Harmony. Business had really slowed down after the holidays. She hoped they got more customers soon, or Logan might have to make some cuts.

"What happened when you went across the street?"

Kate hadn't stopped smiling since she came back.

"You know what happened. He's picking me up after my shift."

"Be careful. I have a funny feeling about him."

Kate laughed. "You sound like Officer Harvey. Maybe he's been rubbing off on you more than you let on."

Chapter Fourteen

Chase rubbed his palms on his jeans as he paced in front of Nick's desk.

"Sit the fuck down. You're driving me crazy," his friend snapped at him.

Chase sat in the chair across from the detective. His leg was bouncing a mile a minute.

"You're vibrating the whole damn place. Why the hell are you so nervous? You've known Harmony most of your life."

"Yeah, but she was always my friend Harmony. Now she's *Harmony*. You know?"

Nick leaned back and grinned. "You got a real way with words there, Harvey. You going to woo her like that?"

"What the hell, man? I thought you were my friend. Clearly, I need to be talked off the ledge."

The door flew open and made a loud bang as it

hit the wall. Both snapped their heads to look.

"Sorry, the wind caught it." Lauren wore a sheepish grin as she pushed it closed.

Chase knew very well that she had been with Harmony, helping her get ready for their date. Their first official date.

Damn, he'd never been so nervous for anything. Not even his academy exam. He'd known he'd ace that. Usually, he was confident with women too. But then again, his longest relationship outside of high school had lasted about two weeks. And that was a week longer than he'd wanted. He'd never been nervous around a woman because he'd never really cared if they stuck around.

But Harmony was different. She was everything to him.

And Harmony had been what Lauren referred to as a 'serial monogamist'. But she'd been single since before their kiss. Until Rance.

Thank fuck she kicked him to the curb.

Now, here he was. He finally had a chance, and he was nervous as hell he was going to fuck it up.

"Wow, are you sweating?" Lauren asked.

"He's nervous as shit." Nick grinned.

Lauren turned to her boyfriend and propped a hand on her hip. "Shit doesn't get nervous."

"Are you sure?"

These two. He'd never seen a couple bicker so much. But it wasn't really bickering. It was their weird version of foreplay. At first, he'd found it entertaining.

Now he found it annoying. Well, more like he wished he had someone to go back and forth with like that.

"I'll deal with you later," Lauren said to Nick. "Harvey, why are you so nervous?"

Well, he might as well be honest. Maybe she would have some advice.

"I'm scared I'm going to fuck this up."

She walked to his chair and rubbed his shoulder, which caused Nick to glare at him. "Why do you think you would?"

Well, damn. He should have known Lauren would want to talk it out. Nick would just tell him 'don't fuck it up,' and be done. But if he did screw this up, he needed Lauren on his side, so he might as well be honest.

"I haven't really seriously dated anyone since high school."

She waved her hand in the air. "I know your history. Harmony filled me in."

"Oh."

"She's not going to hold that against you, Harvey."

"Good. But there's more."

Lauren pulled up a chair and flopped down. "Please don't tell me you've been with any hookers. I'd have to stop the date right now, if that's the case."

"What? No. Why would you think that?"

Lauren looked at Nick.

"Well, you did just give it the big build-up, 'There's more!'" Nick mimicked in his announcer voice, his hands spreading wide.

"I'm trying to pour my heart out, here, and you're being an asshole." Chase let his head fall back as he rubbed his eyes.

"Sorry, you're right. What else is there?" Lauren's hand was now on his leg, rubbing gently. That caused Chase's head to jerk up.

"Honey? Where's your hand?" Nick choked out.

Chase could see the vein bulging on Nick's forehead. Something he'd only seen twice before.

Lauren stared at her hand as if she had no control of it, then yanked it back like it was on fire. "I'm sorry. I was just trying to comfort Chase."

"Only I get that sort of comforting. Understand?"

Well, well. Nick's quite the jealous one. Chase grabbed Lauren's hand. "Don't be jealous of what we have, Nick."

His friend growled as he raised an eyebrow.

"Keep going, Chase. I like him riled up." Lauren bit her lip.

Chase dropped her hand, realizing he'd just been put in the middle of their weird foreplay.

"Dammit! I'm freaking out over here, and you two are... Do you ever think about anything but sex?"

"You're right. We're sorry. What else is there?"

Chase cleared his throat, both to ease the tension, and to shift the focus back to his problem. "I haven't really cared what women thought before. But with Harmony, I care. I mean, I *really* care. I can't lose her."

Shit, he was starting to get choked up.

"Harvey, that's so sweet."

"Yeah," Nick agreed. "You're a real—"

"No." Lauren pointed at him.

His hands flew up in the air. "What?"

"This isn't time for your usual insults. Chase needs our support."

Nick shook his head. "You kidding me? I've been his biggest supporter here."

Lauren turned to Chase. "Just be honest with Harmony like you have been with us," she urged. "She wouldn't want me to tell you this, but she's nervous too."

"Yeah?"

Lauren nodded.

Chase jumped up. "I'm gonna go now."

"Do you need some condoms?" Nick asked as he shifted in his seat to grab his wallet.

"Nick!" Lauren yelled.

Chase stared wide-eyed. "What? Shit. No! Don't be an asshole. This is a first date. Harmony isn't like that."

"First date?" Nick chuckled. "You've known each other forever. The foundation is already there. Plus, I think we can all agree you have the chemistry."

"Goodnight," Chase said pointedly.

He had to get out of there before he said something stupid, like sharing the fact he'd already bought condoms that morning. Not that it was any of their business.

He really needed to not let his mind go there. This was Harmony, and he was going to make sure they went on dates and did this right.

* * *

After knocking on her door, Chase paced the hallway outside her apartment. He'd bought flowers on his way over.

So cliché.

He thought about chucking them, but then the door opened, and with one look at Harmony, his nervousness melted away.

Harmony was stunning. Her red hair was hanging down in loose waves, and her lips appeared even fuller than normal. She wore a blue wrap dress that hugged all her curves. He'd been aware of her curves for years, but this was the first time he could openly appreciate the sight of them.

"You gonna pick your tongue up off the floor and come in?" she teased.

He chuckled. Harmony had trouble with her filter sometimes. That was one thing he'd always really liked about her. No bullshit.

"You look gorgeous," he said.

A blush popped up on her cheeks.

"Thank you."

"These are for you." He held out the flowers.

"Thank you. Come in while I put them in water."

He stepped in and surveyed the space. Nothing had changed since he'd last been here, which was a few days ago. While she was dating Rance.

He needed to get Rance off his mind. He was out of the picture now. Thank God.

When she returned, his eyes went straight to her breasts. The dress was cut low enough to show her ample cleavage.

Damn, stop staring at her like that. This is supposed to be a first date. Take it slow.

"I thought we'd go to the Italian place in Davenport," he told her.

When his gaze connected with hers, heat emanated from her eyes.

He shoved his hands in his pockets to keep from reaching out to her. But when she sashayed across the room—yes, *sashayed*, with her hips swinging—he couldn't hide his arousal.

"Damn, you're so sexy," he growled.

She grinned.

"I'm sorry. I'm trying to be a gentleman here, but I've been wanting you for so long. And that dress..."

Swing. Swing. Two more steps, and she was toe to toe with him.

"Shut up, Chase."

Before he could utter his surprise, her hands were on either side of his face, holding it while her lips crashed down on his.

The feel of her soft lips on his was even better than the last time. Her tongue swept across his bottom lip, and he opened his mouth and deepened the kiss. His arms snaked around her waist, and then one hand moved down to cup her ass. A small moan escaped her mouth.

His mind told him he should slow down, but when her lips moved to his ear, he was a goner.

He moved his hand up and cupped her breast. Then he pinched her nipple through the fabric of her dress. Harmony moaned and pulled him closer.

He was ready to toss her over his shoulder and take her to the bedroom, when his phone rang with Nick's ringtone.

His friend knew he was on this date. Why the hell would he be calling him?

"Is that Nick?"

It had been Harmony's suggestion to set Nick's contact to Eric Church's "The Outsiders." It was a running joke, since Chase had referred to Nick as an outsider when he first came to town. But Chase actually liked the song, so he went along with it. Plus, anything to annoy Nick was always a plus.

"Yeah, I'd better answer. It might be work-related."

He pulled his phone from his pocket and swiped to answer.

"It better be work-related, because I swear to God, if Nick cock-blocked me—"

Chase put his hand up, hoping to stop her from finishing that sentence.

Nick laughed through the phone. "Cock-blocked? I thought this was a first date."

"What do you want?" he snapped.

"Damn. Sorry, man. I did interrupt. I wouldn't have called, except the chief insisted. Something came up."

Chase raked his hand through his hair. "What happened?"

"Some shit went down at the high school. Chief wants us both there. Now. Sorry."

"I'm on my way."

He huffed out a sigh as he pocketed the phone. "I'm so sorry."

She wrapped her arms around his neck. "I've known you a long time. I know when you're called, you have to go."

"You know I'd rather stay here with you," he said.

"Why don't you stop by after?"

"Only if it doesn't go long," he said.

"I don't care what time it is." Her lips were back on his neck.

He took a deep breath and pulled away. "I do. I meant it when I said I want to do this right."

"You're a tease, but so am I."

She loosened the wrap on her dress just enough to expose part of her bra. It was a similar blue to the dress, and lacy.

"Damn, you're evil. A man can only take so much," he croaked out.

"That's what I'm counting on. Enjoy your call."

She winked.

He shook his head as he backed up to the door.

"I think I'll go relieve some of this pressure while you're gone." She disappeared and walked down the hallway toward her bedroom.

He stopped at the front door. Was she going to...? No. Would she?

Then he heard a vibrating sound.

No, she was just messing with him. He needed to leave.

Then he heard a moan.

Holy shit, she was! He ran his hand through his hair and got out of there.

The sooner he got to the high school, the sooner he could get back here to her.

Chapter Fifteen

Chase woke up the next day in a foul mood. He had wanted nothing more than to get back to Harmony's apartment last night. Unfortunately, the high school kids picked the worst night for one of their pranks. And they had to use actual shit, too. Even if he had gotten home earlier, he was in no condition to see Harmony. One whiff of him, and she would have kicked him out despite the fact he'd showered twice.

He checked his phone. Three texts from Nick.

Nick: *Breakfast at the diner at eight?*

He checked the time. It would be tight, but he could make it.

After another shower, he rolled into the diner just after 8 a.m. Nick was at the counter, drinking coffee, and talking to Lauren. Harmony wasn't scheduled to work until lunch, so Chase knew she wouldn't be here.

Lauren spotted him and grinned. "I heard you

had a shitty night."

"Ha-ha."

"What exactly did those kids do?" she asked as she poured him a cup of coffee.

"Thanks." He took a gulp of his coffee. "Didn't Nick fill you in?"

She frowned. "No, he said it would be better coming from you. All he would reveal is that he's calling this the Cock-Block Case. I figured it involved shit, based on how he smelled when he got home."

"Why the hell would it be better from me?" Chase eyed his friend.

Nick laughed. "I figured the name would make it obvious."

Chase let out a sigh. "Fine. Some high school kids unloaded a bunch of shit in front of their school."

"What sick kids would do that?" Nick made a face then tipped his mug of coffee to his lips.

"Farm kids. You forget where you are. They're probably immune to the stench." Chase shrugged. He hadn't been one of the farm kids, but he'd gone to high school with plenty of them. "But they didn't think through their prank."

"How so?" Lauren asked.

He smiled. "Because not only do they have to spend their weekend cleaning up the shit they dumped in front of their school sign, but they get to smell what seeped into the ground for days to come."

"Why would they do that?" she asked.

"Didn't you see the sign at the high school?"

Chase asked.

Lauren shook her head.

"Apparently, for spirit week, the freshmen were supposed to clean the school grounds," Chase said.

She frowned. "They made it harder on themselves?"

He laughed. "No, the seniors dumped the shit. They thought it would be fun to make the freshmen clean that up."

"That's not very nice."

"There's not a lot for teenagers to do here. Anyway, it backfired, because now the seniors get all the cleanup duty."

Nick barked out a laugh. "You said 'doody'."

Chase held up his hand, and Nick high-fived it.

Lauren pointed at Nick. "No. That's not funny."

Chase couldn't hold back his laughter. "Yeah, it is."

"You two are like children sometimes."

"Good thing you love me." Nick leaned over and kissed her.

The bell over the door jingled, but Chase didn't even bother turning around. He knew Harmony wasn't due in, and she was all he really could focus on. He promised he'd make it up to her tonight. He really hoped she wore that blue wrap dress again.

"Hi, Tabitha," Lauren said.

"Harvey, I'm happy to see you here."

Tabitha was one of Harmony's good friends, so she and Chase had become friends over the years by default. He'd known her since high school. She was one of those girls who was always trying to date the popular guy—not because she liked him, but because of what it could do for her status. It never worked, but she kept trying.

"What's up?" Chase asked.

"Ms. Finkle is usually on her porch every morning when I jog by, but I haven't seen her the last few days. Have you? Maybe she went out of town?"

Nick frowned. "Now that you mention it, I haven't gotten a call from her about her cat for several days either. That's unusual."

"She didn't mention leaving town?" Tabitha chewed her lip.

"No. Has she gone out of town before? I didn't think she had any family nearby." Nick glanced at Chase.

"I think she has a son, but he doesn't live around here." Chase remembered hearing that once.

Nick stood up. "Let's go check on her."

Nick called and filled the chief in as Chase drove. The chief insisted they wait for him.

"Why did the chief want us to wait?" Chase asked as they stood on Ms. Finkle's porch.

"They're friends, I think. I'm sure he just wants to make sure she's all right." Nick glanced at his phone. "He should be here any minute."

The chief pulled up, parked, then met them on the front porch.

"I assume you knocked?" Dunin asked.

"No response."

"Door unlocked?" Dunin reached for it, but it was locked.

Nick moved a potted plant next to the door, retrieved a key, then unlocked the door.

"How the hell did you know about that?" Chase asked.

"I'm over here several times a week. I know where her spare keys are, where she stores all the extra cat food, and where she stashes Harmony's blueberry pies that she loves so much."

"I guess I hadn't realized how close you two have grown," Chase said.

"She wanted me to know, in case anything happened to her. She was worried Krinkles would starve."

"You said keys," Dunin asked. "She hides more than one?"

"Yep. I told her it wasn't a good idea, but she insisted this is a safe town, and she's always locking herself out."

Nick opened the door. From their perch on the doorstep, nothing appeared to be out of place. But once they stepped inside, Nick tensed. The chief went upstairs, but Harvey stayed with him.

Papers that had been piled on her kitchen table were now on the ground. There were scratches in her teak coffee table that hadn't been there before. One of the couch cushions was torn, with stuffing coming out.

"I don't see any signs of foul play," Dunin said

as came down the stairs.

"Something is wrong," Nick said. "That cushion wasn't torn the last time I was here."

A loud growl came from the kitchen that made all three men stop.

"What the hell was that?" Chase asked.

Another loud growl.

"That sounds like Krinkles," Nick said as he walked into the kitchen. A beat later, he yelled, "Holy shit!" as he ran past the two men and out the front door.

Following him was a raccoon. Behind the raccoon was a cat.

Chase glanced over at the chief.

"Did you see that? My damn detective just ran out of here, screaming over some little critter," the chief said shaking his head in disgust.

Chase couldn't help the laughter bubbling up. He nearly fell over from the force of it. "I really wish I had that on video."

The chief smiled. "Yeah. Well, I guess we know what caused the damage in here."

He walked into the kitchen, and Chase followed just as Nick returned.

"Be careful, Nick, there might be a squirrel in here too." Chase chuckled.

"Ha-ha. Have you seen the claws on a raccoon? You don't mess with those things."

"Yeah, especially one that is afraid of Ms. Finkle's cat," Chase choked out between fits of laughter.

Moving his gaze from Nick to the kitchen floor,

he saw it was covered in dry cat food. A bag next to the back door had been ripped to shreds. The cat food bowl was empty.

"That must be how the raccoon got in." Dunin pointed to a cat door installed on the back door. "Unless she has a pet raccoon I don't know about." He stared at Nick for an answer.

"No raccoon. But her cat is more like a bulldog than a cat." Nick pushed past the chief and opened the hall closet. "She could be in the house, hiding from the raccoon. I'll check the closets upstairs."

"If that were true, don't you think she'd hear us and call out?" Chase asked.

"Maybe she hasn't heard us." The chief cupped his hands around his mouth, and called out, "Ms. Finkle? Margaret?"

"Margaret?" Chase asks. "How did I not know that?"

The chief shrugged. "Wait here."

Dunin opened the back door. The yard was small, but there was a shed on the property. He made his way to the shed.

Chase stayed put. He had a bad feeling about this.

Dunin opened the shed door, but Chase couldn't see in from where he stood.

"Shit!" Dunin cursed.

Chase ran to him, and Nick was on his heels.

"Did you find her?" Nick asked.

Dunin jumped back. "No, one of those damn

wolf spiders fell on me when I opened the door."

"Et tu, Brute?" Chase asked grinning.

"You having a seizure?" the chief asked.

Chase ignored Dunin's comment.

"Two thirds of our police force are scared of raccoons and spiders," Chase teased, shaking his head. "Good thing you guys have me."

The chief glared at him. "I'm not scared of spiders, the damn thing fell on me and startled me is all. Now let's get back to the house, there's nothing here. Ms. Finkle probably went to visit her son."

"She wouldn't just leave her cat like that," Nick argued.

"Like what? Looks like she left it a whole bag of food. I'm sure she didn't count on the raccoon getting in."

"If she went somewhere, she'd have taken her wallet and keys. She keeps those in her purse, which is usually in the bottom kitchen drawer," Nick said.

"How do you know that?" Dunin asked suspiciously.

"Same reason I knew about the keys. I'm here often."

Once back in the kitchen, Dunin pulled a glove out of his pocket and put it on. Then he made his way to the drawer, miraculously managing not to step on any cat food.

The man must have been trained as a dancer, with some of the moves he pulled off to get there.

When Dunin opened the drawer, Chase felt the

disappointment wash over him.

"Fuck!" Nick yelled.

In the drawer was Ms. Finkle's purse.

Dunin carefully opened the purse and looked inside. "There's a wallet and a cellphone in here."

"She keeps the cellphone off but in her purse in case of emergency. I insisted on it."

Dunin closed the drawer, then ripped off the glove before reaching for his own phone. "I'm calling in the county. Either there's been foul play, or she's wandered off. Either way, we need help."

"Damn it! I should have known something was wrong. I haven't received a call from Ms. Finkle about her cat in days," Nick lamented.

The chief went outside as he made his call. The detective stepped into the living room where he paced back and forth in front of the coffee table.

"She wouldn't wander off. Her mind is fully intact."

Chase knew that was true. No one else in town knew everything about everyone the way Ms. Finkle did.

"That woman has been amazing to me. What if something happened to her?" Nick asked in a panic.

Nick was normally a calm guy. The only other time Chase had seen him so upset was when Lauren dumped him after they had an argument. The man had been a mess. Too much of a mess to even make it to work for a few days.

"Don't think like that. We'll find her."

"Ms. Finkle is kinder to me than my own family. If I'd had any idea she was in danger, I would have been here."

"I know you would have."

Nick frowned as he stared at the floor. "What's that?"

He pulled a glove out of his pocket and put it on as he bent down in front of a recliner. A corner of a book stuck out. Nick reached under the chair and pulled it out.

"What is it?" Chase asked, coming up behind him.

"A yearbook. An old one. Fisher Springs High School, nineteen eight three."

Nick opened it, and they stared at the photos together.

"Look, someone with the last name Rodney. He has to be related to Mr. Rodney. Wait, there are two Rodneys," Chase frowned. "Why does Ms. Finkle have a yearbook from nineteen eight three? I thought she was older."

"She is. She was a teacher there. Two Rodneys... Maybe they were fraternal twins?" Nick mused.

"She taught there? I went to that high school."

"She told me she retired fifteen years ago."

"That was before I was there," Chase told him.

The officer pictured Ms. Finkle teaching at the high school. He wondered if she made up stories about the students the way she did with the local residents now. He chuckled.

"What's so funny?" Nick was frowning.

"I was just imagining Ms. Finkle as a teacher. She probably would have been fun."

Nick cracked a smile. "I'm sure she was." His smile fell. "But why was this yearbook under this chair? She's obsessed with everything being in its place."

A car from the King County Sheriff's Department rolled up. Chase stepped to the door as two officers stepped out of the vehicle.

"That was fast," Chase said.

"They must have been out on another call in the next town to get here so quick," Nick said as he set the yearbook down on the table.

They walked out of the house, and Nick immediately shook hands with one of the officers.

Before transferring to Fisher Springs, Nick had been a detective with the King County Sheriff's Department. Apparently, he'd misjudged a case and almost arrested an innocent man. It was enough that his superior suggested he transfer somewhere else for a while. But instead of transferring back when his head was right again, Nick met Lauren, and fell in love with her and this town.

Chase couldn't imagine ever leaving this town. Yeah, it was small, and they had to call in for backup in cases like this, but the truth was, they rarely saw such situations. He was thankful for that.

"Does she have any family in the area?" the older of the two county officers asked. The name Mills was written on his uniform.

"She has a son, but he lives out of state," Dunin said. "I'll give him a call."

Mills nodded. "Based on the fact her wallet, phone, and keys are still in the house, this doesn't appear to be someone voluntarily leaving on their own."

"It's not like her at all," Nick said.

"You knew her well?" Mills asked.

"I do. No one has seen her in several days. If her son hasn't heard from her, I'm filing this as a missing person report," Nick said.

Mills's cell phone buzzed, and he frowned at the screen. "I have to take this." He stepped away.

The other county officer patted Nick on the back. "How's small town life treating you?"

"It's good. Mostly."

Mills stepped back up to the group, a grim look on his face. "The body of an older woman was found floating in Hawthorne Lake."

Nick went pale as he shook his head. "It can't be her."

Mills went on. "Since that's in Davenport, I thought one of you might want to come, just in case."

Dunin stepped up. "I'll go," he said.

Chapter Sixteen

"Harmony. Just who I was looking for." Logan, the owner of the Lucky Diner, was leaning on the counter, smiling at her.

"Uh-oh," Lauren said under her breath.

Logan chuckled and then winked at Harmony.

His wink did nothing for her anymore. She used to enjoy their flirting and banter, but she also wondered why he never asked her out. It was a good thing he didn't, though, because no one could have competed with Chase.

"Earth to Harmony. Lost in your thoughts again?" Logan asked.

"Sorry."

"Can you take this deposit to the bank? I've got a call with a supplier in a few minutes." He held out the deposit envelope.

"Sure."

Getting a break from the diner was always a good thing, and the bank was only a couple blocks up on Main Street, so it wouldn't take long. Not that they were busy at the moment.

"I'll be right back. Think you can handle the crowd?" she asked Lauren.

Her friend surveyed the diner. One customer was sitting in the corner with a coffee and a laptop. Logan had decided to offer free Wi-Fi to the customers, and slowly, they were getting regulars during the slow after-lunch hours.

"I think I can handle it," she replied with a smirk.

Outside, the bitter cold breeze chilled her to her bones. She practically ran to the bank to warm up.

It was sweet relief once she entered the heated lobby, and her eyes scanned the teller area for Tabitha. At least she could get a moment to visit with her friend. But her friend was very enthralled by someone else.

Jace Callahan.

He was smiling, and his fingers were twirling her hair.

Anger bubbled up inside her, but she realized Kate had never mentioned Jace again. Knowing her coworker, it had been a one-time thing.

Coughing to clear her throat, Harmony marched up to the counter.

Tabitha turned her gaze to her friend. "Harmony, hi. You doing the deposit today?"

Harmony handed her the envelope. "Yep. It's a

good chance to get some fresh air." She turned to Jace. "I'm surprised to see you here."

Jace's eyebrows shot up. "In a bank? What, I don't look like I might have money?"

Harmony didn't even try to hide her perusal as her eyes took in his worn combat boots, black jeans that fit him well, and leather jacket that was zipped up. His hair was messy, but in a sexy way, and he was smirking at her. Yeah, she understood why Kate and Tabitha were into him. He certainly appeared to fit the bad boy fantasy.

"That's not what I meant," she said.

She eyed her friend, who was focused on the deposit.

"I just meant after seeing you at the diner. With Kate."

He grinned wider. "Gotcha. Yeah, I'm not a one-woman kind of guy. I don't hide that either."

"Good for you." She turned back to Tabitha, effectively dismissing Jace.

"You don't like me, do you?" he asked.

"It's not that."

"No?" he arched a brow.

Tabitha handed her a receipt. "Anything else?"

"Thanks." She clutched the receipt and turned back to Jace.

"You remind me of someone. Someone I don't like."

That wasn't a total lie. He reminded her of a guy she'd dated several years ago, who had not been so open about not being a 'one-woman kind of guy'.

"I'll win you over. Just you wait and see. We'll be friends in no time." He winked at her then turned to face the counter. "Tabitha, I have to go, but I'll see you tonight." He strutted out of the bank, and her friend sighed.

"Really?" Harmony said.

What was she doing? She really didn't mean to be rude to Jace, and now Tabitha, but something about him rubbed her the wrong way.

Tabitha shrugged. "I know he's not my usual type but he's hot. Before you go, have you heard? Ms. Finkle is officially missing. A report has even been filed. They hope she's visiting her son, and just forgot to tell anyone."

"They? Is this another rumor? Because I don't want to hear any more town gossip."

"No, it's not gossip. She really is. Nick and Harvey were at her house with the chief, investigating. She's gone."

How the hell did Tabitha know more about where Chase was today than she did?

"Have you heard from Chase today?" Harmony asked.

"No. I'm kind of dating someone from the King County Sheriff's Office, and he mentioned it."

"You're dating someone with the sheriff's department? But you're seeing Jace tonight."

Tabitha shrugged. "Me and the officer are casual, you know?"

No, she didn't know. But if Tabitha was happy, then who was she to complain?

"I gotta get back. Have fun tonight with Jace."

"Don't worry. I will."

Harmony walked a little slower on her way back, disappointed she hadn't heard from Chase all day. Now she knew why — he was busy.

Back at the diner, business had picked up, which made the rest of her shift fly by. By the time the dinner rush died down, Kate had arrived for the evening shift.

Relieved to be done for the day, Harmony went to the back to grab her purse. She checked her phone. Still no messages from Chase. She glanced over at Lauren, whose eyes were welling with tears.

"What's wrong?"

"I got a text from Nick."

"What's going on?" Harmony looked over her shoulder.

Nick: *Ms. Finkle is missing. The body of an older woman was found in Hawthorne Lake. I'm praying it isn't her. I need to see you.*

Several emotions tore at Harmony. Ms. Finkle couldn't be dead. It just didn't seem possible. That woman was the heart of this town. But what was really eating at her was that Chase hadn't texted her.

"Is Chase with him?"

Lauren's fingers flew as she typed out a text. A moment later, she shook her head. "He was, but Nick said he was pretty upset. Shortly after they got back to the station, Harvey left."

Harmony checked her phone again. No messages. She shot Chase a text.

Harmony: *Where are you?*

She leaned back against one of the few lockers that lined the back wall.

"He hasn't called or texted?" Lauren asked.

Harmony shook her head.

"Maybe he went to Zach's," her friend suggested.

"He wouldn't drink while on duty." He'd always turned down even Harmony's wine tastings if he was on duty.

Lauren was typing on her phone again. Then she frowned. "According to Nick, he's not on duty."

Not on duty and not reaching out to her. Would this have bothered her before they'd set up their date? When they really were only friends? Anytime he'd needed to talk, he had always come to her.

"I'm going to Zach's to see if he's there. Call me if you see him."

Harmony threw on her jacket and went out the back door. Zach's pub was only a couple of doors down. Even if he wasn't there, Zach might know where he was.

When she pulled open the door to Zach's, she wasn't prepared for what she saw.

Chase was sitting at the bar, but he wasn't alone. A tall, leggy blond she'd never seen before had her hands all over him.

Hoping this was a one-sided interaction, she entered the pub and made her way to the bar.

"You're right. We should get out of here. You live close?" she heard the woman ask, her gaze making her intention clear. One of her hands was in Chase's hair, the other was somewhere Harmony couldn't see and didn't want to know.

She told her legs to move, but they wouldn't. The last thing she wanted was to see Chase leave with this woman. Her eyes met Zach's. He was behind the bar, and when he took in what she was seeing, he shook his head.

The tears came before she could get out of the pub. At least her anger helped her legs move. Before Chase could turn around and see her, she was down the street and almost to the diner's parking lot.

Now she knew why he hadn't texted her. He wasn't a long-term kind of guy, but she'd thought his intentions with her would be different. But why would they?

"Harmony!"

She halted in her tracks.

Chase. Zach must have clued him in.

It didn't matter. It was too late.

She resumed walking toward her car. She was close, just a few more steps. Raindrops started to fall, and she hoped they might mask her tears.

A hand grabbed her shoulder and spun her around.

"Harmony. Didn't you hear me calling your name?"

Chase was slurring his words.

"You're drunk."

His lips quirked. "A little. Why were you running from me, baby girl?" He snaked his arm around her waist.

Oh no. This was too much.

She pushed him away. "Stop. I'm not your 'baby girl'. I haven't heard from you since you left in the middle of our date. And now I see you about to leave with that blond woman? I'm not an idiot, Chase. And I'm not one of your one-night stands."

He stumbled back. "I wasn't going anywhere with her."

"He's telling the truth."

Out of nowhere, Zach appeared. "That woman was all over him, but he told her he was going home to his girlfriend."

Girlfriend? She felt both hope and fear at being his girlfriend. The idea of Chase with another woman tore her apart, and that scared her shitless.

"I meant you. I hoped to find you," Chase slurred.

"I'm glad he found you, Harmony. I followed him because he's too drunk to be wandering the streets. Can you get him home?"

She nodded, and Zach jogged back to his pub.

"Why'd you let that woman touch you?" she asked choking back a sob.

He stepped closer. "I'm sorry. I told her no, but she wouldn't listen."

Harmony noticed Chase's red-rimmed eyes, and

hair that was messed up, as if he'd been tugging on it all day. They were both soaked from the rain, which was coming down harder. Today's news must have affected him more than anyone realized.

"Can we go home?" he asked as he reached out and moved her hair off her face.

Grabbing his hand, she nodded. "Do you think you can make it back to your place?" she asked warily.

Chase gently pulled her arm as he started walking toward his apartment. She took that as a yes.

Once they got inside, he started stripping his clothes off as he made his way toward the bathroom. First his jacket, then his shirt.

She had to pick her jaw up off the floor. He'd been working out a lot since she'd last seen his bare chest, over a year ago. She'd thought he was sexy then, but damn, her Chase was ripped.

My Chase.

She couldn't stop the smile when she thought of him that way.

He turned and caught her smile. "You like what you see?"

"You've always been cocky, haven't you?" she teased.

He grabbed his junk through his pants. "You have no idea."

That same hand then went for his belt.

"What are you doing?" she asked.

"Getting out of these wet clothes." He winked.

After tossing the belt aside, he sat on the bed and

worked his pants down his legs. It was not the most graceful production, but it was fun to watch. Even his thighs were so much more muscular.

Once his pants were off, he stepped into the bathroom and turned on the shower. He returned, leaning on the doorway into the bedroom.

"You need to get out of those wet clothes." He flashed her his crooked smile.

That smile and those seductive eyes were almost her undoing, until he swayed a little and she remembered he was drunk.

She sighed. "I'd love to get out of my clothes for you sometime, but not until we are both sober."

He bent down and kissed her neck. "Good thing a shower will sober me up. Try not to peek now."

He went back into the bathroom and threw his boxer briefs out the door.

She wanted to peek. Was he holding himself? Was he hard?

This was weird. This was Chase, her best friend. Although, who was she kidding? She'd been fantasizing about him for a long time now.

But no, she wouldn't do it. And he was right about one thing; she needed to get out of those clothes.

In his closet, she found his big, warm robe. She peeled off her clothes and put it on. Then she grabbed a pair of his underwear and pulled them on. They were way too big, but she needed something covering her.

Finally dressed and cozy, she poured him a cup of water to have when he got out of the shower.

Her phone buzzed.

Lauren: *Did you find Harvey?*

She gave her friend a quick update, and then made her way back to the bedroom to find Chase lying on the bed.

Snoring.

Chapter Seventeen

The tapping of rain against the window woke Chase. Why the hell did it have to rain so loud?

When he tried to sit up, his head screamed, and he fell back onto his pillow groaning.

"Looks like you're awake."

He popped open one eye at the familiar voice.

Harmony. But she wasn't in his bed. She was sitting in a chair next to the window, holding a book. She was sexy. Her red hair fell down past her shoulders. Her face was bare of makeup, and she was the most beautiful woman he'd ever seen.

He couldn't stop his stupid grin. But then the memories from the day and night before slowly came back to him.

Ms. Finkle went missing. Then a body was found. The chief later called him and Nick and said he couldn't confirm her identity. They were going to have to match dental records.

The chief didn't have to say any more. He and Nick could fill in the blanks.

When he thought about how much that poor woman must have suffered, he grew nauseated. Angry. He was all over the map.

Harmony shifted in her seat, bringing his attention back to her.

"Why are you way over there?" he whined.

Her eyes lifted from her book. "You needed your sleep. I didn't want to wake you." She waved the book at him.

Pushing up on his elbows, he again tried to sit up. "I feel like shit."

Harmony laughed. "I bet you do. There's water and ibuprofen on your nightstand."

"Thank you." He managed to get the pills and water down before falling back on his bed.

"It's been years since I've seen you that drunk." Harmony moved closer and sat on the bed beside him.

"I had a shitty day."

"Lauren told me Ms. Finkle was missing and a body was found. You think the body is hers?"

He raised an eyebrow. "How many bodies have been found around here over the years?"

Her brow furrowed as she pondered his question. "I don't remember any."

"Exactly. None. Then one is found the same day we discover Ms. Finkle is missing? And when was the last time you saw her?"

"At the diner, the day Jace came to town."

"Wait, who's Jace?"

"Rance's cousin."

Chase shook his head. "You're still hanging out with Rance?"

"No. Jace came into the diner, and Kate was flirting with him, asking him questions. That's when he told us who he was. Ms. Finkle was there, and she asked who his mother was, since she knows Mr. Rodney's family pretty well. Anyway, after Jace left, Ms. Finkle was very concerned. She said there was no one in the Rodney family with the name Jace gave. She planned to go home and look through her yearbooks because she was worried someone was trying to con Mr. Rodney."

Chase's head spun around to stare at her. "Shit. If Jace isn't Mr. Rodney's grandson, and Ms. Finkle dug around, I need to text this to Nick *now*."

Harmony remained beside him while he shot off a lengthy text to Nick. Then he set his phone back on his nightstand and willed the medicine to kick in and give him some relief from the pounding in his head.

"How did she die? The woman at the lake." Harmony's voice was quiet.

"I'm not sure. There'll be an autopsy." He squeezed his eyes shut.

"Why didn't you text me yesterday? And why did you go to Zach's and get drunk? That isn't like you."

"I'm sorry. I didn't text you because I knew I would be horrible company. I couldn't get past the fact the chief couldn't identify the body. What kind of pain do you think she endured for that to be the case?" He sat up and ran his hands through his hair. "I can't get these horrible images out of my head."

Harmony stiffened beside him. "So instead of leaning on your best friend like you always have, you got drunk and let a leggy blond make you feel better?"

Leggy blond?

His eyes shot to hers. "What are you talking about?"

"I heard the woman agreeing to go to your place."

He shook his head. It was slowly coming back to him. "She wasn't agreeing with me. She was being pushy."

"You remember?"

"A little bit. I remember after a few drinks, I really wanted to see you, but you were still working. I told her I was going to see my girlfriend."

He scoffed. "Do you have any idea what it's like being a single guy in this town?" He waggled his eyebrows. "Ouch. Shit. I can't do that right now." He rubbed his temples. "Just know there are a lot of single ladies trying to get a piece of this." He waved his hand over his body.

"From what I've heard, most already have." Her eyes widened, and she slapped her hands over her lips.

Hell, he'd been with a few women in town, but not *most*.

"Well, you heard wrong. I haven't been with anyone since before our kiss."

"No one?"

He swallowed. "Not even when you were dating Rance."

He couldn't even say the guy's name without all his anger boiling up again.

Tears welled in her eyes.

"Harmony, I don't want anyone else," he said softly.

"I didn't sleep with Rance," she said with a sniff.

Chase held up his hand. "I don't need to know. I can't know. The idea of his hands on you...It's too much."

"We never even kissed. Well, he tried to kiss me that last day, but I didn't kiss him back."

Never even kissed? How was that possible? They went out on several dates.

He stared at her in surprise, but her face was turned away, avoiding his gaze.

"Harmony, look at me."

Slowly, she turned to meet his eyes. His fingers itched to pull her to him and kiss her hard, but he was hungover, and his breath probably smelled like shit.

"You're the only one I want. Don't forget that."

Instead of kissing her senseless, he laid his head in her lap and wrapped his arms around her waist. This was new for them, but it felt so right, being so close to her. As best friends, they had hugged now and again, but they hadn't been overly touchy.

"There's more," he sighed.

He really didn't want to tell her the rest, but

she'd find out soon enough from Lauren.

He rolled off of her lap to his side of the bed and landed on his back, staring up at the ceiling. "Lay with me." He waved her over.

She cuddled up against him, and he took a moment to enjoy how well she fit with him.

"A woman went into the county sheriff's office, and said she'd seen a man carrying something large toward Hawthorne Lake two days ago. She thought it might have been a body."

"That's quite the coincidence."

He nodded. "At the time, they took her statement and let her go. Apparently, they often get people coming in and making crazy statements."

"But then yesterday…"

"Yeah, yesterday. I was asked to talk to her. I did, and she gave a description of the man."

"Was it credible?"

He rubbed his hands over his face. "We don't know yet. The problem is this woman described Rance perfectly, a blond man with dark roots."

Harmony sat up. "Chase."

"I know. There are a lot of men who match that description."

She nodded. "Good. I'm glad you realize that."

Pulling her in, he gave her a squeeze before dropping the bomb.

"Well, I realized it *after* I told Dunin what I thought, and he informed me I was biased. The chief accused me of gunning after Rance because he dated you, and he, ah, suggested I take a couple of days off to cool down."

"Oh."

"Yeah."

"How can they lose you for a couple of days during an investigation?"

"The county has officers working on it."

"Okay. So, you went to Zach's?"

He loosened his grip on her, and let his fingers lightly graze her back as they moved up and down.

"You know how I get. I was pissed. It was best I wasn't around anyone."

"But getting drunk in public was all right?"

He shrugged. "I thought I'd feel better after a couple of beers, then I would come see you."

"That didn't work?"

"No. The longer I sat there, the angrier I became. Finally, Zach gave me a shot. Then I ordered a few more. Then—"

It was coming back to him now. The blond that wouldn't take no for an answer. He remembered what she said and laughed.

"What?" Harmony ran her hand up and down his chest.

"I just remembered something from last night. You know the rumors about me?"

She sat up just enough so he could see her rolling her eyes, then she fell back down. "Oh yes, the rumors that you spread yourself?" She laughed. "How the hell did you get those rumors going, anyway? Do you know how many times I've been asked if it's true?"

"How did you respond?"

She laughed. "You really want to know?"

He nodded.

"Depended on my mood. If I was pissed at you, I told people you were no bigger than my finger."

He sat up. "You *what*? Is that why Janelle went from hot to cold at the July fourth cookout a few years back?"

Her lips curved up. "Maybe."

"Why, you—"

Next thing she knew, he was on top of her, tickling her senseless.

"Hey! You changed the subject," she said between fits of laughter.

Chuckling, he stopped his torment, and bent his arms so he was holding himself up with his forearms.

"You said you remembered something from last night."

Leaning down, he gently kissed her just below her ear. "I did. That rumor was why that woman was hitting on me."

Harmony let out a small moan. "Admit you started those rumors," she said as her nails dug into his shoulders.

"I may have." He grinned. "Why are you so convinced it isn't true?"

"Well, I can't say I've ever seen you have a repeat performance with a woman. Must not be too great, huh?"

He pushed up to stare at her and couldn't believe she was smiling while insulting his manhood.

"Really? I have you pinned, and that's how you want to play it?"

She nodded.

"I bet the rumors made you curious. Have you ever tried to get a peek for yourself?"

"How would I do that? Walk in on you in the shower?"

He shrugged. "I thought maybe you noticed sometime when I was hard."

He bent down and gently traced his lips against her neck.

"Yeah right. When would have you been hard around me?"

His head jerked up to meet her gaze, and he arched a brow. "Seriously?"

She nodded.

"Every time I've been around you for the last ten months. And quite a bit before that."

"Yeah?"

"Yeah."

"How long before?"

He shrugged again. "I get near you, and it happens."

To prove his point, he pushed further between her legs, and ground against her.

Her eyes widened as she let out a moan. "The rumor is true."

Only his boxer briefs and her yoga pants

separated them. He couldn't resist, and ground again.

"Chase." Her eyes fluttered closed.

What the hell was he doing?

"I'm sorry." He flipped over onto his back. "We haven't even had our date yet."

She laughed.

He frowned. "I'm not sure what's so funny."

"Well, it's not like we just met. It's more like we've been courting for ten months."

"Courting? Are you reading those romance books again? Is that what that book is over there?" He pointed to the book she'd left in the chair.

She shrugged. "You know what I mean."

"Yeah, except generally, when two people *court*, one of them isn't dating someone else." He played with a piece of her hair between his fingertips before pushing it behind her ear.

"Jealous?" she teased.

"I was, yeah."

Cuddling into him, she wrapped a leg over his, and put her hand on his chest. "If I had any idea how you felt, I never would have dated him."

"I know. Let's talk about something else."

Lifting her head, she stared into his eyes. "Like what?"

"Tonight, I want to take you out. On a real date."

"Okay. I'll let you know when I'm free, I'm photographing a wedding this afternoon."

"Need any help?"

She laughed. "No, you're not really in any

condition. But no worries. Tabitha is helping me."

"That sounds good. I'll rest up so I'm extra ready for our date tonight. And if you play your cards right, you might get lucky." He winked.

She laughed, and he loved the sound. He loved everything about her. He'd never been in love before. Was this what it felt like?

All he knew was he wanted more of whatever this was.

Chapter Eighteen

Harmony's hands gripped the steering wheel as she barreled down the familiar country road. Excitement filled her veins. Tabitha hummed beside her from the passenger seat.

She wished she could bottle this feeling.

In less than twenty minutes, they would arrive at Forester Farms and set up for the first wedding of the year. Well, *her* first wedding of the year. The bride's family had ties throughout the Puget Sound. This could lead to so many more gigs. What she wouldn't do to photograph a wedding on a beach at sunset.

Snapping out of her fantasy, she ducked below the visor and stared up at the mountains. There was plenty of snow on them, and with an early afternoon ceremony, there would be enough light to capture them as a gorgeous backdrop to the wedding party.

"Thank you for coming," she said to her friend.

"No worries. I know this wedding is a big deal. I'm glad to help."

Tabitha had been helping her set up shots since Harmony's kiss with Chase, when he had suddenly found himself less available.

It was so obvious to her now how he felt, but she had been too blind to see it then.

Chase had helped her with photographing her first wedding, three years ago. While she missed him now, she had to admit that Tabitha was made for this role. Her eye for color and texture was amazing.

This year, Harmony was determined to make a real go of it and leave the diner job behind once and for all. The problem was, she was only getting booked for weddings at Forester Farms.

Thank you, Mr. Forester.

He'd known her since she was a baby, and he helped her any chance he could. Now it was up to her to take it to the next level.

"How was your date with Jace?"

Harmony glanced at her friend whose face lit up.

"So good. That man... I swear he's the best sex I've ever had. I hope to see him again soon."

A pit grew in Harmony's stomach. "You heard him say he wasn't a one-woman kind of guy, right?"

She shrugged. "He said that, but I'll change him."

Harmony bit her lip. Her friend didn't need her opinion or judgment. Just because *she'd* been soured on men like Jace didn't mean it would turn out badly for

Tabitha.

When they pulled up, her friend frowned. "One of their colors is yellow? Why?"

Harmony laughed. "Some people like yellow. It's like sunshine."

"Yellow is great for flowers, but not a wedding color."

"Hush. I don't want anyone overhearing you." Harmony got out of the car and started pulling her equipment from the back.

"You're right. Let's talk about something more interesting. Tell me, how was Rance in the bedroom?" She gently bumped her shoulder into Harmony's.

"I wouldn't know, and I'm no longer seeing him."

Tabitha's eyebrows shot up. "Really? What happened?" She grabbed one of the equipment bags from Harmony and followed her up the path.

"There was no chemistry. None."

"Yikes. Well, I guess it is better to know upfront. Does that mean he's available? Or is he, like, an ex and off-limits?"

Harmony laughed. Just because Rance wasn't for her didn't mean he wasn't perfect for Tabitha.

"Go for it. If you two have chemistry, then go crazy."

As they walked to the entrance of the large barn that had been home to many weddings over the years, Tabitha leaned over and whispered, "Even if there's no chemistry, I'd take a crack at him. I'm sure he'd be better than a toy. I wonder if Jace would want to join."

"Toys? Did you bring toys?" A little girl appeared out of nowhere wearing a lacy white dress. Her hair was pulled back into a bun, making her look older than she likely was.

Harmony felt the familiar heat creep up her neck and into her face. "Sorry, we don't have any toys."

When the girl walked away with a pout, Harmony elbowed her friend. "Watch what you say. You never know who is around."

"Right, boss. Time to get to work."

A few hours later, they were wrapping up their final shots at the reception. The bride had danced with her father, the cake was cut, and the bouquet had been tossed.

Harmony should have been exhausted, but instead, she had nervous energy to burn. Assuming Chase didn't get called into work, they'd finally get that real date.

The last thing she should be was nervous. She'd known Chase most of her life, but she didn't know this side of him. The idea of getting a peek into why he was so cocky sent shivers down her arms.

She packed up the rest of her equipment and gave the bride's parents her usual speech about when the photos would be ready, finishing with the note that she would send them a link. The father had been quite inebriated at that point. At least everyone was having a great time.

"Ready?" Tabitha was by her side, holding one of the bags.

"Yes."

As they walked back to her car, the scent of roses floated through the air. The path was lined with bouquets of the fragrant flower. The floral bill for this wedding must have been astronomical.

She couldn't wait for an April wedding, when hundreds of tulips would be in bloom and lining the walkway. At that time of year, the entire property was decorated with a colorful variety of flowers.

Her friend kept shooting her looks.

"What?" Harmony finally asked.

"Do you want to go to Zach's after we get back to town?"

Oh. She hadn't expected that.

"I thought you were going after Rance?" Harmony opened her trunk, and they put the bags in.

"Not tonight. I thought we could hang out. Sound like fun?" Tabitha was staring her down, arms crossed.

Did she know about her date? How could she? No one knew.

"I can't. I have plans."

"Uh-huh. And would these plans involve Harvey?"

"Maybe. Are you mad at me or something?"

"A little, yeah." Tabitha's hands went to her hips.

"Why?"

Harmony's mind raced. She wasn't ready to tell anyone she was going on a date with Harvey. What if it didn't go well? What if there was no chemistry?

What was she talking about? There was more than enough chemistry when she was around that man. It didn't use to be like that, though. Not until that kiss.

"Because the three of us used to hang out all the time. At least, we did until your birthday. Then Harvey started claiming he was always busy. And now I find out you are hanging with him without me. Did I do something wrong?"

"Let's drive and talk."

Harmony needed to buy a minute to come up with a reason she would hang out with Chase and not Tabitha. They got in the car, and she decided redirection was her best option.

"Why do you think you did something wrong?" she asked.

The car was stuffy, so she rolled down her window. After last night's rain, the air was fresh, and it cooled her down.

"I don't know." Tabitha was staring out the passenger window.

"You didn't do anything wrong," Harmony said as she reached for the stereo.

Tabitha turned to face her. I noticed you're calling him by his first name again."

Crap. Think fast.

"I thought he insisted everyone call him by his last name," Tabitha said pointedly.

"He did. But you forget I've known him since long before he became an officer. No one made fun of the name Chase when he was younger."

"I remember. I kind of knew him in high school." Tabitha turned back and stared out her window.

Before her friend could recall her original question, Harmony turned on some music and started singing along. It wasn't long before her friend joined in.

Mission: Redirection successful. Now if she could get Tabitha all the way home without bringing Chase up again, it would be a small miracle.

The song ended, and Tabitha turned the music down, then twisted in her seat to face her. "There's something I've always wondered."

"What's that?"

Please don't be about Chase.

"Why you and Harvey never dated. I mean, you get along well. And I swear that boy had a crush on you in high school."

Everything fell silent as she processed what her friend had said.

"W-why would you say that?" she finally stammered.

Tabitha laughed. "He used to follow you around like a puppy dog."

"No, he didn't. We were best friends." Why was her friend asking her this now? "Why would you think that? Did you have a crush on Harvey in high school?"

She cringed. Did she really want to know if her friend liked him?

"No. He was always like a little brother to me. But lately, something has changed."

They were two blocks from Tabitha's place. Harmony's mind raced, trying to find any topic to get her off this one.

"He's been working out, and somehow, he went from annoying little brother to sexy as hell police officer, you know?" Tabitha sighed. "Plus, those rumors. I heard from Bridgette that they're true. She would know."

"Bridgette? The cheerleader who led the mean girl squad in high school? You talk to her?"

What the hell? Chase slept with that bitch?

That would explain why the woman had been all over him at Harmony's birthday celebration, and the other night at the pub.

Tabitha's house appeared on the left, and Harmony pulled up at the curb.

Her friend explained. "Bridgette works at the hair salon in Davenport. She asked about Harvey, and we got to talking. I found out she has a friends-with-benefits thing going on with him."

"Has?"

"Yep. Well, that's what she said two months ago. That reminds me, I need to get my hair cut."

Two months?

But Chase had said he hadn't been with anyone

since their kiss. Did he lie?

"You all right? You look sick."

"I'm fine. I just can't believe he'd go for someone like her. That's all."

Nausea was overtaking Harmony, and she needed to get out of there.

Chase wouldn't lie to her. She knew that deep down. Right?

But she really didn't like feeling this vulnerable.

"You can't? Bridgette may be a bitch, but she looks like a fricking Barbie doll. She's every guy's wet dream. Anyway, I'll talk to you later. Have fun with whatever you're doing tonight." Tabitha got out and gave her a wave before she went inside and closed her door.

Have fun tonight? Not likely now.

Chapter Nineteen

Chase's head was still pounding, but after he got Nick's text that the autopsy results were in, he had to come in.

When he pushed through the door of the Fisher Springs Police Department, Nick was sitting at his desk, hands in his hair.

"You have the report?" Chase said.

The detective looked up. His expression told Chase all he needed to know.

"You're not supposed to be here. Dunin said you were off for the next couple of days. His order."

"Nick, this is about Ms. Finkle. I can't walk away from that."

He nodded. "The woman found in the lake was murdered."

"Shit." Even though he had been certain of that already, hearing it made Chase want to punch something, hard. "Let me see the autopsy results."

He'd been going crazy, pacing a path at his house since Harmony had left this morning. After she agreed to try another date. He couldn't wait for their date this evening.

But first, he had to know if Ms. Finkle had suffered. He prayed she hadn't.

"I'm still waiting for the ME to email the report, but he summarized the results in our phone call," Nick admitted, avoiding his eyes.

He knew something.

"You spoke to the ME?"

Nick let out a sigh and stood up. "I did. But before I tell you anything else, you need to know the body is not Ms. Finkle."

The heaviness that had been sitting on Chase's shoulders suddenly lifted. "It's not Ms. Finkle? That's great! Well, it's not great for this woman. Why the hell didn't you lead with that?"

"Sorry. I should have. It turns out there were some distinct differences in the dental records, according to Ms. Finkle's X-rays from the old town dentist."

Chase nodded, and silence fell between them.

"Isn't tonight the big night?" Nick asked. "Well, big night, take two. You're finally going on that date with Harmony?"

"Yep."

"Nervous?"

Chase grinned. "Yep."

"Where are you taking her?"

"I figured dinner at Artie's, and then a walk down Main Street."

Nick laughed. "Down Main Street and straight to your place?" He waggled his eyebrows.

"You really have to stop doing that. It isn't a good look for you."

"Oh please, it all looks good on me, and you know it." His friend grinned. "But seriously, just dinner? That's it?"

"What, that's not good enough for you? I haven't done much dating," Chase huffed.

"No, she'll love it. I'm happy for you."

"I hope so."

"She will." Nick nodded.

Dunin came out of his office. "What the hell are you doing here?" His hands went to his hips as he stared at Chase.

Shit. He hadn't prepared for this moment.

His stomach fluttered as he thought fast. "Sorry, Chief. I heard the ME's report was in, and I had to know if the victim was Ms. Finkle."

Dunin grunted. "You heard the report was in?" He turned to Nick. "I wonder how. I wasn't even aware of that."

"Sorry. I was just about to tell you. The dental records on the body were not a match for Ms. Finkle," Nick said as he stood up. "I spoke with the ME. He should be sending the full report any minute."

"It's not Margaret? That's good." The chief nodded. "I mean, it's not *good*. A poor woman was likely murdered."

"The woman was definitely murdered. The ME confirmed that on the phone. Now we have a missing woman *and* a murder investigation," Nick said.

The chief arched a brow. "No, we don't. The county will be working on the murder. We will continue to search for Ms. Finkle. Any luck reaching her son yet?"

"Not yet."

Dunin scratched his beard.

Chase had been jealous of the chief's thick scruff until last year, when he overheard Harmony telling Lauren she was not into men with facial hair. He'd spent most of the last year clean-shaven.

He chuckled, wondering if Harmony had even noticed. He'd have to ask her about it tonight.

Tonight. It wouldn't be long before he would see her smile again.

"What the hell you giggling about?" Dunin bellowed.

That snapped Chase out of his daze.

"He finally has a date with Harmony tonight," Nick told him.

"A date?" Dunin asked.

"Yep. It's been so special to watch them grow up before our very eyes," Nick said with a fake sniffle.

Chase grabbed the tissue box off his friend's desk and tossed it at him, nailing him in the shoulder.

"All right, children, let's behave. Moore, let me know the moment you find Margaret's son."

"Will do."

Dunin was almost to his office when he turned back. "Oh, and since you are so fond of Ms. Finkle's cat, can you take care of it until we find her?"

Nick smiled. "Already done. Krinkles is now staying at the Chanler mansion with me and Lauren and is being well taken care of."

The chief laughed. "Of course, he is. You and that damn cat." He shook his head. "Harvey, now that you know, head home. Get some sleep."

"Will do," Chase said.

The chief slipped into his office, leaving Nick and Chase alone again.

Chase could barely muffle his laughter, so once Dunin's door closed, he stopped trying.
"Damn, that cat owns you."

With a nod, Nick walked around his desk then leaned on it. "Yes, he does. Got a problem with that?"

As intimidating as the detective tried to appear, all Chase could imagine was him holding Krinkles as the cat licked his face.

"Nope. Have fun with that."

"Maybe you should head out before the chief finds you still here. Unless you want to talk about your date some more? Get some pointers for how to handle the ladies?" Nick waggled his brows.

"What did I tell you? Stop doing that. It's not attractive."

"Lauren disagrees."

Chase laughed. "No, I'm good. I'm afraid your pointers would only scare Harmony off."

"You sure? 'Cause I've got skills," Nick said.

"You forget I had a front row seat to your 'skills' last year. You almost lost Lauren for good."

Nick nodded. "True. You'd better figure it out yourself."

A ding from Nick's phone got his attention. "The ME sent the report."

They both walked to Nick's computer as he loaded up the file. The examiner stated there was a wound on the back of the victim's head, indicating she was hit from behind. The ME believed the blow killed her, and she was dead before going in the water, as evidenced by the lack of dirt under her nails or water in her lungs.

"She likely didn't suffer, at least," Nick said.

"But she was murdered."

"I know. The King County sheriff's office is sending a team back out today to see if they missed any evidence. We will find whoever did this."

"How do you know that?" Chase asked.

"My friend Johnson told me. He's one of the officers working on the case."

"Did they question Rance? That woman's description was pretty spot-on."

Nick shook his head. "Harvey, you can't focus only on Rance. You don't even know who the victim is. Look, I did something similar at my last job and that's why I had to transfer out. You need to stay away from this case."

"Why?" Chase yelled. "Because I'm asking

questions?"

"Because you're biased."

"Apparently rightly so," Chase said a little louder.

Nick glanced to the chief's office then back to Chase. "Look, I know you don't like Rance, and I know why. If he *was* the person at the lake, we'll figure it out. But we need to let the sheriff's department question him. They don't know him, so they'll be objective. If you question him, he could get the evidence thrown out at trial."

Nick's explanation made sense, but something still ate at him. However, his friend didn't give him a chance to argue.

"Go for a run," he urged. "Go to the gym. Clear your head. Then take Harmony out like you have been wanting to do for years."

"Years?"

Nick grinned. "I saw the way you looked at her when I first came to town. Way before your kiss."

Chase shrugged. No point in arguing.

"Have a great time. Then tomorrow, we can talk about all of this. Hell, maybe Ms. Finkle will be back."

"I hope you're right."

"But I'm talking late tomorrow. Don't get in your head and mess up your morning." Nick warned.

"My morning?"

"With Harmony."

Chase rolled his eyes. "Why do you keep bringing it back to me and Harmony having sex? You some kind of perv?"

Nick laughed. "No, I'm just sick of you being an asshole. You need to relieve that tension."

"You know what will relieve my tension, is figuring out if Rance is a murderer."

"And the sheriff's office will do that. Hawthorne Lake isn't our jurisdiction, so don't even think about nosing around in their case. Now try to enjoy your date. And whatever you do, don't tell Harmony about this. It isn't public information."

Nick had been right about one thing, though... he needed to let off some steam.

"All right. I'll go to the gym, then take Harmony out. But tomorrow, we talk."

Nick nodded. "Sounds good."

Chase turned to leave.

Nick shouted after him, "Good luck tonight!"

Chase shook his head and kept walking out the door.

Chapter Twenty

"Are you going to bring it up?" Lauren asked as she twirled Harmony's hair around the curling iron.

If it weren't for Lauren, Harmony would have thrown on jeans and a T-shirt for her date with Harvey.

Ever since Tabitha had made it sound like Chase had been carrying on with Bridgette all this time, Harmony had wanted to confront him. But she wasn't going to do it over a text. She'd wait until she saw him. Which meant, despite her best efforts, she'd spent the last couple hours seething. Fortunately, Lauren had calmed her down and was now trying to convince her not to confront Chase when she was upset.

"I have to bring it up. I'm about to jump out of my skin."

Lauren nodded. "For what it's worth, I think Tabitha was wrong. Chase wouldn't lie to you. Plus, since your birthday, he's been spending a lot more time at home."

Harmony leaned in toward the bathroom mirror and applied some mascara.

"How do you know that?" she asked.

"He's been watching all the shows we watch and keeping up. I know that because he always wants to talk about them."

"You've gotten to know Chase quite well this past year, wouldn't you say?"

"He and Nick have grown close. So yeah, I have."

Harmony turned to her friend. "How long did you know Chase had a thing for me?"

Lauren avoided her gaze and was very interested in her tubes of lipstick sitting on the counter. Finally, she shrugged her shoulders. "I suspected for a while, but I didn't know for sure until you told me he asked you out. But I talked to Nick, and he's known for quite a while."

She crossed her arms. "And he didn't say anything?"

"Nope. Not to me. When I asked him why, he told me it was Chase's business to tell. Also," Lauren looked her in the eye, "he wanted to see Chase step up. If he really wanted you, then he needed to work for it. Nick figured if he said anything, you could have gone to Chase."

She was right. If she thought Chase had felt the same, she would have pushed him. And he really needed to come around in his own time.

They walked to Harmony's closet, and Lauren reached for the blue wrap dress.

"I like this one."

"I wore it for our last almost date. I planned to wear this one." She pulled out a deep green halter style dress that fit snugly.

"But now I'm not sure. I don't want to taint the memory of this dress if I find out he's lying."

"Stop it. He's not lying. He is really into you. Wear this dress."

The sound of the doorbell made her jump.

"Put that on. I'll answer the door."

Lauren raced out of the room. Harmony heard her friend greet Chase and lead him to the kitchen.

To avoid her friend's wrath, Harmony put on the green dress. Then she twirled in front of her mirror. She had to admit, she looked good. But she was nervous. More so than she'd ever been around him.

Chase and Lauren were in the living room when she walked in, and she stuttered to a stop.

The man was wearing a suit. She'd never seen him in a suit. The way the jacket fit over his broad shoulders and his arms... Damn, she could see he was muscular with the cut of the jacket. And the way he was staring at her almost had her melting into a puddle right there.

"I was hoping you would wear that blue wrap dress again, but I think this dress is sexier." Chase didn't even try to hide his desire as he scanned her body.

"Thank you."

Lauren grabbed her coat off the coatrack next to the door. "Have fun. Harmony, call me later."

After she left, Chase closed the gap between them.

"Call her later? Does that mean you've already made a decision on how this date ends?" His lips twitched up into a smirk. Then he reached up and ran his hand down her neck to her bare shoulder. Goosebumps appeared on her skin, and she couldn't stop the shiver.

"Why have I never seen you wear a dress like this?"

His eyes were dark. Hungry.

She smiled. "You've never seen me before I went out on a date."

He arched a brow. "You dress like this for all your dates?"

"Wouldn't you like to know?"

"Yes, I would. That's why I'm asking."

"Do you wear a suit for your dates with Bridgette?" she retorted.

Her eyes widened. She hadn't meant to bring it up so quickly, but that's what happened when she let herself stew on something for so long.

He took a step back. "You knew about Bridgette?"

"Everyone knew about her. This is a small town."

Shoving his hands in his pockets, he stared at the floor. "She was a friend-with-benefits."

"She was?"

"She still wants to be. She's having a hard time taking no for an answer. But I swear to you, I cut that off before our kiss."

"Before?"

"After I saw how Nick and Lauren were together, I realized I wanted that too."

"Oh."

"Then you kissed me."

She shoved at his chest. "You kissed me."

"After you begged me."

She grinned. "I did not!"

"Kind of." He tugged her into his arms. "But I wanted to. I'd wanted to kiss you for so long. When you asked me to, I couldn't fight it anymore."

"Then why didn't you bring it up? Chase, why did it take ten months?"

"Why didn't *you* bring it up?" he asked.

She lifted her head to stare into his eyes. "I was scared you didn't feel the same."

He nodded. "That's how it felt for me too."

"I don't know why, but I'm feeling insecure about this. About us. I'm not usually the jealous type." She was becoming one of those women she couldn't stand.

He arched an eyebrow. "Are you sure about that?"

"What? When was I jealous before?"

"Remember in high school, when Ben tutored the new girl?"

191

Ben was her high school boyfriend, and he had been very eager to tutor the new transfer student. She had looked like a younger Gisele Bündchen.

"I remember."

"You were so jealous. I had to talk you out of doing something you'd regret. Remember?"

"Yes. But I ignored your advice, and surprised Ben during one of his tutoring sessions."

"You never told me that. Though you did break up shortly after. What happened?"

She hated talking about this. There was a reason she'd never told Chase. He wouldn't believe her usual line that she wasn't that attached.

"Well, his house had a side door that went to the basement. I used to sneak in that way to see him. When I went in that door that night, and made my way to his basement bedroom, the new girl was there. Naked. On his bed. His face was between her legs."

"Shit. Why didn't you tell me?" He drew her close again and continued running his fingers down her back.

His touch was soothing.

"I'd been with Ben for two years. He never once went down on me, he said he didn't like it. But he liked it quite a bit, from what I saw. It was me that was the problem."

"No. That's not true."

"From then on, I decided I'd date, but I wasn't going to give anyone my heart again."

"What about your other boyfriends?"

"They were nice, but..." She shrugged.

His hand stilled on her back. "You have kept yourself emotionally detached all these years? Is that what you're doing with me?"

"No. I'm the furthest thing from detached when it comes to you, and that scares the hell out of me."

"Yeah?"

"Yeah."

"Me too. I mean, I feel so much for you, it's sometimes overwhelming and scary. But I wouldn't trade it for anything."

She reached out and caressed his cheek. He leaned into her hand, keeping his gaze on her.

He took her hand and kissed it. "We should go. I made a reservation to assure we leave this time."

The flutters she felt in her stomach increased. A reservation meant they were likely going to Artie's. It was the fanciest restaurant in this area.

After a short drive, he turned into his own driveway.

"Forget something?" she asked.

He turned to face her. "How would you feel about a romantic dinner in there?" He used his thumb to point to his house.

Was he being serious, or just messing with her?

"Uh. I know I joked about not taking things slow, but this might be a little too fast." A tingling swept up the back of her neck, and she hoped he couldn't see her flush inside this dark car.

Why the hell was she getting embarrassed? Oh

yeah, because she was imagining having sex with her best friend. This was *Harvey*. But then he flashed her his crooked smile, and her nervousness melted.

She wanted this man.

"Are you sure about that?" he teased. "Because the way you're looking at me right now, I have to question your words."

He chuckled as he brushed her bottom lip with his thumb. "As much as I do want more, I really do mean dinner. I'm serious about us, and I want to do this right and take you on dates."

"I want that too."

He nodded toward his house. "I've got takeout from Artie's in there. I realized, when I went for a run around town earlier, that everyone has questions about the body found in the lake. I'm afraid that if we went out, I'd be dodging busybodies the entire time."

He had a point.

"Yeah, people have been asking me too. They think because we're friends that I know everything."

He took her hand in his. "Are you okay with this?"

She squeezed his hand. "Yes. Now let's see what you ordered for me."

Chapter Twenty-One

The date night in was a great idea except for one part. Chase hadn't made a plan for what to do after dinner, and he only had one thing on his mind. But he had told her he would date her, and he meant it.

But between the little touches and heated looks she gave him; it was taking all his self-control not to kiss her senseless.

Not that he was any better. Throughout dinner, he used any excuse to touch her, even if it was just pushing some hair out of her face. The way she shivered at his touch turned him on even more.

By the time she suggested dessert, he had to shove his hands in his pockets to maintain control. The other night at her place, if Nick hadn't called, he wasn't sure either one of them would have stopped.

After placing the leftover dessert in the refrigerator, he turned around to find her inches from him.

"Hi," he said. His lips curved up as he kept his eyes locked on hers.

"Hi." She cupped his face, pulling him down until their lips met.

His lips brushed against hers, and her hand snaked behind his neck in an attempt to draw him even closer. Then she swept her tongue across his bottom lip. His lips parted, and she deepened the kiss, causing him to moan.

Damn, he couldn't resist her. Why did he keep trying?

His arms went around her waist, and he walked them backward until her ass bumped into the kitchen counter. He hoisted her up onto it and positioned himself between her legs. She used them to trap him and pull him closer.

His hand was in her hair as he kissed down her neck. Her heartbeat fluttered against his lips. Her fingers found the top of his pants, and one finger dipped below his waistband.

The feeling of her skin on him lit him on fire.

He pushed his body into her, knowing full well she could feel how much he wanted her. But when her hands went to undo his belt, the reality hit him.

He grabbed her hands.

"What's wrong?" she asked.

"I don't want to go too fast." He was breathing hard. He'd fantasized about being with Harmony for so long he couldn't believe it was finally coming true.

"Confession time." She hopped down off the counter and smiled at him.

"Okay," he said. This moment already had him anxious, and he never knew what she might say.

"It doesn't feel fast to me, because—"

"Because we've known each other so long? I know but seeing each other like this is new." He wrapped his arms around her and pulled her close. He could not stop touching this woman.

Placing her hands on his chest, she squeezed. He cocked an eyebrow.

"What I was going to say is it doesn't feel fast because I've thought about it for so long. I've been masturbating to thoughts of you for over a year."

Holy shit. Over a year? He was now at full command. "I'm sorry. I need you to repeat that." His voice was gravelly.

"Remember about a year ago, we went sledding and slid into a puddle?"

"Yeah, then we went back to my place to change clothes. We wrapped up in blankets to warm up."

"There was a moment when you stripped down to your boxer briefs… Damn, Chase, you're a sexy man. I was so turned on. Do you remember I took a shower? I said it was to warm up."

His jaw dropped. "Are you saying you masturbated in my shower? Fuck, that's hot." He backed up to lean against a wall.

That's when her gaze moved down. Yep, no denying how he felt.

"I want you, Chase."

The heated stare she gave him broke his resolve. In two strides, he was standing toe to toe with her. His lips crashed down, and he lifted her, but this time, he carried her to his bedroom, where he gently lowered her until her feet were on the floor.

Spinning her in his arms, he unzipped her dress as she untied the halter top. It fell to the ground, and he stumbled back.

"You aren't wearing underwear or a bra."

She spun back to face him, smiling. "I can't with this dress. It would show."

He drank her in. The reality beat every fantasy he'd ever had about her.

While he stood dumbstruck, she quickly worked the buttons of his shirt. He pushed his jacket off his shoulders, and tossed it on a nearby chair, never taking his eyes off her.

"You okay there, Officer?"

He let his shirt drop to the ground, and then cradled her face in his hands.

"You're so beautiful." He leaned his forehead down to hers.

This was really happening. They were finally going to be together.

"Chase, you're shaking. What's wrong?"

He smiled and shook his head. "Nothing's wrong. I've never felt like this before."

"It's the same for me." Pushing up on her toes, she kissed him softly.

Suddenly, something snapped, and all the fantasies he'd had about her, and all the sexual frustration that had built up, exploded.

"Lie on the bed," he commanded.

"What?" She blinked at him a few times.

"Lie on the bed and open your legs nice and wide for me."

"Oh my God, are you into bondage?"

He chuckled. "No, not really. But I am into making sure you come several times tonight."

Her pupils dilated as she stared at him. "You really that confident you can do that?"

She backed up until she reached the bed, then lay down.

Quickly taking off his pants, he left his boxer briefs on. Then he lowered himself over her.

He nipped at her ear. "You don't think I can?"

He kissed down her shoulder, lightly biting, and, her hips bucked up.

A familiar red blush crawled up her neck and flushed her face.

He sat up just a little and stared at her, but she avoided his gaze.

"Look at me," he said.

She turned her head to him.

"Do you trust me?" he asked.

She nodded.

"Good. Then trust me when I tell you I'm going to make you come on my face." He leaned down and gently bit her nipple. "Then on my cock."

"Damn, Chase. I've never seen this side of you."

"I'm just speaking the truth, babe. You don't like it?"

He kissed his way down to her stomach.

"I love it."

He chuckled. "Good to know."

Then he kissed his way down to her inner thigh and used his thumb to trace circles on her other thigh.

"Chase, please."

He glanced up at her. "Please what, baby?"

She stared at him, licking her lips.

"I'm gonna need to hear you say it," he rumbled.

"Lick me," she said quietly.

He never would have guessed her to be so shy. He was going to have fun with this.

Using his tongue, he licked her inner thigh.

"Chase."

He could hear the frustration in her voice.

"Yes, babe?"

He ran his fingers over her wet slit. Damn, she was wet.

"Yes," she moaned.

"What do you want me to do, Harmony?"

She bit her lip. "I want your mouth on me."

He wasn't going to make her beg.

He dove in, licking and sucking while she writhed on the bed. When her fingers gripped his hair, he knew she was close.

"Chase!"

She moaned as the orgasm took her.

Damn, she was the sexiest woman he'd ever seen.

When she came down, she reached for him and pulled him up over her. "That was amazing." She kissed him.

"What will be amazing is when that sweet pussy of yours comes all over my cock."

She wrapped her legs around him and drew him close, slipping her fingers beneath the elastic of his boxer briefs. "I need you now."

He stood and removed his underwear before easing over her. The next thing he knew, her fingers were wrapped around him, stroking him.

"Fuck, Harmony."

How could everything about this woman feel so much better than anyone else?

"The rumors are true." She grinned.

"They are."

He righted himself above her again, and then reached into his nightstand drawer to grab a condom, and quickly rolled it on. After lining up at her entrance, he locked gazes with her, then pushed inside.

"Jesus, Harmony. You're so tight."

She froze.

"Does it hurt? Shit, I didn't mean to go so fast. I couldn't hold back."

She shook her head. "It's fine. Just give me a minute."

He crushed his lips to hers while making sure not to move any other part of himself. Her hands wove into his hair, then as their kiss deepened, her hands moved to his ass, bringing him toward her.

Taking her cue, he withdrew then slowly pumped in again.

"Faster," she commanded.

Every time he pulled out, she grabbed his ass and pushed him in harder and harder. She was so responsive.

He reached down and found her clit, rubbing small circles over it. That was all she had needed, as she cried out just before crashing into her second orgasm.

Feeling her spasm around him, he could no longer hold back his orgasm and he let it go.

She kept her legs wrapped tightly around him. They stayed like that for several minutes as they caught their breath.

Finally, he pushed up. "I'll be right back."

He took care of the condom, and came back to bed, curled her into his arms, holding her tight.

His mind was racing. That had been, hands down, the best sex he'd ever had. And now he couldn't wait to do it again.

Chapter Twenty-Two

Chase could hardly contain his grin as Nick entered the police station. "Morning," he managed to say with a straight face.

Nick nodded as he walked past.

"What the fuck?" the detective shouted from his desk.

Chase couldn't fight off the laughter that bubbled up.

"A fucking stuffed raccoon?"

Chase tried to stand up to walk over to him, but he couldn't contain his snort. "Did this one scare you too?" he managed to eke out.

The chief came out of his office and assessed the situation. His gaze went from Nick, who was holding the raccoon and glaring at Chase with his hands on his hips, to Chase, who was unable to contain his laughter.

"Now, that's actually funny." The chief shook

his head with a grin. "Might be too soon, but it is funny." He slapped Nick on the shoulder as he walked by. "Lighten up, Moore. This one won't bite you."

The chief chuckled as he made his way to the door. Over his shoulder, he said, "I've got a meeting. I'll be back soon."

"Shithead," Nick said to Chase.

The officer leaned back and put his hands behind his head.

He and Nick had been going back and forth, teasing each other, but he had to say this was one of his better ideas.

The door opened, and his gaze followed, expecting to see the chief returning to grab something he forgot. Instead, a familiar man stepped in. Familiar, but he couldn't quite place him.

"Can I help you?" Chase was up and on his feet. Their town was so small, they didn't have any employees to screen visitors.

"I hope so. My mom's missing."

Chase shot Nick a look.

"What's her name?" he asked.

"Margaret Finkle."

"I can help you," Nick said. "Please have a seat." He motioned to the chair on the opposite side of his desk.

Chase opened his mouth, but Nick arched a brow. After the fiasco with Mr. Rodney's caretaker, it was better that Nick handle this one.

As the man sat down, Chase opened a file on his

desk and pretended to read it while listening to the man tell Nick about his mother.

"You're Ms. Finkle's son?" the detective asked.

"Yes. My name is Dave Finkle. Do you know her?" The man stopped and shook his head. "Of course, you do. Sometimes I forget how small this town is. And my mom would have made a point to get to know you. She always likes to know what's going on with everyone."

That was her son's way of saying she was a busybody. She was in everyone's business, but most wanted her there.

"I'm glad you came in. We've been trying to locate you. Your mom has been missing for over a week. We found her wallet and keys at her house. She also left her cat behind and I know for a fact she would never do that."

Dave paled and Chase rushed to his chair, concerned he might faint.

"Her wallet and keys were at her house?" the man gasped. "No, I thought, maybe she just forgot to call."

Dave stood up, shaking his head. "Was there any evidence that she was taken?"

"Please, sit down." Nick gestured to the chair.

Dave sat down.

"When was the last time you spoke with her?" Nick asked.

"Sunday before last. I remember because I had taken that Monday off, and I was going to go on a hike.

We discussed it."

Nick shot Chase a look, then asked, "Where did you hike?"

"In the Olympic National Forest. I went with a friend. Anyway, I normally talk to my mom on Sundays. This past Sunday, I called, but she didn't answer. She didn't call me back either. I've left messages with her the last three days, and she hasn't called me back. That isn't like her. Then this morning when I called, it said her mailbox is full. I went to her house, but she's not there. She'd never leave her cat."

No, she wouldn't. It was a good thing Nick had taken the critter home.

"You're saying she's been missing over a week?"

"Yes, we tried to reach you but the address and phone number we had for you were for a prior residence and we couldn't get forwarding information," Nick said.

Tears welled in Dave's eyes. "I had to move last month, and I didn't have anything lined up. I've been crashing on a friend's couch until my situation improves."

"Improves?" Chase asked.

"I was laid off. I lost my apartment and my cell phone was disconnected."

Nick leaned back. "That explains why we couldn't reach you."

Dave leaned forward, letting his face fall into his hands. His shoulders shook up and down as he wept. He sniffled as he looked up.

"I was hoping she was simply caught up with her friends and too busy to call me back."

"I realize this is hard, but I need some information for the report," Nick said softly.

Dave nodded.

"Does your mom have any identifying marks?"

"She has a tattoo on her lower back."

Nick's eyebrows shot up. "A tramp stamp?"

That caught Chase's attention. He sat down and pulled up the report from the medical examiner.

Dave smiled. "I told her not to get it there, but when she turned sixty, she insisted. It was an anniversary gift my parents gave to each other. He got a matching tattoo as well on his chest. He passed a few years later and I hated the fact she was living here by herself, but she said she was fine. And I know she has a lot of friends."

"She does. She's very well liked here. I visit her several times a week. Her cat escapes all the time, and she can't crawl under the house to get it. I lure him out with tuna fish."

Dave laughs. "That sounds like her. Her and her damn cats, she always has at least one." He shook his head.

Nick's face was pale. Chase hadn't realized how hard this would be for him. Ms. Finkle had become like a mom to him.

The photo he'd been waiting for finally loaded on his computer.

"Can you describe the tattoo?" Chase

interrupted.

"It's two rings intertwined followed by their wedding anniversary."

"Two rings?" Nick asked.

"Wedding bands. They're gold. And the date next to it is August fourth."

Nick glanced up from the computer. "No year?"

Dave chuckled. "No, Mom didn't want everyone to figure out how old she was."

It took all of Chase's willpower not to show any emotion.

Nick's phone buzzed, and he glanced at it. "Sorry, I have to take this. Harvey, can you finish up?"

"Sure."

He took Nick's seat and typed all of the information in, checking to make sure everything was complete. After a few minutes, he had everything he needed.

"I want you to know that we've been searching everywhere for her. She does have a lot of friends and they have all come out and helped too. Let me give you my card." Chase pulled a card from his shirt pocket and turned it over. "I'm writing the name of the woman who's been leading the town effort on the back. She's very close with your mother."

Chase offered him the card and the man took it and put it in his wallet. "Thank you. I'll call her right away. I'm really hoping my mom is with a friend. When she gets focused on something, everything else falls away."

Dave stood, and Chase extended his hand to shake, then he watched as Ms. Finkle's son walked out the door.

Back at his computer, he pulled the image up again. It was a photo of a tattoo that looked like it could have been two rings followed by some words.

Making his way to the kitchen, he found Nick sitting at the one table, head in his hands.

"Hey." Chase sat across from him.

He didn't need to ask how he was doing. The sorrow was written all over his face.

Nick shook his head. "Where could she be? Between us and her friends, we've searched all over. Even though I knew better, part of me hoped she was with her son."

Dammit. Nick hadn't seen the photo from the ME with the tattoo. Chase didn't want to tell him. Fuck. She was a fixture in this town.

He stared at the floor, unable to meet Nick's gaze when he gave him the news. "The body found in Hawthorne Lake had a tattoo that matches Dave Finkle's description."

There, he'd said it.

After a couple beats of silence, he glanced up. Nick sat stunned, staring at him.

"No. No, the dental records confirmed it wasn't her." The detective stood up so fast, his chair fell backward. "That unidentified woman lying in the cold locker is *not* Ms. Finkle," he boomed.

Chase stood. "Let's go talk to the ME, just to be

certain. Then we should try to talk to Mr. Rodney again."

Nick frowned. "What's the point? Last week, he had no idea who he was, much less if he had money socked away somewhere."

Chase licked his lips. "You're right. We should track down one of his kids. They'd know about the money and if Jace is who he says he is."

"Do you think the yearbook was pushed under her chair because she was hiding it?" Nick asked.

The chief stepped into the kitchen. "You two getting along again?"

"We always get along," Chase said.

"Not always." Dunin crossed his arms.

"Ms. Finkle's son Dave was just here, filling out a missing person report. Chase and I are going to run down some leads." Nick arched his eyebrow at Chase, his way of telling him not to mention the tattoo. No reason to mention it until they knew more.

The chief let out a sigh. "Did you find out where the hell he has been?"

"He said he got laid off last month and has been crashing on a friend's couch," Chase said.

Dunin nodded. "Alright. Let me know if you uncover anything new."

"Will do," Nick said.

Chase drove them to Davenport, where the ME's office was located.

This was a drive he was familiar with. For many months, he had driven to see Bridgette. They'd had a nice friends-with-benefits setup for a while, but he ended it shortly after Nick and Lauren got together. It had become clear to him he wanted more, and there was no way in hell it would be with Bridgette. She was a gorgeous woman, no denying that, but she was the shallowest person he'd ever met. Hell, he'd only gone out with her because she'd come on to him. She wouldn't give him the time of day back in high school, so it was an ego boost when she finally would.

Of course, the lack of men around town didn't hurt his chances there.

What had he been thinking? Now that he had Harmony, he realized he'd been living in a gray world. Nothing compared to her vivaciousness. Yes, they'd been friends and he'd enjoyed her company, but everything was different now. He saw color everywhere.

"You all right over there?" Nick asked.

Chase glanced over. "Yeah, why?"

Nick smirked. "Nothing." Then he reached down and turned the radio on.

Turning the radio off, Chase glanced at his friend again. "You can't do that. What's going on?"

Nick turned in his seat to face him. "When you think no one is looking, you get this dorky smile on your face."

"Dorky? I don't think so."

"Lovesick. That better?"

Chase growled. He wasn't lovesick. He was happy with Harmony, yes, but not lovesick.

"I'm happy to see you two together. It's about time you stopped dicking around."

The county building came up on his right, and he parked the car at the curb.

"I wasn't dicking around."

Nick arched a brow.

"All right, I *used to* dick around, but that was back when I didn't have a chance with Harmony. No one else compared."

"And now that you're together?"

He didn't even fight the smile. "It's better than I ever imagined."

"Hold on to that, especially when this job gets shitty. Hold on to the good."

Nick hadn't shared too much of his past, other than that he'd been in the military and then joined the police academy. But Chase suspected Nick had seen things he wished he hadn't. Now his advice...

A few moments later, they were sitting with the medical examiner. Chase had first met the man about five years ago at a party. He was older and, if Chase recalled, an avid runner. Since he didn't have many occasions to cross paths, as dealing with bodies was rare in Fisher Springs, they hadn't talked since.

"Lucky you caught me." The man sat down at his desk and took a bite of his sandwich. "I'm leaving early today."

"I'll be quick," Nick said. "I know we already ruled out the body from Hawthorne Lake as being Margaret Finkle based on her dental records, but we just found out Ms. Finkle had a tattoo that might match."

Chase watched his friend as he described the tattoo. He never once wavered with emotion. He was in full business mode. How did he do that when the body he was discussing might belong to someone he cared so deeply for?

The ME's voice pulled him from his thoughts. "You just described the tattoo that is on the body. That's a pretty unique tattoo. Maybe we should take a second look at the dental records."

The ME spun in his chair to face his computer and typed. Then he turned the screen around so they could see it.

"On the top are the dental X-rays our forensic dentist took. On the bottom are the ones we obtained from Margaret Finkle's dentist in Fisher Springs. You can see here that Finkle's canine teeth are much shorter. There are other variations as well. The forensic dentist's report said he was certain these two X-rays did not come from the same person."

"You said Finkle's canines were shorter?" Nick asked. "Do you mean these?" he pointed at his own.

"Yes. Those are canines."

"Then something's wrong. Ms. Finkle used to joke about how easy it was for her to eat apples because she had vampire teeth. And she kind of did. I'm sure someone around town or her son has a photo we can show you," Nick said.

The ME leaned back in his chair. "You think the X-rays we received are wrong?"

"I'm concerned they are," the detective said.

"Who is the dentist in Fisher Springs?" Chase asked.

The ME clicked a few times and pulled up a name.

"Here, I'll write it down for you. I believe your chief was the one who obtained the X-rays and brought them over."

The ME handed Chase the paper.

"Dr. Robert Kieves." Chase stared at the name. "That's not the name of the dentist I know in town."

"Well, let's go meet him." Nick stood. "Thank you."

Chapter Twenty-Three

"I'm happy you were able to stop by. I feel like I never get to see you anymore." Lauren poured wine into two glasses before handing one across the kitchen table to Harmony. She sat down and took a sip while admiring the redecorated kitchen. "You've made a lot of changes."

Lauren laughed. "I had to for my peace of mind. Everything in here reminded me of Grace."

Grace Chanler was Lauren's step aunt and was thankfully out of the picture now. Lauren was the proud new owner of the Chanler mansion. Over the past year, Lauren had made significant progress in making it feel much more like her and Nick's home.

Lauren jumped up and clapped her hands. "I bought new hand towels!"

"Towels?" Harmony grinned.

"I know it sounds simple, but I love them

because Nick picked them out. And a couple of months ago, Chase hung the pot rack over the island. Did I not tell you about it? Has it been that long since you've been here?"

Chase installed a pot rack? The image of that man wearing a tool belt and no shirt was hot.

"Earth to Harmony." Lauren snapped her fingers in front of her friend's face.

"What?"

"Where did you go?"

Harmony grinned. "Just imagining Chase wearing a tool belt."

Lauren laughed. "That's probably better than the image I actually saw. Nick couldn't figure out how to install it. He's not the most handy. He called Chase over to help. After they argued, like they do, Chase finally took over and installed it for us."

Harmony took another sip of her wine. Those two men took shots at each other all the time, but it was usually good-natured. They had become best friends after a rough start when Nick first came to town.

"I figured you would be busy this week, finalizing the photos from the wedding. How did that go, by the way?"

Yes, the wedding. It seemed like so long ago now. Fortunately, she'd already worked on those photos and sent them to the couple.

"The wedding was beautiful, as they all are at Forester Farms. I really hope you and Nick get married there."

Lauren waved her hand. "We aren't going to do anything that big. I'm thinking maybe the two of us run off to Hawaii and get married."

"I haven't met Nick's family, but from what I've heard, that wouldn't go over too well."

"You're right. But neither one of us is willing to have a big church wedding like his mother wants, so likely anything we choose will disappoint her."

Harmony's phone buzzed on the table. The screen lit up with Chase's face and she couldn't help the huge grin that spread across her face.

"It is so good to see you smile like that," Lauren said.

"I'd better take this. He's working on that case and might not get another chance to call."

"Of course."

Lauren stepped away from the table, farther into the kitchen.

Harmony answered her phone. "Good afternoon."

"Hey, sexy."

Even through the phone, this man's voice caused her to squeeze her thighs together.

"Will you be working all night?"

"Actually no. That's why I called. I'll be done in about two hours. Do you want to hang out?"

Yes!

"That sounds good," she said casually.

"All right. I can swing by and pick you up."

"I'm at Lauren's. Can you pick me up here?"

He chuckled, and she could imagine the lines by his eyes when he smiled.

"You two having happy hour?"

"Yep."

"All right. Just don't get too carried away. I have plans for you later, and you'll need your energy."

"What plans?"

She took a drink of wine to keep from laughing. She knew what he was thinking but was curious what he would say when pressed.

"Plans that involve my head between your thighs."

She spat out her wine. "Holy shit, Chase."

He laughed. "Too much?"

She grabbed a napkin off the table and cleaned up. "No, just unexpected. I guess I never really knew this side of you."

"Just thinking of you brings up so many dirty thoughts."

"Yeah?"

"Yeah. And I can't wait to share every one with you."

"You want to share some more now?"

He chuckled. "I never knew you liked dirty talk."

"There is a lot you don't know about me," she said, hoping her voice sounded sultry.

"Mmm. Is that so?"

"If you play your cards right, I might let you get to know more."

He growled. "Tonight, I'm going to get to know you really well, babe. I'll see you in a couple of hours."

"I'm looking forward to it."

She ended the call. "Damn that man!"

"Someone has it bad." Lauren walked into the room, carrying a bowl.

"Yeah. I do."

Lauren set the bowl down. It contained a variety of cut vegetables and a dip in the middle. "That's a new hummus recipe I made today. Let me know what you think."

Before Harmony could try the dip, her phone buzzed again. This time, it was a text.

"It's amazing either of you get anything done." Her friend rolled her eyes.

Butterflies took hold of Harmony's stomach. She knew Chase was busy, but that didn't stop her from wanting to talk. But the text wasn't from Chase.

"It's from Rance." She frowned. Why would Rance text her?

"What does he want?" Lauren narrowed her eyes.

Harmony swiped her screen to read the message.

Rance: *Are you free to meet now? I need someone to talk to about my grandfather. I just need a friend.*

Lauren came up behind her. "Tell him to come to my place. I'm here, so he can't try anything."

Her suggestion sounded good. Harmony didn't want to be rude, but she didn't want to encourage him either.

Harmony: *I'm at Lauren's. Can you stop here?*

Rance: *Thanks. I'm on my way.*

"I can't imagine how hard it must be to take care of Mr. Rodney." Lauren refilled her wine glass. She held up the bottle to Harmony, who nodded, so she filled her glass too. "Do you think he really wants to discuss his grandfather?" She quirked an eyebrow.

"Sure. What else would it be?"

"Really?"

"Oh, pfft. We had a few dates that were bland. He's not trying to win me back."

"If you say so."

Harmony leaned back and watched her friend. Lauren was sitting in the chair across from her, but her leg was bouncing.

"What's going on?" She tipped her chin toward Lauren's leg.

Her friend stopped the bouncing. "Sorry. Too much nervous energy."

"Nervous energy?"

Lauren let out a sigh. "Nick's been so busy with this case that, well, it... um."

"Spit it out!"

"It's cut into our sex life."

"Oh."

"Yeah."

Harmony frowned. "Honeymoon is over, huh?"

"What? No! No, it's just Nick was really attached to Ms. Finkle, you know? And he feels like he should have been able to do something."

"What could he have done?"

"That's just it. Nothing. But he's stubborn, and I can't get that through that thick skull of his. But I don't want to push, either. People need to grieve in their own way."

"I'm sorry. You've dealt with so much loss lately."

"I'll be fine. I have you and Nick. What more could I want?"

The front doorbell rang.

"If that's Rance, that was quick," Lauren said as she walked into the living room.

Harmony followed.

Her friend opened the door, and there stood Rance.

"Lauren, good to see you again. Harmony! Thank you for agreeing to talk."

"Let's sit at the kitchen table." Lauren led him to the table. Once Harmony sat down, Rance took the chair next to her. Lauren sat across from Rance.

He clasped his hands together. "I needed someone to talk to. I've been home with grandpa for a few days straight, and it's hard, you know? One minute, he's lucid and talking about old times, and then the next, he's yelling at me, asking who I am and why I'm in his house."

"You need a break. You can't do it all yourself," Lauren said.

He nodded. "Jace is there now. He said he'd help

more."

"That's good." Lauren reached for a carrot and dipped it in the hummus.

"Why did you fire the caretaker?" Harmony pinned him with a stare. "I get you wanted to be there, but it sounds like you still need her."

Rance grabbed a bell pepper strip and chewed it slowly, staring at Harmony.

An awkward silence took over as they waited for his response.

"You're right," he said finally. "I didn't realize how bad off he was, and I thought I could handle it myself. I was wrong."

"Then call his caretaker back."

"I'll think about it. Hey." He nudged Harmony's shoulder but was staring at Lauren. "Any chance I can get a tour of this place? I'm curious how many bedrooms it has."

Lauren's gaze met Harmony's. Harmony gave a slight nod. What harm could there be? It sounded like he needed something to take his mind off his grandfather for a while.

"All right." Lauren jumped up out of her chair. "This is the kitchen, and through here is a reading room."

Then she led them upstairs and gave a quick tour of the master bedroom and a guest room. Soon after, they passed a closed door.

"What's in there?" Rance asked.

"We don't go —."

Rance entered the room. Harmony stepped in behind him, and noticed several boxes marked 'William' on one side of the room. On the other side…

Holy shit.

"What the fuck is that?" Rance jumped back.

"Those dolls belonged to my aunt," Lauren said.

The wall was covered with creepy dolls on shelves. How had Harmony not seen them before?

"Why do you keep them?" she asked.

Lauren shrugged. "I need to go through everything in here. I just haven't felt up to it yet.

Harmony didn't blame her friend one bit for leaving this stuff out of sight. She'd had a hell of a time; it would take anyone a while to deal with all of that.

Throughout the tour, Rance had asked Lauren many questions. The odd thing was, they were all questions about her.

"Lauren, did you go to college?"

"Lauren, do you have a second job like Harmony?"

"Lauren, what do you do for fun?"

Harmony stepped in between them as they returned to the kitchen. Her friend's expression said it all, *save me.* "And that's the house," she said.

Rance nodded and looked around. "What about the garage?"

"I didn't cover outside, did I?" Lauren asked. "Let's go."

They followed her out the front door and stood in front of the garage.

"I don't have the garage door opener on me. But I can tell you that it is what you'd expect in there."

"It's awfully big." Rance crossed his arms while his gaze roamed over the expanse of the garage.

"Yes. Lauren's stepdad stored his cars in there."

"Cars?"

Rance's face lit up.

What was it with the guys she knew all getting hot and bothered over cars?

"Yes. Collector cars."

"*Collector* cars? What a coincidence! Lauren, if you need any help selling them, I can help you out. I actually know a few collectors looking to buy."

Why did Rance's lip quirk up? That was his tell. He was lying. But why? Now that she thought about it, he'd hardly spoken of his grandfather at all. Did he even want to talk, or was he still trying to get to know Lauren?

"Oh, well, that's not—" Lauren stammered.

Harmony cut her off. "Thank you, Rance. She'll think about it."

Lauren arched a brow at her.

"I think Rance has asked enough about you for one day," she said to her friend.

"Any chance I could get a peek at the cars?" He rubbed his hands together, then took a step toward the window on the side of the garage.

Harmony reached out and grabbed him by the arm. "Actually—"

Before she could finish her sentence, a car pulled

into the driveway. She spun around to see who it was, twirling Rance around with her.

Nick's piercing eyes stared her down through the windshield as he pulled in closer.

She glanced at the passenger seat, but thankfully, Chase wasn't there. She was holding on to Rance. This looked bad. But it was innocent.

Nick parked the car and got out, scowling in their direction. "Am I interrupting something?"

She could feel the daggers he was shooting at her.

Dropping Rance's arm like it was on fire, she stepped away from him. "No, not at all."

Nick grunted and marched over to Rance. "Harvey is my best friend, and if I catch you sniffing around his woman again—"

"You'll what?" Rance was in Nick's face.

Harmony was shocked. Rance had always been so mild-mannered, a gentleman. This caveman attitude took her by surprise.

Lauren pulled Nick away. "Nick, don't."

He let her lead him away, but he glared at Harmony over his shoulder. "You'd better not hurt my boy."

Her eyes welled. She had no intention of hurting Chase. Nick had simply misunderstood what he saw.

"Is what he said true?" Rance asked. "Are you that cop's woman? You said you two were just friends. Was that a lie?"

Using her sleeve to wipe the tears from her

cheeks, she turned to Rance. His face was flushed red.

"We were just friends. But then something changed."

Rance laughed. "Something changed? After, what, fifteen years? Yeah, I'll tell you what changed. He was threatened by me. I just hope for your sake you know what you're doing."

He stomped to his car and then tore out of the driveway.

Chapter Twenty-Four

The moment he stepped out of his truck and onto Lauren's driveway, Chase sensed the tension. Nick and Lauren were standing on the porch, while Harmony stood at the bottom of the stairs with her hands on her hips.

He knew Nick was a mess after they had discovered the body was Ms. Finkle's. Despite the fact they were waiting on confirmation from the ME in the morning, the moment they had the correct dental records, they knew.

But he wasn't sure why Harmony and Lauren were so tense, considering they'd agreed not to mention any of this to anyone.

"Everything all right?" he asked as he moved from his truck to the porch steps. His arms naturally snaked around Harmony's waist.

She turned in his arms and that's when he

noticed her eyes were wet.

Nick shook his head. "Yep. I'll be inside." Without so much as looking in Chase's direction, he went into the house.

"Nice to see you, Harvey," Lauren greeted. "I'll leave you two alone."

After her friend left, Harmony continued to stand still.

Chase pulled her into his arms. "What's going on?"

She shook her head. "I don't think Nick's in a good mood."

"He said something that upset you? I'll talk to him." He moved toward the house.

Before he could pass her, she took hold of his arm. "No. He's upset. Let's just go."

He studied her for a moment, then took her hand and led her to the truck. "Do you mind if we go to Zach's tonight?"

"Sounds good to me."

As they drove, the events of the day ran through his mind. Harmony picked up on his silence.

"What happened today? Nick wasn't in a good mood, and you're in your head."

He shook his head. "It was a bad day. I'd rather talk about something good, if you don't mind."

He would keep his promise to Nick to not discuss the case. Besides, there was no point until the ME was able to redo the dental check with the correct X-rays he and Nick had obtained this afternoon.

"Valentine's Day is coming up. I know in the past, you've been sort of anti V-day, but I thought it might be nice if we went out," Chase said staring straight ahead.

Feeling her eyes on him, he glanced over.

She was staring at him, eyes wide. "I'd love that."

"Good. Because I have some ideas."

As he usually did, he parked at his house and then ran around to help her out of his truck.

"Those shoes are sexy," he told her as she stepped out.

"Thank you."

"Also, I've missed you."

Before she could respond, his hand went behind her neck, and he bent down and pressed his lips to hers. What he meant to be a quick kiss turned deeper when she sighed, and he took the opportunity to sweep his tongue into her mouth.

This woman could kiss.

Her hand snaked into his hair, and she gave it a little tug. He moaned, and his other hand cupped her ass.

"Get a room, Harvey!"

They broke apart as a teenager rode by on a bicycle laughing.

"Is that Tom's boy?" she asked.

"Yep. He's a pain in the ass." The tension he'd just started to release came back.

Harmony intertwined her fingers with his.

Every time they touched, it felt so damn good.

"Let's go get you a drink so you can unwind, and then we'll come back here where I'll *really* help you unwind." She winked.

He laughed. "You're a goofball, you know that?"

"That's what you always tell me."

He did, but now it meant more.

She tugged on his hand and they walked the short few blocks to Zach's.

"How was your day?" he leaned in to ask.

Normally, they would have rehashed whatever she and Lauren had talked about. But since their relationship had changed, their conversations seemed to too.

"Good. I always enjoy hanging out with Lauren."

"You mean drinking with Lauren?"

She stepped in front of him, stopping him in his tracks. "We do other things together."

He arched a brow.

"We talk about you."

He laughed. "Do you now? I should have known you can't keep your mind off me." Leaning forward, he gave her a quick kiss.

Rain started to fall, and they quickened their pace.

Once inside the pub, Chase ordered two IPAs, then set them on the table as he slid into the booth across from Harmony.

"Harmony! It's great to see you again so soon."

Rance had come out of nowhere and was now standing next to their booth.

"Again?" Chase asked her.

Rance took that as an invitation and sat down next to Harmony. "I'm sorry I left so quickly. I had to process everything, but now that you're here, I want to thank you again for being such a great listener today. I don't know what I would do without you."

Chase watched as Rance moved his hand on top of Harmony's and gave it a squeeze.

She had seen Rance today. Why hadn't she mentioned that? He'd asked about her day, and she'd only mentioned Lauren.

"When did you two see each other today?" Damn, despite his effort, he couldn't keep the growl out of his voice.

The way Harmony's eyes widened; he knew he sounded like some possessive prick. But dammit, Harmony knew his family history, and she knew he would be sensitive to this. Why didn't she mention she'd seen him? And she'd 'listened' to him? This wasn't a passing meeting at the diner.

"Just a little bit ago, at Lauren's. I asked Harmony if I could see her, and she said yes." Rance turned and grinned like a fool at Harmony.

She said yes. Did she still have some kind of feelings for this guy? Why would she agree to see him? They weren't even friends... or were they?

He realized suddenly there was a lot he didn't know about her.

He must have worn his confusion on his face, because her gaze finally met his, and she shook her head.

"He needed someone to talk to, and I figured since I was with Lauren, he could stop by."

His jaw ticked. He drained his beer then stood up to get another. "I'll be right back."

Unfortunately, luck was not on his side today, because he found himself at the bar standing next to Jace. The cousin. He'd met the man the other day when he'd run into him and Tabitha coming out of the diner. Now, instead of relaxing with a beer, he was sandwiched between the two suspects in Ms. Finkle's murder.

"Officer Harvey, right?"

Well, so much for ignoring this guy.

Drawing a deep breath to calm himself, he turned. The man was a few inches shorter than he was, and older. He wore a gray sweatshirt with the sleeves pulled up, exposing tattoos. The man likely had sleeves of tattoos. He wore black jeans and combat boots. Give the man some eyeliner, and he could pass for the lead singer of Green Day, with his long hair sticking up in all the right places.

"You here with Tabitha?" Chase asked.

The man grinned. "Nah. Just my cousin, Rance. It seems you've gotten to know him well, since he was dating your girl and all."

Chase pivoted on his heel to face Jace. "I make a point of knowing everyone in this town."

"I bet you do."

Zach poured him another IPA and set it on the counter.

"I'm sure I'll see you around." Chase gave a tight smile before he made his way back to his table, where Rance was still sitting too close to Harmony.

At least she didn't look happy about it.

"My grandfather mentioned a woman had gone missing. Says she was a high school teacher. You find her yet?" Rance asked.

He studied the man. Was he trying to fish for information because he was guilty? Nothing about his demeanor gave off any guilty vibes, but then, some people knew how to hide that.

"No." Since Rance brought it up, maybe he could find out some information of his own. "Have you ever met Ms. Finkle?"

"Finkle? That's an unfortunate name." Rance chuckled. "No. Never have."

He glared at Rance, but the man didn't notice.

"Hey, isn't that Jace at the bar?" Harmony asked.

"Yeah. I should probably get back to him." Rance stood up.

"I thought you said he was with your grandfather. Who's with him now?"

Rance paled.

Jace conveniently came up behind him. "Neighbor offered to sit with him so we could go out."

"Yeah, we should probably get back. I'll call you sometime." Rance was looking directly at Harmony.

"Or not," Chase said.

Rance's eyes ping-ponged from Chase to Harmony. "Yeah, Harmony mentioned you two are a bit more friendly now. Funny how you stepped up once I was in the picture."

"What the hell are you saying?" Chase glared at him while he chugged half his beer.

Rance shrugged. "Just curious if you're really into her, or if you just like controlling women."

Chase glared at Rance counting to ten in his head to calm himself so he didn't do something stupid. Controlling? Never. The truth was he'd just been too chickenshit before.

Jace must have sensed Chase's loose hold on his anger because he pulled on Rance's arm. "Let's go." Thankfully, he followed, leaving Chase and Harmony alone.

After they were out of earshot, Chase couldn't help himself.

"Want to tell me why you didn't mention seeing Rance today?"

Red crept up Harmony's neck to her cheeks. Yeah, she knew she'd been caught lying. Well, lying by omission, but that was the same thing to him.

"I didn't think it was a big deal, because Lauren was there."

"Give me a break," he said as he finished off his second beer.

"You're angry."

"You think? You know my history. I thought

you were the one person I could count on to be honest. Be faithful."

The moment the words slipped out of his mouth, he regretted them. They'd never spoken about being exclusive. But they weren't a normal dating couple. Of course, she would know they were exclusive, right? After her jealous outburst here the other night...

Wait.

"Was this revenge for the blond hanging on me the other night?"

Shit, why hadn't he thought of that? But no, Harmony had a short fuse, but she wasn't vengeful. Was she?

Her eyebrows shot up. "How dare you? No! I was just being nice to Rance, and I didn't think it was a big deal. But then when Nick got home and saw Rance, he tore into me." Tears fell down her cheeks.

Damn, way to go. Now she's crying.

"Nick tore into you?"

She nodded. "When he saw Rance, he asked what the hell he was doing there. Rance took the hint and left while Lauren tried to calm Nick down. Nick accused me of using you, but he was wrong. I didn't tell you about Rance because I didn't want you to think that too. I'm sorry."

He moved over to her side of the booth and wrapped her in his arms. "I would never think that."

"I won't talk to Rance anymore," she promised. "I'll make that clear to him."

He felt like an asshole. He should tell her she

could be friends with whoever she wanted. But dammit, staying away from Rance really was in her best interest right now, so he kept his mouth shut, and just squeezed her tighter.

Chapter Twenty-Five

Harmony winced when she saw her reflection in the mirror. Mascara had run beneath her eyes, giving her a raccoon appearance. She'd never been a cute crier like Lauren. She hadn't even realized she'd cried that much, sitting at the table with Chase.

After wiping away the offending black smudges, she exited the pub's bathroom. Instead of turning left to go to the front to find Chase, she heard a familiar voice to her right. The men's room door was open.

"Focus, this isn't about the girl," the familiar voice said.

"I know. She isn't the priority now, but later, she will be."

She swore the second voice had been Rance's.

"No. She won't. If you keep bothering her, that cop boyfriend will really be up in our business. The last thing we need is a cop snooping around."

Jace. She was sure that was Jace. Snooping around? What were they up to?

"Let's go before the cop sees us. I don't want to have to further explain who's watching grandpa," Rance said sarcastically.

As she heard their footsteps approach, she dashed back into the women's bathroom until they had passed.

What the hell had she just heard? Bile rose in her throat, and nausea took over. Something was wrong, she could feel it.

After a count of three, she stepped out.

The hallway was empty except for the large, framed photographs that lined both walls. It was her favorite part of the pub. Each photo showcased a different part of the forest around Washington state.

She squinted at the name signed at the bottom. Katie Thiel. The name was familiar.

Harmony found Chase at the bar, talking to Zach. At least he was smiling now. Maybe they could salvage this night after all.

When she walked up, his gaze flitted to her. His crooked smile was back, and it went to his eyes. Those familiar creases were there as he took her in.

"Ready?" Chase asked.

"Yes."

He took her hand and led her out to the street. The winter wind was blowing harder than usual tonight, and she was shivering.

"I overheard two men that I think were Rance

and Jace," she said. "I couldn't see them, but Jace said they didn't need a cop snooping around. Do you know what they are up to?"

Chase stared forward. "No but thank you for telling me. I'll keep an eye on them." Then he turned to her. "Can we not talk about Rance anymore tonight?"

She reached for his hand. "Sure."

They made their way to his front porch, and he winked at her as he fetched his keys out of his pocket.

That wink. This man. She pressed up onto her toes and kissed him.

Just that one small touch, and they exploded. He deepened their kiss with his tongue, and his hand was on her ass. He somehow managed to unlock the door, and they parted long enough to get inside. But her plan to jump him went up in smoke when a familiar voice spoke.

"Chase, honey, I'm so glad you're back!"

Chase's mom. On his couch. Right now.

Damn, her timing couldn't be worse.

"Mom, have you been crying?" he asked.

When his mom stepped into the light, Harmony saw the telltale wet streaks streaming down her cheeks.

"I had a fight with Gus. We're done. You were right all along. He was just like the rest."

Harmony did her best to not frown.

This was what his mother did. She'd date a man who wasn't good for her, he'd disappoint her, she'd cheat on him, then they would break up, and she'd cry on Chase's shoulder.

Danielle Pays

In high school, Harmony had told Chase it wasn't appropriate. But he'd said his mom had no one else to turn to. But what made Harmony so angry was the fact that the woman's relationships never worked out for the same reason: she'd been caught cheating, or the guy suspected. Although, the type she dated, she was pretty sure it was a mutual activity.

"Harmony, it's good to see you. It's been too long. I'm sorry to interrupt your plans, but I'm happy to see it's you two. I was half-worried Chase might bring back a date, and here I would be." She laughed.

Chase chuckled uncomfortably.

"Speaking of, I haven't seen my son in a while. Are you seeing anyone special?"

He speared his hand through his hair and avoided Harmony's gaze. "Um. Mom, I don't want to talk about my dating life."

What the hell? Why wouldn't he tell his mom about them? She'd probably be thrilled. Unless she was just another one of his flings. Was that what she was? A friend-with-benefits?

Her stomach churned, and her face warmed. If she didn't get out of there, she was going to be sick. How could she have been so stupid?

From out of nowhere, Chase's mother had her hand to Harmony's forehead. "Are you feeling all right? You look flushed. I think you might be getting sick."

"I am feeling sick." She glared at Chase, but he avoided her stare.

He remained where he was. He didn't reach for

her, didn't explain.

They were new. Maybe that was why he didn't say anything. But no, they'd known each other too long. This wasn't that kind of new. This was huge. She'd told everyone about them because she was so excited. Hell, her parents knew, as did Lauren, Kate, Tabitha. There wasn't anyone she'd kept this from.

Had he even told any of his friends? Maybe Nick only knew because Lauren had told him. And Zach knew all her friends, so he could have heard it from one of them.

She had to get out of there.

"I need to go. I'm sorry about your boyfriend."

She ran out and was almost to the road when a hand wrapped around her arm and twirled her around.

No, she didn't want him to see her cry. She'd been a fool, thinking they were something they weren't.

"Harmony, don't go." He was breathing hard. "I don't know why I said that. It's just my mom. She's, you know."

"Yeah." His mom was someone important to him. She got it. "She needs you. I'm going to head home."

"Maybe I can drive you."

"No. It's a short walk. I'll be fine."

His mother appeared in the doorway. "Chase, I'm going to help myself to a drink. I hope that's all right."

When his mother had 'a drink,' she had more like ten. He was in for a long night of babysitting her.

Harmony took this chance to get away.

"I'll see you later." She turned and took off before he could stop her.

Two blocks later, she realized this had been a bad idea. The wind had picked up, and she was shivering so hard, she could barely walk straight. Add to that she was wearing heels that she could barely walk in on a good day.

When she turned off Main Street, it grew darker and colder. Fisher Springs was a small town and safe. Usually. Except, Ms. Finkle was missing. What had happened to her?

She really hoped the woman would return from some fancy cruise with stories to tell, just like Bella Daniel.

An unfamiliar car pulled up beside her, and she jumped. How had she not heard that coming?

She picked up her pace. Her heart raced. The headlights cut through the darkness, and up ahead, she saw garbage cans out on the sidewalk, waiting for tomorrow's pick up. Most houses had porch lights on, but their light didn't fall all the way to the street.

A humming drew her attention to the car. The window rolled down. One glance, and she saw it was Jace. She stopped.

"Need a ride?" he asked.

A couple of the times she'd been out with Rance, Jace had popped up. Although she didn't really know him, two of her friends had no problem trusting him. Although, after overhearing him in the bathroom, she wasn't as sure.

"What happened to Rance? You were just at the pub with him."

Jace smiled. "He's still at the pub. The neighbor called and asked if I'd bring some food from the diner. I was driving back home with it when I saw you walking."

Well, that was plausible. Mr. Rodney's house was in this direction.

"I don't bite, I promise." He grinned. "Well, unless you want me to."
Screw it. It was cold and she could barely feel her feet. She was about to become a statistic if she stood outside any longer.

"Sure. It's not far."

After a nod, she walked around and got into the car. When she got in, the heater was cranked up all the way. She placed her hands in front of the vents to warm up.
The car smelled of his cologne and faintly of cigarettes.

"You could have frozen to death out there," he said.

"I wasn't thinking about that. Thanks for the ride."

"Where to?" he asked.

She gave him directions, and he pulled away from the curb.

"You can have my hot chocolate if you'd like. Looks like you need it more than I do."

She glanced down at the cup holders to see a cup

near him. It looked like one of the diner's to-go cups. The diner had the best hot chocolate.

"Thank you."

She reached down, grabbed it, then took a sip. Damn, that was good. It sent her stomach growling. She hadn't eaten since lunch and assumed she and Chase would order a pizza in, but that plan had gotten trashed to hell.

She stole a glance at Jace. "Do you dislike Harvey as much as Rance does?"

Jace laughed. "Well, Rance dislikes him for obvious reasons. I don't dislike him, but I'll side with my cousin anytime."

"Have you and Rance always been close?" That was good. Sounded casual.

"No. But we've grown close recently."

Short answers. She needed more.

"What's your family like?"

Jace smiled and stared straight ahead.

"Oh, turn right here. Sorry."

Jace turned.

"It's the apartment building on the left."

To prevent her fingers from fidgeting from nerves, she found herself taking several more sips of the hot chocolate. Jace continued to stare at the road and ignored her last question.

"What apartment number?" he asked as he parked.

"Two-oh-one."

Before she could think of another question, he

was outside her door, opening it for her.

"Such a gentleman."

When she stood, she wobbled a little. Funny, she'd only had one drink.

"Let me help you to your door."

"That's not necessary."

"If anything happened to you, I'm sure your boyfriend would have my hide for leaving you like this. Just to the door. I promise."

Her boyfriend. Yeah right. He didn't care as much as she'd wanted him to.

"Okay."

No harm in him walking her to her door.

Chapter Twenty-Six

"Chief, you have a minute?" Chase followed Dunin into his office the next morning.

Dunin took off his coat and hung it up on the back of his door. When he spun and got a glimpse of Chase, he frowned. "What the hell happened to you? You look like shit. I thought I told you to go home to rest."

"Long story."

He wasn't about to tell the chief that he'd screwed things up last night with Harmony. He was still kicking himself for not telling his mom about her. But he knew his mom, she'd have their wedding planned by the end of the week. Discussing the 'M' word with Harmony was not something he was ready for. Hell, he never imagined he would even get married. Not after the way his parents' marriage had blown up. Why would anyone subject themselves to that?

But then he thought of Harmony. He knew she wanted marriage and kids. They'd talked about it one night, after one of her relationships had blown up in her face. She hadn't been upset about losing the guy, she said. It was the loss of an opportunity to have it all.

After he'd calmed his mom down and she'd fallen asleep on the couch, he'd tossed and turned. If he couldn't give Harmony what she wanted, then what was he doing? Was he preventing her from finding true love? Then he'd spent the rest of the night imagining her walking down the aisle with another man, and the thought had him so fucking furious, he couldn't sleep.

And that was why now he stood before his chief, looking like shit.

"Does it have to do with Ms. Finkle? You have some news for me from yesterday?"

"I do and you're not going to like it. We had the wrong dental records." Chase handed the file to Dunin. "That *was* Ms. Finkle's body in Hawthorne Lake. The ME came in early this morning to look over the new dental records. He confirmed it." He pushed his fingers into his hair and tugged to calm himself. "I'm sorry. I know she was a friend."

"What do you mean new dental records? How?" The chief stood, a red flush creeping up the back of his neck. That was a telltale sign he was pissed. The poor man had been through a lot.

After their visit with the town dentist to retrieve the records yesterday, they returned to the station to find Dunin talking with his son in his office. Nick had heard Dunin was having troubles with his son, Joey, again. Chase texted Joey to find out what was going on, but he never heard back. Joey hadn't responded to any of his texts since he'd been fired as the town detective for drug use. He'd hoped that Joey would reach out for help. Whatever Dunin was discussing with his son, Nick and he agreed, they wouldn't interrupt.

"Nick and I went to visit the dentist that provided the X-rays to the medical examiner."

The chief held up his hand. "Wait. Back up and explain why you thought you needed to do that. The last thing you guys told me was that Ms. Finkle was missing, and you were going to track down some leads."

Chase explained that Ms. Finkle's son mentioned she had a tattoo, and he remembered the ME's report indicated there was a tattoo on the body.

"After we confirmed the tattoo, we asked to see her dental X-rays. But when Nick noticed something was off about the X-ray, we went to visit the dentist."

He shook his head at the memory. "The man has been retired for something like ten years. He had all these files in his garage, and the boxes had spilled at some point, and he'd just tossed the files back in. It was a mess. I don't know whose X-rays he gave you, but they weren't Ms. Finkle's."

"You're saying the body is Ms. Finkle?" the chief asked.

"I'm afraid so."

The chief put his fists on his desk and leaned on them. "Why would someone murder her? She's such a kind woman."

"That was the other part of our day. Rance's cousin came to the diner about two and a half weeks ago, and Ms. Finkle had questioned him about his mother. According to Harmony, she didn't like his answer, and said she was worried someone was trying to con Mr. Rodney."

The chief chuckled. "Well, if someone is trying to con that man, they are barking up the wrong tree."

"Actually, she might have been onto something. We caught Donald in a lucid moment, and discovered he inherited a large sum of money several years ago. According to him, it just sits in a few bank locations. He said money ruined his father, and he wasn't going to fall into the same trap."

"A *few* banks? How large a sum are we talking?"

"Ten million dollars."

The chief whistled. "I can see Margaret's reason for concern. How the hell did I not know about that?"

"Harmony—" His voice cracked merely saying her name.

He coughed and tried again. "Harmony mentioned Ms. Finkle said she was going to check her yearbooks to verify the Rodney family after the cousin, Jace, said his mother's name was Laura. Ms. Finkle knew that was wrong. That day we were at her house, Nick found a yearbook shoved under a chair in the front room. At the time, we just thought it was odd. Now I'm thinking she hid it when someone surprised her."

"That's quite a leap, Harvey."

"It is. But we went back to her house yesterday and discovered two yearbooks missing. Both were years that Mr. Rodney's daughter would have attended Fisher Springs High."

The chief fell back into his chair. "Huh. Well, you know the library keeps a copy. You can see if there is anything odd about those years."

"Already tried that. The library was missing three yearbooks."

"You think someone is trying to hide something?"

Chase nodded. "I do. The yearbook shoved under Ms. Finkle's chair matches one of those missing from the library."

"And?" The chief crossed his arms.

"The cousin gave the wrong name. The daughter's name is Susan, not Laura."

"Run me through how you figured this out."

"In the yearbook from Ms. Finkle's, Mr. Rodney's twins were sophomores. Mr. Rodney had one son, then he had fraternal twins, one boy and one girl. The girl's name is Susan. Jace said his mother's name was Laura. He was lying and Ms. Finkle had the proof."

"Maybe Jace's mother married one of the Rodney boys."

"It's possible but the fact all those yearbooks went missing is suspicious. Nick and I will double-check with the county records for marriages, and I'm going to see my grandma. She knows the family too."

The chief grabbed a stress ball and started to

squeeze. "You think Jace killed Ms. Finkle?"

"That's the current theory. But we can't rule out Rance, either. If Jace isn't really Rance's cousin, then Rance may not be Mr. Rodney's grandson, either."

"Who the hell are they, then?" Dunin scratched his beard. "Well, find out, but don't let on that you're investigating them. Sounds like they could be dangerous."

"Will do, Chief."

Chase made his way out of the office and ran into Nick. "I know someone who might know a bit about Mr. Rodney's family." He grinned.

"Who?"

"My grandma."

He called her to set up their visit. Then he checked his messages. No text or anything from Harmony. But why would she reach out to him after last night?

He quickly wrote out a text.

Chase: *I need to see you tonight.*

Immediately, bubbles appeared. Wasn't she working? How could she respond so fast?

Harmony: *I can't.*

She was still pissed. He couldn't blame her, but he had to see her.

"Are you going to stare at porn on your phone all day, or are we going?" Nick had snuck up beside him.

"Jackass."

"Hey, isn't that what you called me after we

met?"

He couldn't help but laugh.

He had called him jackass. He'd come in and taken over Joey's job which rubbed him the wrong way. But Chase was finally able to admit that Joey had lost the job himself when his addiction got the best of him. If it hadn't been Nick, the chief would have hired someone else to take his son's place.

Chase drove them to his grandma's house. The door flew open before they could knock.

His grandma stood in the doorway, wearing her usual outfit of a sweater and jeans. But instead of the smile he expected, she stood with her arms crossed, glaring at him.

He had no idea what he'd done wrong, but it was time to put on his charm.

"Grandma, it's nice to see you." He gave her his biggest grin.

"Oh, don't you smile at me, boy. How long has it been since you've come to see me?"

"Too long."

"Damn straight it is. Now come on in." His grandma caught sight of Nick. "And who is this handsome fellow you brought with you?"

They both stepped into her house. Not much had changed in all the years she lived here. The walls were the same color, and the curtains were the same as when Chase was a boy. Well, they might be a little lighter now, from being bleached by the sun. Even her brown couch and chair were the same. On her wall, she had several photos of Chase through the years.

"Nick Moore," he introduced himself. "I work with your grandson at the police department."

His grandma eyed Nick up and down "Then why aren't you wearing a uniform too?"

Nick chuckled. "I'm a detective, and I've always worn a suit for work."

"Uh-huh. Well, you can call me Carol."

She motioned to the kitchen table, which sat adjacent to the living room. "Well, sit down now."

"I'm guessing you're here because of your mom and her latest mistake. I'll tell you what I told her. It's good Gus is gone. God, I don't know where I went wrong with that girl, but she can't pick a decent man to save her life."

Chase sat and shook his head. "Actually, I don't want to discuss my mom."

She waved her hand in the air. "Good. No point. What brings you by?"

"We're here to ask you about Mr. Rodney and his family. We need to know the names of his children."

She leaned back, frowning. "Well, I guess you can't really ask Mr. Rodney, can you? That poor man. As if losing his wife wasn't bad enough. Now he's been cursed with this." She shook her head.

A whistle came from the kitchen, and his grandma stood up.

"I'm making tea. Would you boys like some?"

"Yes, please," Nick replied.

"Let me get that for you." Chase jumped up

before his grandmother could move further.

"Thank you," his grandma said with a smile.

He placed tea bags in three mugs and poured hot water into each. Then he carried them on the tray his grandma kept on the counter.

"Here you go." He set the mugs on the table.

"You know I was best friends with his wife, Maria, back in high school," she said. "She was very popular, and beautiful with her long, shiny, dark hair. I remember everyone loved her hair."

Chase knew he had to cut his grandma off, otherwise she'd go down the wrong memory lane. "Was there anyone named Laura in his family?"

"Laura?" Carol sat back with a frown. After a moment, she leaned forward again. "No. I'd remember that, because I just loved that girl Laura Ingalls Wilder in that show *Little House on the Prairie*. Do you remember...ah, you're too young. Anyway, Laura was one of my favorite names."

"Was there anyone with a name that sounded similar?" Nick asked.

"No. Donald and Maria had three children. David was the oldest. Then they had the twins, Susan and Ron. Here, let me write it down so you have the names."

She went over to a nearby desk and pulled out a piece of paper and a pen. Then she sat back down at the table and drew out the Rodney family tree.

When she was done, she spun it around and pushed it toward Chase. "No one named Laura. No L names at all, actually."

He stared at the information. His grandmother had filled in the next generation as well. Rance was the son of Ron. There were no children listed under David. But she had written that Susan had a son named Jace.

"Are you certain about the name of Susan's son?" Chase asked.

"I am. I helped organize the baby shower for her. It was her first child."

"Thank you. This helps tremendously." Chase pocketed the family tree, then glanced over at Nick, who was frowning.

"Now we have motive," his friend said under his breath.

"Okay. Now that we have that out of the way, it's time we play cards." Carol clapped her hands together, and then went to her desk to retrieve a deck.

"Cards?" Nick asked.

Carol sat down and smiled. "I hope you brought some money."

"Grandma, we're on duty. We can't play poker right now."

She arched a brow. "I'm an old woman. You can give me one game."

Nick chuckled. "I'm sure we can play one game, but I only have three dollars on me."

Carol shuffled the cards and dealt them like a pro. "That's all right this time. Next time, you will be more prepared."

For only having thirteen dollars between the

three of them, the game went on for longer than expected. Once his grandma brought out muffins that she had made earlier that morning, Nick was a goner.

After thanking his grandma, they walked out to the car. Chase still had no response from Harmony.

"I need to stop at the diner," he said.

"Sounds good. I'm hungry."

Chase laughed. Nick had already eaten three muffins.

They made their way to the diner for lunch. To his surprise, Harmony was not working. According to Logan, she'd called in sick.

Harmony never called in sick.

Dammit. He had to fix this. Nick would understand that he needed to go see her.

While Chase paid for lunch, Nick leaned back in his chair, chewing on his lip.

"What are you thinking?"

"Whether Jace and Rance are even related and why they're really here."

"You already know my opinion on Rance. Mr. Rodney was adamant no one in his family was blond." Chase stood and grabbed his jacket from the back of the chair. "As for the why, we know ten million reasons why."

"Just to be sure, we'd better run a few more searches. There must be a photo somewhere online of Rance Rodney."

Chase sighed. His issues with Harmony would have to wait.

Chapter Twenty-Seven

Before she opened her eyes, the pounding headache had her seeing stars. What the hell happened?

Slowly, she pried her eyes open. She wasn't in her bed. Where was she? Directly in front of her was a gray wall. Pushing up, she realized she was on her couch, facing its back cushion, and had her favorite blanket pulled up to her shoulders. At least she was home. But that didn't explain the pounding headache, or why she was on her couch.

Closing her eyes to dull the pain, she went over the last things she remembered. Chase's mom. Her asking if he had a girlfriend. Him saying he didn't. The memory gutted her just like it had last night. Then she remembered walking back to her place. It was so cold. Too cold. Jace. He gave her a ride home. But she couldn't remember walking into her apartment, or why she was on the couch.

Turning to her other side, she nearly jumped out of her skin when she saw Jace sitting in the chair across from the couch.

"Good morning, sleepyhead." He smiled.

Self-consciously she pulled the blanket up higher. Wait, what was she wearing? A quick glance under the blanket, and she let out a sigh of relief. She was fully clothed in the same clothes she'd worn out last night.

Jace was still smiling at her.

"Jace? Why are you in my apartment?"

He rubbed his face and pushed his hands into his already messy hair. "Do you remember last night?"

"I remember you gave me a ride, but I don't remember inviting you inside."

He chuckled. "I walked you to your door because you were swaying. I was worried about you, so I helped you inside."

"You were worried about me? You don't even know me."

He stood and stretched his hands up in the air while he yawned, revealing even more ink on his stomach. How many tattoos did this guy have?

"That's true, but my mom raised me to be a gentleman, and I wasn't about to leave a drunk woman standing on the curb."

The pounding in her head was too much, so she leaned back. "That was to my door. Why are you inside?"

"I helped you to the couch, but before I made it

to the door to leave, you stopped me."

She arched a brow. None of this sounded like her.

"You asked me to have a drink with you because you didn't want to drink alone."

Okay, that part did sound like something she would say. She wasn't one to drink alone. And after what happened with Chase, she could see that she would want a drink.

Pointing at the coffee table, he explained, "Then you opened up that bottle there, and started taking shots. You offered me a couple as well."

Her eyes went to the table where a half-empty bottle of whiskey sat, along with two shot glasses. What the hell? She never drank whiskey. That was Chase's bottle he kept there for nights they hung out at her place. That wasn't very often, since her apartment was smaller than his house. But she was pretty upset last night. Maybe she did drink. She certainly felt like she'd been up most of the night drinking.

"I offered you a drink of whiskey?"

Jace fell back into the chair. "No. You offered to open a bottle of wine, but then I saw that sitting on your counter, and said I would prefer the whiskey."

"Oh."

"You said it belonged to Chase."

All right, she would say that.

"How many shots did I have?"

He laughed. "I don't know. I kind of lost count."

"And you slept in that chair and I slept on the

couch?"

He leaned forward, wearing a grin. "Nothing happened between us, if that's what you are worried about."

"Good. I was, yes."

She attempted to sit up again and glanced out the window. The sun was peeking out of the clouds, but in the wrong location in the sky. What time was it? Well, if she drank too much, she would have slept in, but how late?

"What time is it? I've got to get to work." She jumped up.

"It's four in the afternoon."

She froze. Four? How could she have slept that long? How late did she friggin' stay up?

"Don't worry. I called the diner this morning and told whoever answered that you would be out sick today."

"You called in sick for me? How the hell did you know I was supposed to go in? And they were all right with that?"

His lips curled up. "You mentioned last night that you had work today. After you stayed up all night, I figured it wasn't for the best. They probably thought I was that boyfriend of yours."

For the best? Who the hell was this guy?

When she saw her phone on the coffee table, she reached for it. Jace made no move to stop her. That was good at least. Although, if he had intended to harm her, he would have already.

There were six texts from Chase. He wanted to see her. He was sorry about last night. Then she had responded.

"When did I respond to a text?"

According to the time stamp, it was sent this morning.

"Before you passed out."

Chase sent more texts after that, letting her know something came up at work, but he'd come to the diner when he was done. But she wouldn't be at the diner, which meant he'd come to her place.

Jace needed to leave.

"Thank you for helping me home last night, but if you don't mind, I'd like to be alone now."

"No worries. I understand. I just wanted to make sure you woke up this morning."

Her eyebrows shot up. Woke up?

He ran his hands up his face. "That came out wrong. What I meant was, I was concerned you might have drank too much last night, and I wanted to be here in case you puked or something. You know?"

"I do. And thank you for that." She walked toward the door, hoping he would take the hint to leave right away.

Fortunately, he stood and grabbed the jacket he had tossed on the back of the chair. As he slowly inserted each arm in the jacket, she braced herself on the wall next to the door.

Why did her head have to weigh so much? It was a struggle to hold it up. And why did he have to move so slow? Just put the damn jacket on outside!

Shower. Food. Bed. She couldn't decide what order she wanted to do those in. Food? Yes. Food first. Then shower. Then bed. That made sense.

Good Lord, now he was zipping his jacket?

Finally, he moved toward the door. She opened it as he approached.

"Thank you again for last night."

Jace's gaze moved to the doorway as he smiled. "Anytime, Harmony. Excuse me."

Her head whipped to the doorway to find Chase; his hand held up like he was about to knock on the door.

His eyes took in her clothes. His brow furrowed, and his gaze moved to her hair. He then turned in the direction Jace had gone.

When she leaned out the door, she saw what he saw. Jace's clothes looked rumpled. His hair was a mess.

"It's not what it looks like," she assured him.

Chase growled. The man *growled*.

Shit. Shit. Shit.

She knew what he'd gone through with his parents' divorce, when he learned it was because his mom had cheated. And then cheated on every boyfriend since. This was probably why he didn't do relationships.

He couldn't think this about her.

"Chase, seriously. Look at me."

His gaze met hers, and pure, deep anger like nothing she'd seen before emanated through his eyes.

"Jace slept in that chair," she turned to point at it. "And I slept on that couch, under that blanket. Jace said he only stayed to make sure I didn't puke in my sleep."

Chase's hands were clenched by his sides. He took one and ran it through his hair, pulling, causing his hair to stick up.

"Why the fuck was that man in your apartment?" His voice was incredibly calm and did not match his body language.

He'd never been this angry at her. She could feel it coming off him in waves.

"After I left your place, I was walking home. It was cold. Jace drove up and offered me a ride. Then he said I swayed when I got out of the car. Apparently, I'd had more to drink than I realized."

Chase stepped inside and stood toe to toe with her. "You had one beer."

"That's what I thought, but—"

He pushed past her into her apartment and stopped next to the coffee table.

"You two drank my whiskey?"

"Jace didn't want wine, so he—"

"You invited Jace into your apartment and offered him wine. After we had a disagreement?"

Shit. This looked so bad. But it wasn't.

Wait, what did he say?

"Disagreement?" she repeated.

"Yeah. We had a disagreement. I'm sorry I couldn't talk about it right then, but my mom needed me."

"Oh no you don't. What we had was not a

disagreement. You didn't want your mom to know that I was anything to you. That hurt."

"Look, I wasn't ready to tell my mom. She would have started planning our wedding and asking us when we were getting married." He spiked his hand through his hair again as he started pacing.

She could feel the nervous energy rolling off of him.

"And the idea of ever marrying me is just too much? I get it. You've always made it clear you are not a relationship guy. Stupid me. I thought somehow what we had would be different than one of your friends-with-benefits arrangements." Tears rolled down her cheeks.

He pointed at her. "No. I see what you're doing. You're redirecting."

She threw her hands in the air. "What?"

"You invited Jace up to your apartment for a drink after we had a... well, you know. How could you do that? You know cheating is my sore spot, Harmony. How could you?"

"Nothing happened with Jace. If you can't believe me then you need to go. Please leave." She held open the door.

He stopped pacing and faced her. She turned her gaze outside. Looking at him would be too much.

She wanted him to take her in his arms and say he was sorry, that he'd made a mistake and yes, he wanted her forever. But instead, he took her suggestion and walked out her door. He didn't look back.

The pounding in her head came back hard. She sank to the floor.

Chapter Twenty-Eight

The baseball smashed the bottle, sending it flying. It should have made him feel better, but it didn't. Chase took another pull of his beer. All of this usually made him feel better, but nothing was working tonight.

"Harvey? You back here?" Nick rounded the back of the house. "I saw your truck in the driveway, and since you weren't at Zach's, I figured you must be around back. Either that, or I was going to have to consider you might be ignoring me." He chuckled.

Chase threw another baseball at the next empty bottle he had lined up. Nailed it.

"What's going on?" Nick asked.

Chase drained his beer and set the empty bottle on the fence post.

"I went to see Harmony. Found out why she hadn't responded to my texts. She was too busy with Jace Callahan. No, wait. She did respond to one, telling me she couldn't see me. Now I know why."

He threw the ball as hard as he could, knocking that bottle back into the woods too. He was grateful to have the green belt behind his property. It proved useful for times like these.

"What do you mean she was busy with Jace?" Nick growled, hands on his hips. "Did you tell her he's a suspect?"

"Hell no, I didn't tell her. After I left you earlier today, I went to see her. Before I had a chance to knock, she opened the door. And Jace was leaving."

"All right, but that doesn't mean anything happened—"

"As she was opening the door, she thanked him for last night."

"Shit."

"Yeah. Last night, we came back to my place, and my mom was here."

Nick helped himself to a beer, sitting on the outdoor table. During the last year, Chase had opened up enough about his family that Nick knew this was a beer conversation.

"My mom has always known Harmony is my best friend, so she didn't think a thing of asking if I was seeing someone."

Nick groaned. "Please tell me you said yes."

"I said I didn't want to talk about it. Harmony left angry."

"What happened when you went after her?"

After opening another beer, Chase leaned

against the table. "I followed her outside, but after she yelled at me and stormed off, I didn't follow her."

Nick closed his eyes and said something under his breath.

"What?"

"Harvey, I love you like a brother, but you can be a real idiot sometimes."

Chase set his beer down and pushed off the table. "I found my girlfriend with another man in her apartment, and you are chewing *me* out?"

"Yes. And I like how now you admit she's your girlfriend. Why didn't you tell your mother?"

"Was my girlfriend. I can't be with someone like that."

Before Nick could respond, Chase jogged to the fence line and went through the gate. He retrieved the three balls. He'd get the glass in the morning when it was lighter out.

"What's her side of the story?" Nick asked when Chase stalked back.

"She said Jace found her walking back to her place and gave her a ride home. Then when she got out of the car, she swayed, so he helped her to her place. That can't be right, though, because she only had one beer with me. There was no swaying."

"That's odd. Did she say why he was in her place?"

Chase relayed the rest of her story as he lined up new bottles on the fenceposts. Then he threw the balls one after the other, hitting each bottle.

"You have quite the accurate throw. You should have been a pitcher."

"I was. High school baseball team."

"You're good. Why didn't you pursue it?"

Chase went back to the table and finished off his beer. A guy like Nick who'd grown up with more money than he knew what to do with wouldn't understand. Chase wasn't good enough to get drafted out of high school. He wanted to go to college and pursue college ball with the dream of having a chance of getting drafted then. But when the time came, the money just wasn't there for college. Chase followed the only other option he felt he had and joined the police academy right after graduation.

"Long story. I've got other things on my mind right now."

"Has she called you?"

Chase reached for his phone. He'd left it on the table. Since he'd left Harmony's, she'd sent text after text, and he got tired of the damn thing buzzing in his pocket.

"Sent a lot of texts."

"What do they say?"

"Basically, this is a misunderstanding. It isn't what I think. And she's pissed I jumped to conclusions. La da da da da." When he turned back from his phone, Nick was holding a baseball.

"Do you mind? It looks fun."

Chase shrugged.

Nick did some sort of weird arm wind-up

motion and then tossed the ball at one of the bottles. It missed. He reached for another ball and tried again. The whole attempt was so ridiculous that Chase couldn't help but laugh.

"Sorry, man. I don't mean to laugh, but I'm guessing you weren't a baseball player."

Nick grinned as he faced his friend. "No. Hockey."

Chase chuckled. That made sense.

"What?" Nick asked.

"I can see you playing hockey. You've got the size and attitude for it."

"Attitude? Why does that feel like a backhanded compliment?"

Chase held up his hands. "We both know you're a confident guy. But you could use a few tips when pitching."

His phone buzzed again on the table, and Harmony's name lit up the screen.

"You going to answer that?"

"Nope."

"You're more concerned that she might have slept with Jace, rather than the fact your girlfriend ended up tipsy after being in his presence, and then he managed to stay the night there. And that same guy is our number one suspect in a murder investigation?"

"Well, when you put it like that—"

"Like I said—idiot. Look, you've known her longer than I have, but from the moment I met her, I could see she was crazy about you. I even told Lauren it was just a matter of time before you two got together. I don't think for a minute she stepped out on you with Jace."

"Yeah?"

"Yeah. And I know for a fact she's been crying on the phone with Lauren since you left, so I've heard her side of the story a few times now."

"Then why the hell did you make me repeat it?"

"Because I'm concerned about what Jace was up to. I wanted to see what you thought."

"Do you think he gave her something? Drugged her?"

Nick shrugged. "I can't say for sure, but I did talk her into getting her blood tested."

"What? You're just now telling me this? Why do you think she was drugged?"

"She gave Lauren a blow-by-blow of what happened last night. She doesn't remember anything after Jace picked her up, and she woke up with a bad headache. Now, it could be that she actually drank those shots, although that doesn't explain the lack of memory prior to drinking."

"But he was there when I came by, and it was after four in the afternoon."

And you didn't see their rumpled clothes, her guilty expression, and the fact she willingly got in a car with him after our fight.

"She told Lauren she'd woken up shortly before you arrived. She was trying to get Jace to leave when you arrived."

271

He let everything Nick said sink in. Why had he let her walk home by herself? Fisher Springs had been a safe town, and it had given him a false sense of security.

His stomach churned as he thought about what Jace could have done if he drugged her. But did he drug her?

"You said she went for a blood test?" he asked.

"Yes, I think she's there now. I called the hospital to let them know she was on her way."

"How long until the results are in?"

Nick shrugged. "A few days, maybe a week."

Chase fell back in a chair and scrubbed his hands over his face. He could wait a few days. If the test came back positive, they'd deal with it together.

"Wait a minute." Chase shot up. "Why did Jace pick up Harmony? Was he watching her? Did she call him? He was with Rance at the pub when we left. Did he follow us? And if he drugged her, why?" Chase asked.

After grabbing his beer and finishing it off, Nick sat down. "That's what we've got to figure out."

Chapter Twenty-Nine

Harmony stared at the bruise on her arm as Nick explained a plan he had. The bruise developed shortly after the nurse stuck her with the needle.

It hit her all over again that she'd had to give a blood sample. Nick suspected she'd been drugged. She'd told him Jace didn't do anything to her sexually, so what the hell would be the point of drugging her? But she had to agree it was odd she didn't remember more of the night.

Had Rance put Jace up to it? Was it some elaborate scheme to break up her and Chase?

Chase. She squeezed her eyes shut. He'd immediately assumed the worst. He knew her better than that, dammit! Why didn't he think something was off, like Nick did?

"Harmony?"

She glanced up to see Nick staring at her. "Did

you hear anything I just said?"

"Sorry, can you repeat it?"

"For the record, I don't agree with this plan," Lauren said.

Nick retrieved a glass from her cupboard and filled it with water.

"Here, drink this."

He was being too nice. He definitely wanted something. She arched a brow at her friend, but Lauren was too busy glaring at Nick to notice.

"Just say it," she said, rubbing her temples. "What do you want?" Ever since she woke up with Jace in her apartment, she'd been getting recurring headaches. She hoped like hell they would stop soon.

"Do you have any idea why Jace picked you up that night?" he asked.

"It was cold out."

"And do you think he just happened to be driving by at the right time?" Nick crossed his arms.

"He said he was bringing food home for whoever was watching his grandpa. He was driving in the direction of his place."

Nick pulled up a chair and sat across from Harmony. "I understand Jace was at Zach's when you left, and then somehow he went to the diner, bought a hot chocolate and now, according to you, food, and then found you walking on the street. Is that right?"

"That's right." She crossed her arms defensively. Nick was trying to help but she felt like she was being interrogated.

"I think he got the hot chocolate to keep him awake as he spied on you and Chase." Lauren said. "Then you leaving was an unexpected opportunity."

Nick reached out and grabbed Lauren's hand. "Lauren, I appreciate you want to help, but we can't jump to conclusions."

"I'm not jumping. It's possible. Harmony, you said he mentioned food. Do you remember smelling food in the car?" Lauren asked.

Harmony took a sip of water as she thought over Lauren's question. "I remember smelling the hot chocolate when I held it." She imagined herself back in his car. "I could also smell his cologne and I thought cigarettes."

"Jace smokes?" Lauren asked.

"Not that I've noticed," Nick said.

"See, that proves it. If there had been food, she would have smelled it," Lauren leaned back and crossed her arms.

"Huh, that's a good point," Nick conceded as he jumped back up and paced.

"She might be onto something. Part of me wondered if Jace wanted to cause trouble between me and Chase so I'd go back to Rance. Maybe he had been watching me."

"You think Rance put him up to this?" Nick asked.

Harmony shrugged.

"Grown men do shit like that?" Lauren asked.

"We really don't know these guys, so it's

possible," Nick said.

Harmony sighed. She just wanted to go back to bed and stop thinking about Chase. "Nick, you said you had a plan. What is it?"

He nodded. "I think Jace is lying about being Jace Callahan."

Harmony laid her head on the table. It was pounding too damn much to keep trying to hold up. "Why would he do that?"

"We found out Mr. Rodney has some money stashed away. We think he's trying to con the man out of it."

Harmony lifted her head and drank down the water sitting in front of her. "That would be a really shitty thing to do."

"Yes, it would," Nick said.

"Wait, is Rance in on it? Does this mean Chase was right, and he isn't Mr. Rodney's grandson?" she asked.

"We don't know yet. But since you're friendly with Jace, I think he'll talk to you," Nick said. "All you have to do is meet up with Jace somewhere public, on Main Street perhaps. Then strike up a normal conversation, and ask him how Mr. Rodney is doing, how his parents are dealing with it. Questions like that. I want to see how he answers. My guess is he slips up and maybe gives something away."

"Jace did mention he likes to get coffee from the bakery in the mornings. I could take my laptop and hang there for a bit."

Lauren stood up. "I don't like this. We aren't using Harmony to get information out of Jace. He's a suspect in a missing persons case, Nick. We're not putting her in harm's way. Besides, none of this would be admissible in court."

"I'll do it," Harmony announced.

Lauren sat back down, staring at her. "You will?"

"I'll go in the middle of the day and stay in public. It'll be fine." Harmony yawned. "Now, if you two don't mind, I'm tired."

"Sure. Thanks again." Nick leaned in and gave her a quick hug.

"You call me if you need anything, okay?" Lauren asked.

Harmony nodded.

Nick's cell phone rang. After glancing at it, he held it up. "I need to take this."

He answered as he walked through the door. "Chase, what's up?"

Harmony squeezed her eyes shut. She couldn't escape thoughts of Chase. A week had passed since she'd seen Chase, but he was all she could think about. At first, she sent him texts trying to explain what happened with Jace. But the more she thought about it, the more pissed off she was that he left her so easily. He knew her history with her parents and if anything would crush it, it would be his leaving her. Yet, he did it anyway.

Chapter Thirty

Harmony fidgeted while waiting at the bakery for Jace. Part of her couldn't believe she had said yes to Nick's plan. But at this point, she would do anything that would help her to stop thinking about Chase. Right now, she needed to focus on what she would say when she saw Jace.

"Hey stranger."

Shit. Too late.

She glanced up to find Jace, arms crossed, grinning at her. She'd been so caught up in her head, she'd almost missed him.

"Hi." She flashed him a grin.

Jace plopped down into the chair opposite her, setting his coffee on the table. He was still grinning at her.

"What?"

"You're cute, you know that?"

She gave him a quick perusal. He was an attractive man, if you liked the gritty, tattooed type.

"Are you dating Tabitha?"

He cocked his head. "No, I thought I told you I was more into the one-time thing."

Ah, a player. Not surprising. Apparently, all the men in this town were incapable of having feelings for a woman. Although, Tabitha likely wasn't looking for anything long-term with him either. But none of that mattered. What mattered was that she was supposed to find out about Jace's family.

"I thought you said you weren't a one-woman kind of man."

He shrugged. "Same difference."

What difference did it make to her? She didn't have to date him. No, she needed to do what she came here to do.

"How's your grandfather doing?"

He stared at her while he took a sip of coffee.

"About how you'd expect. Rumor has it you and the cop broke up."

"Something like that. He didn't take too well to the fact you were in my apartment, and we looked..."

"Like we had sex?" He was grinning again, putting his dimple on full display.

She could see how he might charm some women, but not her. If he really did hurt Ms. Finkle, she was going to find out.

"Rumpled."

He shrugged. "Sorry. I'd be upset if I were him

too."

"You don't seem that sorry."

He reached across the table and put his hand on top of hers. "I really am. And to show you how sorry I am, here. Take these."

Four concert tickets landed on the table.

"They are for the Blake Shelton concert on Valentine's Day."

"What? Why?"

"I can't go, and I'd hate to let these go to waste."

She glanced at the tickets. The seats were decent. But wait, it was for February fourteenth.

"Thank you, but I'm not sure I'd get anyone to go on that date."

She was certain Lauren and Nick had some sickeningly romantic plan. Chase had been planning a surprise, but that was off the table.

"Take them anyway. Ask your friend Lauren and her boyfriend. And if you haven't made up with that cop yet, then bring a date. You'll feel better than wallowing in a bakery." He stood. "I've got an appointment. I'll catch you later."

Wallowing? She wasn't wallowing. Well, actually she was but she hadn't realized it was obvious to others. But now what the hell was she going to do with these tickets? Maybe she should go by herself. It would be better than sitting in her apartment, crying all night.

She watched Jace through the window as he crossed the street. Dammit. She hadn't gotten any information, which meant she'd have to come back and try again.

After packing up her laptop, her phone buzzed with a text from Nick.

Nick: *Your blood test results came back positive.*

Harmony: *So I was drugged?*

Nick: *Yes.*

Jace had drugged her. Her hands shook as she tossed the strap of her bag over her shoulder. He could have really hurt her. But he didn't. So why the hell did he drug her?

Thank goodness he hadn't sent that text before she saw Jace. One look at her and he would have known something was wrong. She rushed back to her apartment. It was a typical cold and crisp February morning. Pulling her scarf tighter around her neck, she managed to get to her building without seeing anyone. That was probably for the best since she was still pretty shaken by the time she got to her building.

But when she got to her door, she skidded to a stop and let out a small gasp.

Sitting against her door was Chase. He had his phone in his lap. Likely playing video games. He said it calmed him.

He must have heard her, because he glanced up and smiled his crooked smile. His hair was a mess, and he had bags under his eyes.

Good, he wasn't sleeping either.

"Hi," he said.

"Why are you here?"

"I think we should talk."

His eyes were red-rimmed. Had he been crying? She'd never seen him cry. Not even when his childhood dog died. Always the stoic one.

"You hurt me," Harmony said simply.

He ran his hand through his hair, pulling it. There was no doubt he was upset too.

"I'm so sorry, Harmony. You are the last person on earth I ever want to hurt. I should have been upfront with my mom and I should have listened to you about Jace."

He stood up and took a step toward her.

She stepped back. Distance was what she needed right now.

"Harmony, please don't do this," he begged.

When her gaze met his, it nearly broke her heart again. So much pain radiated from his eyes.

"I know what you're doing," he said. "You're putting your walls back up. I'm not your parents. I'm not going to leave you."

But you already did.

"Did you get my blood test results?" she asked.

"Yeah, they came in an hour ago. Jace drugged you," he said reaching for her.

Tears welled in her eyes as she took a step back.

"You came after you saw the test results? You still don't trust me." She pushed past him and unlocked her door.

"Harmony, wait. That's not true," he pleaded.

After opening her door, she stepped inside.

Without turning to face him, she said, "Please leave. I can't do this."

Then she closed the door and collapsed on the other side, crying.

"Harmony," he pleaded through the door.

A few minutes later, she heard him sigh, then his footsteps as he walked away.

Thank goodness she didn't have to work today. There was no way she could.

After grabbing the pint of chocolate ice cream she kept hidden in her freezer, she curled up on the couch. Her spoon had just hit the bottom of the container when someone knocked on her door.

No one just *popped by*. It had to be Chase, and she couldn't deal with him anymore today.

"Harmony, it's Lauren."

Without even a glance in the mirror, she let her friend in.

Lauren's reaction confirmed she likely had makeup running down her face from all the crying. "Oh, honey." She swept her up in a big hug. "Chase told me what happened. He's a wreck. You're a wreck. How can I help?"

Harmony shrugged. "I don't think anyone can do anything. I just need time to heal."

"Heal? You really are breaking things off for good?"

Harmony sat back in her spot on the couch and curled up in the blanket she kept on the back.

"I have to. One misunderstanding and he left. I

can't do this. Chase could destroy me," she reasoned.

Lauren sat down on the other end of the couch. "What's the plan, then? You'll find some guy you only like, get married, have a family?"

Harmony flinched. "There's nothing wrong with that. At least I won't be a bumbling mess."

Lauren shook her head. "Wow. I thought I knew you, but I guess I don't, because the Harmony I know isn't a coward."

She sat up straight. "I'm not a coward, I'm being practical."

Her friend arched a brow. "Practical isn't running from the love of your life."

She swallowed hard.

Love. After what happened with Ben in high school, she swore she'd never fall in love again. But now she had. Even more reason to end it now.

"I've made my decision, and it's final. This is how it has to be."

Lauren's sad puppy dog eyes were not helping her right now.

"I'm tired," Harmony grumbled as she rose. "It's been a rough morning. I'm going to take a nap."

After putting the small amount of ice cream back in the freezer, she returned to the living room to find her friend standing at the front door.

"For the record, I think you're making a mistake. Yes, love is messy and complicated, but it is so worth it. You and Chase belong together. We can all see it. Just give it time."

Lauren turned and left before Harmony could tell her time wouldn't help. She'd still feel the same.

Chapter Thirty-One

"I don't know about this." Chase paced the driveway.

He knew Harmony, and she was not a fan of surprises. Not this kind, anyway. Yes, it had been a few days since he'd shown up on her doorstep begging her. But Harmony was stubborn. When she made a decision, she stuck to it. He could use all the help right now convincing her she was wrong.

"Get in the damn car already." Nick motioned to the open door that led to the back seat.

"You really think ambushing Harmony is the way to go?" Chase asked.

"It's plan B, but it will work."

"What was plan A?"

Nick looked up at the sky and muttered something, then stared Chase down. "Plan A was to lock the two of you up in a room and not let you out until you both admitted you are in love and can't live without each other."

Chase backed up. "Whoa now. What exactly are you two planning to do tonight?"

Steam was practically coming out of Nick's ears, so Lauren stepped between them.

"We told you. We're going to pick up Harmony and all go to the concert. She has four tickets."

"She agreed to go with me?" Chase asked.

Lauren glanced over her shoulder at Nick. "Well, not exactly. But she did agree to go with us. And we might have told her Nick's friend Luke wanted to go."

"Who the fuck is Luke? She thinks she's going on a date?"

"No. Luke is my very attached friend."

"Then why the hell would he be with you on Valentine's Day?"

Nick looked at Lauren. "He makes a valid point."

She rolled her eyes. "She didn't ask."

Chase paced back and forth. "This is going to be a disaster. She probably has a date lined up. Someone meeting her there."

"No, she doesn't."

"Did she tell you that?" he asked. *Please say yes.*

"She's in no condition to date someone. She's an emotional mess. Like you."

He opened his mouth to argue, but she was right. He was irritable at best and had probably pissed everyone off by now.

"All right. I'll go," he relented. "But if this goes badly, you're to blame."

Chase climbed into the back seat, and Nick followed.

"Why are you getting in the back?" Chase asked him.

They were crammed in like sardines in the tiny back that was not made for anyone more than six feet tall.

Nick closed the door and nodded to Lauren, who'd gotten into the driver's seat. As they got on the road, Nick replied. "The plan is for Harmony to hop in front with Lauren. The car will already be in motion before she notices you're in the car."

What the hell?

"You have to trick her to be near me?" This was worse than he thought.

"No, we had to trick both of you. Quite exhausting, actually."

Chase shook his head and stared out the window. What if they were wrong, and when they pulled up, she was waiting there with Rance?

The thought made him queasy. He rolled the window down; certain he was going to throw up.

"You okay?" Nick asked.

He gulped the fresh air coming in. "Yeah. I'll be fine," he lied.

As they approached her apartment building, Harmony was standing on the road talking to some man.

No, that wasn't 'some man'. That was Jace.

"What the hell is he doing here?" Nick asked.

Same question Chase had, except he suspected he knew.

Jace wasn't clean-cut like Rance. Jace was a bad boy, especially now that he was a suspect. What better way to get over one man than to have a fling with a guy like that?

He shook his head. No, Harmony was smart. She'd never get caught up with someone dangerous.

Lauren parked at the curb and got out.

"I'm sure it's not what it looks like," Nick said.

Chase punched the driver's headrest. "I should go. Make this less awkward than it already is." He reached for the door handle.

"Wait, he's leaving."

Turning his gaze back to the curb, he watched Jace walk backward as he said a few words. He couldn't quite make them out. Then Lauren got in the driver's seat, and Harmony in the passenger seat.

Lauren had the car started and moving before either of them had seatbelts on.

"Slow down!" Harmony said. "What's the rush?" She was focusing on getting her seatbelt latched.

Lauren had gotten hers locked. "Jace happened to walk by while she was standing there, and they were just talking."

Harmony's head jerked around. "Does it matter?"

That's when she turned her gaze to the back seat.

The smile she'd been wearing dropped the moment she saw Chase. Then she took in Nick wearing a shit-eating grin.

Chase could see the moment she knew she'd been had.

Turning back around, she slumped in her seat. "You know I don't like surprises, Lauren."

"I know, but we didn't have another choice."

Harmony turned to face her friend. "You didn't have another choice? Really? Or was this your idea?" She turned her glare on Chase.

He shifted in his seat. "No. I wanted to see you, but not as part of an ambush."

She turned back around and didn't talk for the rest of the drive.

When they finally parked, he couldn't wait to get out of the car. Maybe he could get a private moment with her, and they could talk this through. But by the time he walked to her side of the car, she was halfway to the entrance of the stadium.

He ran to catch up. "Harmony, wait."

He grabbed her shoulder, and she spun around. "Why are you here?"

"I'm here to stop you from running scared. What we have is real, and you know it."

Tears welled in her eyes. "What we *had* was a great friendship. I'm sorry I agreed to cross the line. I can't go there, don't you see? One misunderstanding and you left. You left me Chase. My biggest fear and that crushed me. Between your distrust and my fears, it's just a matter of time before we implode again. It's a risk I can't take. Maybe some day we can go back to being just friends."

She turned and walked away, leaving him wondering how he was supposed to go on, with the hole she'd left in his chest.

Lauren jogged ahead to catch up with her.

Nick was at Chase's side. "Hey, let's skip the concert and get a drink."

Chase nodded. His mind was reeling too much to form words.

Nick led him back to the car, and the next thing he knew, they were pulling up at a local bar. It was crowded, but he didn't care as long as he could get a drink.

About three shots in, he turned to the detective. "If we are both here, who's helping Dunin tonight?"

That was one problem with a three-man police force. They usually didn't get to take time off together unless they stayed right in town, ready to herd goats, or whatever the latest need was.

"He said he'd call me if anything crazy came up."

Chase nodded.

Nick placed another shot in front of him, but Chase noticed Nick hadn't had any.

"You're not drinking?"

Nick held up his soda. "Nope, I'm the driver and, like I mentioned, on call for Dunin."

"That's right."

Chase took the last shot, hoping the burn of the alcohol would help dull his pain.

"What the hell am I going to do? I can't live without her," he groaned.

He wasn't normally so dramatic, but what the hell did it matter at this point? Without Harmony, he was a miserable ass. Nick already knew that.

"Give her time."

Chase shook his head. "Time? She's says I left her. And she was right. I knew her issues with her parents. Now she says I'm not worth the risk. Wants to be just friends again."

He glanced around the bar. The idea of going to bars again, dating. It all turned his stomach.

As he looked around the room, he noticed most people were coupled up. That was odd. It was a bar on a Saturday night. Then he noticed the decor.

Holy shit. Harmony had mentioned it was Valentine's Day. How could he forget so quickly? He had been wrapped up in his own problems.

"Shit, I'm sorry, Nick. We ruined Valentine's Day for you and Lauren."

He shook his head. "No, you didn't. We went out and celebrated last night."

"You did?"

Nick took another drink of his soda. "Yeah, we figured you two would likely screw this up, so just in case, you know." He flashed him that smile that showed off his dimples.

He'd heard Lauren go on about it before. Nick

must think it worked on everyone. The guy was being nice, so he'd spare him his thoughts.

Nick was right. He and Harmony had ruined this night for everyone.

"One more drink, then we need to pick them up," his friend said.

Chase closed his eyes. "Great. Another long car ride in silence with Harmony."

But that wasn't meant to be. When they returned to pick up the girls, Harmony wasn't there.

"Where is she?" Nick asked Lauren.

"She ran into a friend and asked for a ride."

Chase clenched his fists, and a wave of anger washed over him. A friend? Had she gone home with some guy to avoid him? To drive the stake in further?

Nick glanced back at him in the rearview mirror as he asked, "Who was this friend?"

"Someone she went to high school with. She lives in Fisher Springs too," Lauren explained.

She. Not a he. Chase melted back into his seat with relief.

Lauren turned back to face him. "Give her some time, Chase."

Time. Again with the time. Why the hell were they so hopeful when, for him, all hope was gone?

Chapter Thirty-Two

Harmony's heart pounded as she knocked on the door. The text from Rance inviting her over this morning was the last thing she'd expected to see. But after her failed meet-up with Jace at the bakery, she had a chance to find out more about their family.

"Just a moment," someone called from inside.

The door opened, and there stood Mr. Rodney, wearing a robe and nothing else. An open robe.

Dear Lord, is this what happens when men age?

She quickly glanced up at Mr. Rodney's smiling face. Then she glanced at a chair on the front porch. "Ah, I think your robe is, ah..."

Mr. Rodney glanced down. "Sorry about that. It comes undone sometimes." He tied it up. "How can I help you?"

"Harmony!" Rance stood behind him. "She's here to see me, Grandpa."

Mr. Rodney turned to him. "Who are you again?"

Rance rolled his eyes for Harmony's benefit. "I'm your grandson, remember?"

Mr. Rodney shook his head. "No, that's not possible. No grandson of mine has blond hair."

The memory of what Chase told them at Zach's came back to her. What were the odds the man would say that twice in his state?

"I poured you a bowl of your favorite cereal in the kitchen. Why don't you go back and have some?"

Mr. Rodney moved past Rance, muttering, "No blonds in my family."

"Sorry about that," Rance said as he closed the door behind him. "Let's sit on the porch."

They each sat in a chair.

"What's going on?" Harmony asked.

"I'll be honest. I want you back." Rance smiled at her as if he was certain she'd say yes.

Her eyebrows shot up. "You what?"

"I do. I really like you, Harmony, and I think you really like me too. I know you were confused about your friend. I'm sure him turning up everywhere and acting jealous confused you, but I heard you two are done. Is that true?"

She nodded, unsure how to answer his initial question.

Why would he think they should date again? It hadn't been good the first time.

The front door opened.

Rance turned. "Grandpa—"

"No, it's me," Jace said as he popped his head out. "Can you come help me a minute? With Grandpa?"

"Sure." Turning to Harmony, Rance said, "I'll be right back."

"Hi, Harmony." Jace flashed her a toothy smile.

"Hi." She took several deep breaths to calm her nerves. The worst thing she could do now is giveaway that she knew he drugged her.

Act normal.

When Rance and Jace went inside, she pulled out her phone. Her hands were shaking from seeing Jace and she was still processing what Rance had said. He wanted her back? She needed to talk to Lauren about this.

When she pulled out her phone, she discovered several missed messages from her.

Lauren: *Where are you?*

Lauren: *Someone broke into my garage last night. It was empty, so nothing was stolen. They didn't get in the house, as far as we can tell.*

Lauren: *Nick thinks someone was looking for the cars that used to be in there.*

Harmony quickly responded that she was on Rance's front porch because he'd asked her to come by.

Her phone rang. Lauren.

"Hey, Lauren, I'm sorry about your garage."

"It's Nick."

"Oh, Nick?"

"Get out of there now."

"What? Why?"

Nick sighed into the phone. "He's a suspect, Harmony. He could be dangerous."

"Harmony, I'm sorry I left you out here. Why don't you come in?" Rance was at the door.

"Don't do it, Harmony," Nick warned from her phone.

Rance wanted her back. He wasn't going to hurt her. Besides, if there was any chance he was trying to con Mr. Rodney, someone needed to get in there and see what was going on. She was in the perfect position to do so.

"Thank you, Rance, I'd love to come inside," she said into the phone before ending the call. At least they knew where she was.

Following him into the house, she noticed nothing had changed from the last time she was here. The day Chase had stormed in with a search warrant. It seemed so long ago now.

As they went to the family room in the back, they could hear Mr. Rodney singing. Once they rounded the final corner, they got a full view of the old man dancing, with the robe wide open again.

"Goddammit! Grandpa, stop showing us your bits." Rance flinched. "Sorry. I didn't realize. Let's go to my room, okay?"

"I told you, they aren't bits! Salami and potatoes!" Mr. Rodney shouted at them.

She closed her eyes, trying to get the vision of Mr. Rodney's 'salami and potatoes' out of her mind.

As they walked up the stairs, Rance looked over his shoulder and smiled.

She froze. What the hell was she doing? This man just said he wanted to get back together, and now she was following him to his room? Talk about sending the wrong impression. She had to let him know she didn't want the same thing.

But before she got the chance, Jace was behind them, at the base of the stairs.

"Rance, sorry, but I need you again."

"Really?" he asked.

Jace shrugged his shoulders. "Harmony, can you wait in Rance's room? I won't keep him long."

"Sure."

She walked into his room and surveyed the room. He had a bed, a dresser, and a desk. Something on the desk caught her attention. A yearbook that appeared to have been cut up, and a pair of scissors lying next to it. Odd.

She lifted the cover of the yearbook. Nineteen eighty-four. Fisher Springs High School. Why would Rance have this?

Doing the math quickly in her head, she supposed it could have belonged to his parents. But when she saw what was cut out, she knew that wasn't right.

Next to the yearbook was a photo of a woman, and the name Susan Rodney.

Holy shit.

Rance was cutting up old yearbooks. Jace had

said his mother was Laura. Ms. Finkle knew that was wrong, and said she was going home to look at yearbooks. Had Rance taken these from her? If he did, what did he do to Ms. Finkle?

She took a deep breath. No, that was quite a leap. Rance was a nice guy, wasn't he?

She opened the front cover hoping to discover who this yearbook belonged to. She frozen when she saw it.

Property of Margaret Finkle.

Her hands shook as she set the yearbook back on the desk. Chase had been right about Rance this entire time. She had to get out of there before the two *cousins* came back.

Slowly, she walked down the stairs. She heard their voices in the kitchen.

"Tonight?" Rance asked.

She quietly went down two more stairs.

"Can't you wait a few more weeks?" Rance asked.

Step by step, she was careful to be quiet. Although, if she did make a noise, she likely wouldn't hear it over her heart beating out of her chest.

After what seemed like an eternity, she made it to the door, and her hand was on the doorknob.

"No. I can't," Jace replied. "Those idiot cops keep snooping around. It doesn't help that you keep going after that redhead."

The voices were getting louder. They were walking this way.

She yanked the door open.

"Hey, I really like her," Rance pleaded to Jace.

"Too bad. You're not here to fuck —"

She ran down the porch steps and to her car.

"Harmony, wait!" Rance must have seen her through the open door.

She yelled over her shoulder, "I'm sorry, Rance. I don't feel the same way. We can only be friends."

Without looking back, she dove into her car and drove.

This was too much. She needed to get to Lauren and Nick. No, she had to go to the chief. The police station was close. But she had to tell somebody.

Keeping her eyes on the road, she grabbed her phone out of her purse. At the next stop sign, she quickly dialed Lauren.

"Harmony? Thank God. Did you really go into Rance's place?"

"I did, and I saw something I don't fully understand. I'm on my way to the police station."

She tugged on the seatbelt to get it on, but it was stuck. Unwilling to slow down, she just tugged harder.

"What did you see?" Lauren asked.

"A Fisher Springs High School yearbook."

After another unsuccessful tug, she glanced down and saw that she'd managed to close the door on it.

"Harmony, it's Nick. What exactly did you see?"

Before she could answer, a car came out of nowhere as she crossed the intersection.

Veering hard to the right, she braced for the inevitable impact. Then came the sound of metal on metal, glass flying all around her.

"Harmony?!?" she heard Lauren scream.

Then silence.

"Harmony?"

Was that Chase? She tried to get her eyes to open, but they wouldn't cooperate.

"Harmony. Please wake up, baby."

I'm trying!

"Any change?"

That sounded like Lauren.

"No."

"Go home. Get some rest. I'll sit with her," Lauren said.

"If she wakes up..."

"I'll call you right away."

Why couldn't she open her eyes?

"Don't wake up, Harmony."

The voice was familiar. Why couldn't she open her damn eyes?

"Don't wake up."

Sleepy. She felt so sleepy.

Chapter Thirty-Three

From Chase's viewpoint in the doorway, she looked so pale and frail. Each day, he'd gone into work hoping it was the day she would wake up. It had been three days since the accident, and she was still in a coma.

He strode across the room and fell into his usual chair, taking her hand in his.

"Why weren't you wearing a seatbelt?"

According to the woman who lived across the street from Mr. Rodney, Harmony had run to her car and taken off faster than a bat out of hell. Lauren said she'd sounded scared on their call. What had happened inside that house? Why the hell was she even there?

He hoped like hell Lauren was right, and Harmony had only been there to get answers. If she wanted to be with Rance again...

He couldn't go there.

He squeezed her hand.

"You're a fighter Harmony. I need you to fight to wake up now."

He squeezed her hand.

"You don't let anything take you down. Remember that time you put a frog in Lizzie's purse?" He laughed, remembering the day. "I never heard a girl scream so loud."

Lizzie had been one of the popular but mean girls in their high school, and one day Harmony had had enough. Somehow, she not only got the frog in the girl's purse, but made sure Chase took the blame.

He'd give anything to have her playing pranks again.

"Come back to me, baby. I need you. You have been the bright star in my life all these years. I'm sorry it took me so long to see that. But now that I have, I'm not letting you go."

Footsteps approaching caught his attention. Doctor Martin stepped into the room, holding a chart.

"Doctor, any change?"

She glanced up and smiled. "Officer Harvey, good evening." She glanced back at the chart. "No, I'm afraid there's no change. All we can do now is wait and hope she wakes up soon."

"You hear that, Harmony? You need to wake up."

"Officer?" The doctor was standing close, but on the other side of the bed. "Go home and get some rest. There's no need for you to be sleeping on that cot. If she wakes up, I'll call you."

"Thank you, but I can't leave."

"She's lucky to have someone who loves her so much."

Love. He'd never told her that he loved her. No, he had been too busy living in denial, and wasting time.

"You know the drill. Let the nurse know if you need anything." Doctor Martin left.

It would be just him and Harmony again tonight. Lauren had spent the day with her, leaving once her shift started. Nick understood Chase wanted this time alone with her. But there were two others who should be there, and they weren't. Harmony's parents.

He'd known when he called them and discovered they were in Hawaii that they wouldn't end their vacation early. They never did.

One thing he knew for sure, if *he* ever had kids, he wouldn't ever let them feel unwanted. Harmony tried to put on an act like it didn't bother her, but he saw through her armor. How could it not hurt?

After getting the cot set up, he stretched out and reached for her hand.

The last few nights, he'd made sure he held her hand. Usually, at some point, a nurse would come in and force him to move so they could check her vitals. It was worth it, though. With her hand in his, he'd gotten some of the best sleep he could recall.

Even more proof that they belonged together. As soon as she woke up, he was going to make sure that was exactly what happened.

"I love you, Harmony."

He gave her hand one last squeeze and closed his eyes.

★ ★ ★

Her eyes flew open and then she scrunched them shut.

Why was it so bright in here?

Slowly, she tried to open her eyes again. What was that beeping sound?

Turning her head to the right, she discovered a monitor.

Wait.

When she tried to turn to get a better look, something pulled on her arm. Glancing down, she saw a needle protruding from it, like they kind they used at the hospital. Why was she in the hospital?

She tried to sit up, but her head was pounding, so she quickly abandoned that idea.

A nurse walked into her room.

"Why am I here?" Harmony asked.

The nurse jumped. "You're awake? That's wonderful! Let me get the doctor."

She ran out of the room, and a minute later, returned with another woman in tow.

"Good morning, Harmony. My name is Doctor Martin."

"Hi, I remember you. You were my friend's doctor when she was poisoned last year. Was I poisoned?"

"No. Can you tell me the last thing you remember?"

Harmony ignored the pounding in her head and tried to think.

"I was driving to the police station when a car came out of nowhere. I swerved, but I don't think I got out of the way."

"No, you didn't. It was a pretty bad accident. You're lucky you don't have more injuries. It was a hit and run."

"Hit and run?"

The doctor flashed a light into her eyes, and Harmony winced. "You're actually in pretty good condition, considering you weren't wearing a seatbelt. Hopefully you'll learn from this and wear one next time."

Next time?

"I always wear a seatbelt. This was the only time—"

"Harmony! You're awake." Lauren rushed to her side. "Thank God. We've all been so worried."

Harmony tried to sit up again.

"Please relax." The doctor was at her other side. "The collision knocked you unconscious. We didn't know why you wouldn't wake up, but now that you have, we need to run a few tests."

She nodded. "How long was I asleep?"

"Four days," Lauren answered quietly.

Four days? She would have sworn the accident

happened only an hour ago.

"What about Rance and Jace?" she asked.

Lauren squeezed her hand. "We'll talk later. I'm so happy you're awake."

After many tests, the doctor determined she was fine. No one could explain why she'd slept so long. Either way, she was happy to be discharged.

"Chase will be so happy you're awake. He slept next to your bed every night," Lauren explained as she drove them to her place.

"Every night?"

"The first day, he was there for twenty-four hours. Nick had to pry him away. He was pretty upset… We all were. We almost lost you."

"Who was the driver that hit me? Was it Rance?"

"Sadly, there were no witnesses. But Nick and Chase suspect Rance or Jace based on your last phone call."

"I never made it to the police station. What happened with Rance and Jace and the yearbook?"

Lauren glanced away.

"Lauren?"

Her friend squeezed her hand. "I'm afraid that, without your statement, Judge Milton wasn't willing to sign a warrant so nothing has happened. The judge brought up the last warrant he signed had been for a woman that turned out wasn't missing."

"So because Bella Daniels came back to town, Rance and Jace are walking around town free?"

Lauren nodded. "And Jace is dating Tabitha. She

has been holding no details back when she tells me about him."

"Yeah, I saw him flirting with her at the bank a while back. Wait, you said dating?"

"Yep, and you're lucky because you have been spared the stories of them having sex in the bank. She thinks it's hot, but all I can think of are all those surfaces the public touches. It's gross." Lauren shook her head. "No. I can't think about it."

Sex in a bank? More than once? "Jace told me he was a one-time kind of guy. So why is he sticking with Tabitha? And how could they have sex in a bank? Banks have cameras."

"I asked that too and I couldn't believe what she told me." Lauren held up her phone to reveal a text conversation between her and Tabitha.

"This morning she responded and said she turns them off."

Harmony swallowed down the bile that was trying to creep up her throat. Nausea was closing in as she closed her eyes. "Jace talked her into turning off bank cameras? Did you tell Nick?"

Lauren frowned. "I was going to go to the station and tell him in person after I checked on you. Nick's been really busy, and I wasn't sure how long it would take for him to read my texts."

"Please text him now. He needs to know now. I have a really bad feeling about this. Why has Nick been extra busy?"

Lauren grabbed her phone from her purse and

her fingers flew over the screen. "I sent the text. As for why Nick's busy, he's been covering for Chase."

"Chase hasn't been going to work?"

Lauren smiled. "He has, but, Harmony, he's a wreck. You know he's in love with you, right?"

"Love?"

She was certain he'd loved her as a friend, but he's in love with her? She hadn't been sure he was capable of romantic, forever love.

"Yes, love. What are you going to do about it? Because as soon as Chase can leave the station, I guarantee he'll be driving straight to my house to find you."

What *was* she going to do about it? About her Chase being in love with her?

She knew now that she didn't want to keep pushing him away. She wanted him, all of him. She was going to wrap her arms around him and never let him go.

"I hope that smile means what I think it does," Lauren grinned.

"It does."

Chapter Thirty-Four

Chase had not been expecting the scene laid out before him. He'd received a call about a man wandering in the street. He didn't think that man would be Mr. Rodney, or that he'd be wandering around in his open robe. Someone needed to get that man some underwear.

"Mr. Rodney," Chase said as he walked up to him.

A woman was standing in a nearby yard with her hands on her hips. "Disgraceful!" she yelled. "My poor daughter has been scarred for life!"

"Salami and potatoes!" Mr. Rodney shouted.

"Donald, can you go back into your house, please?" Chase ordered.

The old man made his way onto his front porch. The door had been wide open when Chase arrived, and the driveway was empty.

Wait, empty?

"Do you know where Mr. Rodney's grandsons are?" he asked the neighbor.

"No idea, but I can tell you, I heard yelling coming from that house late last night. It woke me up. I looked out the window and saw both of them get into a car and tear out of here."

"What time was that?"

"Just after two a.m. I remember because I couldn't get back to sleep. Now if you'll excuse me, I need to get back inside and check on my daughter."

Mr. Rodney had been alone since last night?

"All right. Thank you, ma'am." Turning his attention back to the old man, he said, "Let's get you back inside. Have you eaten?"

"Eaten? No. I don't think so."

After helping the old man back inside, Chase called the chief and filled him in on what was going on.

While he was on the phone, he heard Mr. Rodney shouting from the office.

"No! No! No!"

How had he moved so fast? He had just been sitting at the dining room table, eating.

Chase rushed to the office.

Donald was standing behind his desk. It looked like someone had pulled the drawers out and emptied them. There was no way Donald could have just done this; they hadn't been in the house long enough. Somehow, Chase hadn't seen that when he walked inside.

"What's happened?" he asked.

Donald looked up, his eyes welling with tears. "My keys are gone."

"What keys?"

The man handed him a plain white envelope. It had been torn open. When Chase flipped it over, his breakfast churned in his stomach. The envelope was from their local bank.

"What was in here?"

"I told you. My keys!"

Please stay lucid.

"Donald, what did the keys go to?"

"My safe deposit boxes. I knew they were looking for it."

"Who?" Chase pressed.

Donald flopped onto the desk chair, shaking his head. "Those two idiots pretending to be my grandsons. I overheard them talking about finding my keys. How the hell did they know I had safe deposit boxes at the bank? They must have gone through the entire drawer. I kept them hidden in the false bottom."

Chase placed his hand on the old man's shoulder. "What's in your safe deposit boxes?"

"Everything. Absolutely everything. She said it would be better than those risky investments I'd made."

Chase turned around and found a stack of bank statements on top of the desk. He quickly scanned them and saw that the man only had a small amount in his account.

But he had millions. He wouldn't keep it all in safe deposit boxes... would he?

"Donald, did you keep your money in safe deposit boxes?"

He stared up at Chase with his brow furrowed. "Where did my cereal go?"

Chase sighed. "In the kitchen."

After Donald left the room, Chase called the chief and told him what Mr. Rodney had said.

"Who the hell is 'she'?" Dunin demanded.

"I don't know, but I'm going to find out."

The chief agreed to call the bank and see what he could find out on his end.

After hanging up, Chase tracked down the number for Bella Daniel, because he couldn't leave Donald alone. Thankfully, she agreed to come over.

Before she arrived, the chief called back.

"Harvey, you need to get to the station. Tabitha came in and wants to talk to you. It's a police matter."

The doorbell rang, and Chase saw Bella through the glass.

"I'm on my way."

★ ★ ★

Once he entered the station, the chief called him into his office. Tabitha was sitting across from Dunin, crying. Kate was sitting beside her, holding her hand.

"Please tell him what you told me," the chief said gently.

"Harvey, I think Jace drugged me."

Fuck.

"I don't know why he would. We've had sex many times. I thought that was why we were meeting up last night. When I got into his car in the bank parking lot, I was cold, and he offered me his hot chocolate. The next thing I know, it's morning, I'm in my own car several blocks from the bank, and my head is pounding. It's just like what Harmony said happened to her."

"God dammit!" Chase yelled.

Dunin coughed while glaring at Chase. He knew what the glare meant. Calm the hell down.

"Tabitha, tell Chase why you met at the bank," Dunin urged.

Tabitha's face flushed red. "I know it was wrong, but when I was with Jace, he talked me into things. I swear, I've never had sex that good. I was powerless."

Chase glanced at the chief, who rolled his eyes.

"What did you do?" Chase asked.

"I've been seeing Jace for a few weeks. A few nights ago, he said he had a fantasy about doing it in a bank."

Now he had a visual of Tabitha and Jace having sex. It wasn't pretty.

"And you thought this was okay?" he asked.

Tabitha pushed her hair behind her ear. "Well, like I said, the sex was incredible. I wasn't thinking straight."

"Don't they have cameras all over the bank?"

She nodded. "I agreed to turn off the camera to

the lobby."

Chase raked his hand in his hair. "You turned off the bank cameras?"

She nodded again. "It was only the lobby camera at first. But then the next night, he talked me into turning off another camera. He followed me, and now I think he was watching how I did it."

"Why do you think he would do that?"

She sniffled, and Dunin handed her a tissue.

"I'm afraid he robbed the bank," she admitted. "Why else would he drug me when we could have had sex? Plus, my master key is missing."

"Master key?"

"It gets me into the vault and the safe deposit boxes."

Dunin closed his eyes. "You've got to be kidding me," he muttered under his breath.

"The master key alone could get into the safe deposit boxes?" Chase asked.

Tabitha shook her head. "No, you need two keys. The master key and the key each individual box owner has."

He looked at Dunin. "Have you talked to the bank about Mr. Rodney's boxes?"

Dunin nodded. "I did. All five are empty."

"No!" Tabitha cried. "I'm so sorry."

"Let's start at the beginning. How did you two meet?" Dunin asked.

"He came into the bank a few weeks ago and

started flirting with me. At the time, I didn't think much of it. He asked about safe deposit boxes. I thought he wanted one."

"He didn't." Chase shoved his hands in his pockets, trying not to show Tabitha how frustrated he was with her.

"Then he asked me how secure they were. I showed him that they were in the vault, and you needed two keys."

"Where did you put the key when you were done? Did he see?" Chase asked.

Her fingers went to her neck. "I kept it on a chain around my neck. The chain is gone too."

Chase bit his tongue to keep from commenting. He knew Tabitha wasn't the brightest. Hell, he'd been friends with her since high school, and was fully aware of the situations she'd gotten herself into. But this was too much. The woman had no common sense.

The chief rubbed his beard. "I think that's enough for now. Kate, can you take Tabitha to the hospital for a blood test and exam?"

"Of course."

"Harvey, get back over to the Rodney house. I'll send Moore too. Start looking for any clues where those two men impersonating his grandsons might have gone. See if anyone in the neighborhood happened to catch their license plate. Check in with the woman you talked to earlier. I'm going to have to call the FBI in on this, now that the bank's involved."

Chase checked his phone on the way out. No text

from Lauren. He'd planned on spending his morning by Harmony's bedside. No one knew why she wouldn't wake up. But dammit, once she did, he was never going to let her go. He'd convince her they should be together.

Outside, Nick was just getting out of his truck when Chase walked out.

"Let's go," he said to Nick.

"Where?"

"I'll fill you in on the way."

He explained the morning's events as they drove.

"Dammit," Nick cursed. "We have to find them. They aren't going to get away with what they did to Ms. Finkle."

"We'll find them," Chase assured him. "Dunin's calling in the FBI. They won't get far."

* * *

By the end of the day, the Federal Bureau of Investigation had taken over and effectively dismissed Chase and Nick. Chase didn't mind because he had gotten a text from Lauren letting him know that Harmony had woken up.

He was about to head to the hospital, when Lauren told him she was going to be discharged soon and would be at Lauren's.

He was thankful she'd woken up. The thought of never again seeing those chocolate eyes of hers was too much. He was hopelessly in love with her, and he couldn't wait another minute to tell her. He couldn't waste any more time. At least she'd be safe at Lauren's until he could get to her.

During the four days she'd been in the hospital, when Chase wasn't at her bedside, he'd been focused on finding evidence to prove that Rance or Jace had hit her. He knew in his gut it was one or both of them. But he kept running into one dead end after another. There were no witnesses, and no traffic cameras in their small town. Milton wouldn't grant him a warrant without hard evidence. Now the two suspects had fled, and he was sure they would have destroyed any evidence by now.

As they walked down the pathway, away from Mr. Rodney's house, he heard an agent yell out, "Hey, Pat! You would love this Chevelle. Well, minus the banged-up hood." The agent laughed from inside the now open garage.

Chase stilled. He turned and locked eyes with Nick.

"Banged up car?" Chase asked.

They moved quickly, entering the garage from the driveway.

The front end of the large car was smashed. The damage was consistent with Harmony's collision.

A younger agent was feeling the dents. "That can be fixed. Nice thing about these older cars."

"Please stop touching the evidence," Chase shouted.

The man laughed. "We're investigating withdrawals from a bank. This car isn't evidence."

"We have reason to believe it may have been involved in a hit and run on one of our residents."

The agent lifted his hands and backed up. "Sorry."

Chase took out his phone and snapped some photos. The chief walked by the garage door.

"Chief!"

Dunin turned around.

"I think this might be the car involved in Harmony's hit and run."

Dunin walked around to the front of the car. "It does look suspicious. What do you think? Mr. Rodney got a hold of the keys and didn't realize he hit her?"

Chase chewed on that for a moment. Lauren had said Harmony had gone into his house and found a yearbook. She had just been about to tell Nick something more when she was hit.

"No. My money is on Rance and Jace," he said. "I think Harmony saw something she wasn't supposed to. I'll go bag the keys for this, and we can dust it all for prints. We'll need to dust this for prints too."

The chief took two steps away before he spun around. "I'll do it. You and Nick might be too close to this one."

"Actually," Pat interjected, "we'll do it. Anything in this house is now under FBI jurisdiction. Plus, we can then rule out our junior agent's prints." Pat glared at the agent that had earlier had his hands all over the car.

"All right. Send us the report on that as soon as possible," Dunin said.

Chase stared at the car. It was huge and old. Sturdy. He was amazed it hadn't done more damage to Harmony's car. She'd veered away at just the right moment to lessen the impact to her.

There was no doubt in his mind, whoever had been driving this car was intent on killing her. It had to be Rance or Jace. Or hell, maybe they had both been in the car.

Another agent walked into the garage. She had dark, short hair and piercing blue eyes.

"Pat?" she called out.

"Yes, here."

She handed him an evidence bag. "We found a vial labeled 'SP-117'. I need you to personally run this to the lab for testing."

Pat held up the bag. "How the hell would anyone here have gotten this?"

"I'll worry about that. You find out if it's real."

"Sure thing, boss," he said.

As he was leaving, the agent turned to Dunin. "Chief Dunin?"

"Yes."

"I'm Agent Jessie Doyle. We found the registration for another car that seems to be missing. We just put out an APB for the car and those two men. We should have them soon."

Dunin stepped forward. "That's good to hear.

What's in that vial?" He jerked his chin in the direction Pat left.

"You know I can't officially answer that, Chief. However, I will tell you that it's a very potent truth serum. But this stuff is nasty. The person who ingests it also suffers memory loss and headaches. It sounds like this might be what was given to the bank teller."

"And to Harmony," Chase said.

"I feel for them. We also found a second drug that's not as potent but appears to have been illegally obtained. It's a sedative. We thought perhaps they used this to keep the old man sleeping."

"A sedative?" Chase looked at Nick. "That might be why Harmony wouldn't wake up."

"Yeah, but that would mean either Jace or Rance was in the hospital room with her. Alone," Nick said.

If they had wanted her dead, she would be dead.

The reality of how close she came hit Chase all over again.

Chapter Thirty-Five

Chase drummed his fingers as Nick drove them to the Chanler mansion. He couldn't remember ever feeling this nervous.

"It's too bad the FBI took over the case. I'd love to be the one to arrest those two assholes," Nick said.

"Yeah." Chase stared at the text from Lauren. He'd reread it a dozen times.

Lauren: *Harmony woke up!*

Unlike Nick, he was happy the FBI took over. But he was still nervous to see Harmony. When Nick turned down the long driveway, he broke out in a sweat.

"You all right over there?" his friend asked.

"Yep," he lied.

"Do you know what you're going to say to her?" Nick parked his truck and stared at Chase.

"Nope."

"All right then. Let's go."

Nick hopped out of the truck, but Chase sat frozen. The detective came around to his side and opened the door.

"Do you not want to do this?" he asked.

Chase stared at the house as if he could see Harmony through the walls.

"What if she says no?" he asked.

That was all he'd thought about since he'd found out she had been released and was here. What if she still said no to him?

"Well, then you leave knowing that at least you tried."

Chase's head snapped to Nick. "That's your brilliant advice?"

He laughed. "I'm not particularly good with all this feeling shit, so yeah, that's my advice. You get hurt; I'll get you drunk. Deal?"

Chase raked his hand through his hair. "Fuck. Here goes nothing."

He hopped out of the truck, and they made their way up the porch steps. Nick reached for the door then turned back.

"Ready?"

"As ready as I'm going to get."

"You were all gung-ho earlier. Where's that Chase?"

"Hiding."

Nick laughed as he opened the door. When they walked in, they could hear Lauren talking.

Chase made his way to the kitchen, and his eyes

found Harmony. Despite the fact she'd just spent nearly a week in the hospital, she was stunning. All he could focus on was her staring at the table, and his own heart beating in his throat. Time seemed to stand still. Then she glanced up.

He couldn't breathe.

Please don't run from me again.

She didn't.

She stood up and faced him. "Chase?"

Chase. Not 'Harvey'. She looked so pale and small, he had to hold her.

Crossing the room, he pulled her into his arms and held her tight.

At first, she stood frozen, but then slowly, her arms moved up his back until she held on just as tight.

"Harmony, I was so scared. You were lying there so still, and you wouldn't wake up."

"I thought I heard you talking to me. You were talking to me, weren't you?"

"Every night, baby. Every night."

"I'm sorry I put you all through that."

He pulled back. "What? No. This isn't your fault."

"It is. If I hadn't gone to see Rance, and if I hadn't seen that yearbook—"

"What yearbook?" Nick interrupted, stepping forward. "You never got to explain before the accident."

"It was in Rance's room."

"His *bedroom*?" Chase asked.

She'd gone to his bedroom.

The image of her with Rance sliced him like a knife. He dropped his arms and took a step back.

Coming here was a bad idea. He didn't want to hear this.

He took another step back.

Harmony grabbed his arm. "You need to stop jumping to conclusions. It's not what you're thinking." Her grip was firm.

"Start from the beginning," Lauren told her.

Harmony explained she'd received a text from Rance, but before they'd had a chance to talk, Jace kept pulling him aside, and finally asked her to wait in Rance's room.

"That's when I saw the yearbook on his desk. It was from Fisher Springs High School, and a photo of Susan Rodney had been cut out and was laying on the desk. I flipped through the yearbook, and that's when I saw a stamp on the inside cover that said, 'Property of Margaret Finkle'."

"This was in Rance's room?" Nick asked.

"Yes."

"That Jace asked you to go to?" Nick asked again.

"What happened when Rance came upstairs?" Chase asked.

He stared at her hand that was holding his arm. He couldn't bear to look her in the eye. How far was she going to let it go with Rance? How far did she want it to go?

"He didn't. I saw the yearbook and freaked out.

I left as quietly as I could. As I was leaving, I heard Jace yelling at Rance about the cops sniffing around."

"They didn't know you left?" Nick asked.

Harmony shook her head. "Not until I was stepping out the front door. Rance saw me. He ran after me, but I ran to my car as fast as I could. Then I called Lauren and was on my way to the police station when I was hit."

"We suspect either Rance or Jace hit you," Nick said as he paced the kitchen.

"Chase." She squeezed his arm.

He finally looked at her.

"Rance said he wanted me back. I said no. I only went there to see if I could find anything that would help find Ms. Finkle but maybe he didn't take my answer all that well."

Chase squeezed his eyes shut.

"How could you go knowing Jace had drugged you?"

"I hoped he wouldn't be there. I know it was dangerous," Harmony said quietly. "I'm sorry."

"Mr. Rodney allowed us into his house this morning. There was no yearbook in Rance's room. We don't know what he did with it," Chase said. Then he pulled Harmony in tight. "I have to tell you something about Ms. Finkle."

Nick's phone rang. "It's Dunin." Bringing the phone to his ear, he said, "Moore here."

Keeping his gaze pinned on Chase, he nodded. "Uh-huh. That's good. What about Jace?"

Another pause.

"Uh-huh. And the money?"

His hand went to the back of his neck, and he rubbed while the chief talked.

"I'm with him now. I'll let him know." He ended the call.

"Rance was arrested in California. The cops down there are holding him until the FBI can take him into custody."

Fuck, Chase couldn't wait until this guy was out of the picture, and out of Harmony's head for good.

"If only I'd asked him directly if he was here to take care of his grandpa. We would have known sooner," Harmony said.

"Why? Do you really think he would have told you the truth?" he asked.

"No, but I would have known if he was lying, and maybe I could have dug further."

"Harmony, it isn't your job to investigate these guys. It is ours." He motioned between himself and Nick.

"I know, but when Rance lies, he has a tell. I could have used that to get more information."

Chase took a step back. "Rance has a tell?"

As soon as Harmony explained Rance's lip twitch, Nick called the chief to relay the information. After he was done, he pocketed his phone.

"Maybe that will help the FBI."

"You said Rance was arrested. How did he get caught?" Lauren asked.

Danielle Pays

"He crashed into some trailer. Jace managed to get out of the car and disappeared."

"And the money?" Chase asked.

"Still missing." Nick's gaze fell to Chase's arms, which were wrapped around Harmony again, and he gave him a grin. "Lauren, let's go upstairs and give them a moment."

She smiled at them both. "Take all the time you need."

After they left, Chase pulled back just enough to stare into Harmony's eyes. He loved this woman, and he had been a fool to not let her know sooner.

He cupped her cheek with one hand. "From the moment you walked out of my house after seeing that text, I haven't been able to think of anything except you. My biggest regret is not telling you the moment I realized... I love you, Harmony. I have for a long time. And I know you're scared. I'm scared too. But I'm not going to let your fear or mine ruin what we have."

The swell of emotion building in his chest was too much, and he felt his eyes well with tears. He took a deep breath, trying to get his emotions under control. What the hell was happening?

"Chase, you're crying?"

He shook his head.

Oh, who the hell was he kidding?

He touched his forehead to hers. "I feel so much for you, and then you were in that accident. We thought we might lose you, and you wouldn't wake up."

He shook his head again, remembering the

feeling, as if someone had reached in and ripped his heart out. She'd looked so helpless, lying in the hospital bed.

"Goddamn, I love you so much, but if you aren't ready, that's fine. Well, no, it's not fine. But I'll make sure you see every day that we are meant to be together. Because I know you, Harmony. I know you love me too."

His mouth was dry, and his heart was thundering in his chest as he waited for her response.

"Chase." Her gaze met his, and her eyes were wet.

Please let her feel the same. He couldn't bear her rejection right now.

Then her fingers brushed away the wetness from under his eyes as she smiled up at him.
"I love you, too."

His eyebrows shot up. She'd said it.

"I've been in love with you for a long time, Chase. I've just been too scared to admit it. I've been too scared to open up and let myself feel. But when I woke up in the hospital, all I could think about was you. I need you, and I want you. All of this has made that clear to me. I don't want to go another day without you in my life."

"Does this mean we can start over?" he asked.

Her arms wrapped around his neck. "I don't know about starting over. I kind of like what we have." She let out a sigh. "All that time we wasted by not being honest with each other. I don't want to waste any more time."

"Neither do I. Let me take you back to my place. We can watch a movie, or just rest together. I know you're still recovering from your injuries. I just need to be near you."

She grinned. "I'd like that."

"Yeah?"

She nodded, then pulled him down until his lips crushed hers.

Chapter Thirty-Six

Chase: I'll be there in one hour. Can't wait to see you.

One text had her nerves on edge. Her stomach was in knots. But why? This was just a date with Chase. They'd spent most of the last forty-eight hours together. Well, until he'd left this morning for work.

Before he left, he'd asked her to wear her blue wrap dress tonight. She had no idea what he had planned.

Now here she was, in the dress he'd requested, nearly an hour after he'd sent that text, and she was a mix of nerves and excitement.

A knock at her door made her jump. Taking a deep breath, she opened it. Chase was holding flowers and wearing the same suit he'd worn for their first date. The way it fit across his shoulders and down his arms had her drooling.

"Hi, these are for you." He handed her a

beautiful bouquet of roses.

"Thank you." She accepted it, and her gaze swept up and down his body. "How have I been so blind to how sexy you are?"

A blush crept up his cheeks, and she couldn't help smiling. She couldn't recall ever seeing him blush.

"I wouldn't say you were blind. You weren't ready."

"And you were?"

He shook his head. "Neither of us was, but we are now." He leaned down and kissed her softly.

"Mm. Let me put these in water."

In the kitchen, she grabbed a vase, filled it, and placed the roses inside. They were beautiful and smelled wonderful.

"I love these. Thank you."

He came up behind her and wrapped his arms around her waist. "I'm glad you like them. How are you feeling? Does your head still hurt?" His lips skimmed her neck, up to her ear.

"It's much better today. But since I still get dizzy from the concussion sometimes, I opted for flats."

He glanced down and took in her footwear. "Still sexy." He kissed her neck.

"We might not leave if you keep that up," she warned him.

"Well, we do have a reservation to get to." His hands skimmed her hips as his lips moved to the other ear. "But we can be a few minutes late."

She spun around to face him. "A few minutes? Is

that really all you got?"

"That's all it would take for me to have you screaming my name," he said, grinning.

"Damn, you are the cockiest man I've ever known. You really think you could —"

Before she finished her sentence, Chase had dropped to his knees and was kissing his way up her thigh.

"Chase." Her voice was already husky.

He grinned up at her. "I know I could."

His fingers brushed up until he reached the small bit of cloth between her legs. She twitched at his touch, already so sensitive.

Chase groaned. "You're so wet. I must taste you."

After moving her panties to the side, his tongue swept up to her clit, and her eyes nearly rolled to the back of her head.

Damn, this man was skilled. And he made good on his promise. Not even two minutes later, he had her on the edge.

"Scream my name when you come," he demanded.

"Damn, Chase. I love this side of you." She gripped the kitchen counter for support.

"I want to feel your pussy come on my tongue."

He continued to suck and work her until her orgasm overtook her.

"Chase!" she screamed.

He kept lapping at her until the spasms stopped.

Then he stood up, and all she could do was stare as she caught her breath, and hope she'd be able to stand soon without support.

"Let's go," he said.

She threw her head back and laughed. "I can't walk."

"I'll carry you."

"Let me make you happy first."

He drew her into his arms, pulling her away from the counter. "Later. For now, we should go on our date." He leaned down and kissed her.

Tasting herself on his lips turned her on even more. Despite knowing him for so long, she'd never known he was so talkative and demanding in the bedroom. Now that she knew, she couldn't get enough of this man.

* * *

When they drove out of Fisher Springs and past Davenport, she became confused.

"Where are we going?"

Harmony was familiar with the highway they were on, but there wasn't much out this way.

"You'll see." Chase winked.

A few minutes later, they pulled into the parking lot of what appeared to be an old warehouse.

"Should I be worried?" she asked, glancing around for any clues.

"No. You'll like it. I promise." When he gave her his crooked smile, she melted.

"Okay."

They approached the warehouse, and Chase banged on the closed door. As they waited, she could hear a frog croaking in a nearby swamp.

The door swung open with a loud squeak.

"Chase! We're ready." A man she didn't recognize ushered them in. "This way."

They followed the man down a hallway into a room.

"Oh!" she exclaimed.

White Christmas lights decorated the ceiling, and in the middle of the room was a table set for dinner.

"I had this planned for us for Valentine's Day, but as you know, that didn't work out. My friend Troy was nice enough to let me reschedule for tonight."

She walked farther into the room, taking it all in. There was only the one table, but there was room for a few more.

"What is this place?" she asked, twirling around.

"Welcome to the area's new escape room."

She turned to Chase, excited. "This is an escape room?"

She'd always wanted to try one. She'd read about them online and sent Chase every article she could. He must have remembered.

He chuckled. "No. This is a dining room. Please, have a seat." He pulled out her chair for her. "Once we're done with dinner, we will walk to the other side of the warehouse, where the escape room is set up."

"Are you serious?"

He nodded as Troy entered the room.

"Would you two like some wine?" their host asked.

"Yes, thank you," Chase said.

Troy set two wine glasses on the table and filled them with red wine. When he stepped out, Chase leaned forward.

"Troy is the owner, and the escape room doesn't officially open for another week. But he agreed to let us try it out."

"I can't tell you how excited I am. But there's a dining room too?"

Chase took her hand in his. "Actually, no. This was being used as storage. Troy helped me set it up. And the food is actually delivery."

As if on cue, Troy walked in carrying a box of delivery pizza.

Her heart swelled for this man. "Is it what I think it is?"

After Troy set the box on the table, Chase opened it.

"Mm-hmm. Your favorite. Hawaiian... but only on one half, because let's be serious for a moment, I can't have pineapple ruining a perfectly good pizza."

She laughed. "Perfectly good? I'm afraid your half is ruined with those mushrooms."

His eyes were as big as saucers. "What? Pepperoni and mushrooms make the perfect pizza."

She shook her head. "No. Putting fungus on a pizza is way worse than adding pineapple. Anyone would agree with me."

He arched a brow. "Want to bet on it?"

"I would, yes."

He pulled out his phone and typed away, then showed her he'd sent a group text to her, Nick, and Lauren, asking whether pineapple or mushrooms was the better pizza topping.

Nick: *What happened to your date? She left you already?*

Lauren: *If you are texting while on a date, I'm going to hunt you down and shove that phone where the sun doesn't shine.*

"Damn, I can't say I've seen that side of Lauren." He frowned.

Harmony laughed. "She might be small, but she's tough. How else could she put up with Nick?"

He laughed with her. "You're right."

Harmony: *No worries. Date is going great. Just a little disagreement over the pizza.*

"Figure I'd better save you from a night of phone calls."

He placed a slice of pizza on her plate, and then one on his. "Good call. I have plans for you, and interruptions would be bad."

"What kind of plans?"

"Plans that involve me ripping off that lace thong of yours and seeing how many times I can make you come."

She almost choked on her pizza.

Damn, she wasn't used to his dirty talk.

"Too much?" he asked.

"No. I love it."

He leaned over and gave her a quick kiss. "Good."

His phone buzzed.

Nick: *Whatever she wants is what you will like. Just do it.*

They laughed, and then finished dinner.

At the escape room, Troy explained the theme of this escape room was the Mayan Ruins. Then he gave them instructions and explained what to do if either one of them panicked.

Once inside, she marveled at the winding corridors as they walked through and found a tomb. The detail in the décor was amazing, and she almost felt like she was really in the ruins. Troy gave them clues over a walkie talkie and they worked together to solve as many as they could.

Despite being a police officer, Chase was not particularly good at the game, which made it more fun for her. But their time ran out before they escaped.

"What did you guys think?" Troy asked when he met them at the entrance.

"I had a blast. That was really fun. Hard, but fun," Harmony said.

"Yeah, I'll be recommending at least four people to a group for this one."

"Thank you again for letting us try it out," Chase

said.

As they walked to the car, she squeezed his hand.

"Thank you for this," she said.

"I'm glad you liked it. It was fun, but also frustrating."

"Take me home and I'll help you work that frustration out," she said.

He threw his head back and laughed. "You're perfect. You know that?"

Chapter Thirty-Seven

"Earth to Harvey." Nick stood in front of Chase, snapping his fingers in his face.

Chase batted them away. "What the fuck, dude?"

"I've been calling your name for five minutes. I had to get your attention somehow."

"Five minutes? I doubt that." He reached for the coffee on his desk and drank it down.

"I'm happy for you. I knew you and Harmony would get it figured out eventually."

The past couple of weeks had been bliss. Yeah, that was a cheesy term for it, but it fit. He'd never been happier. He'd spent every night with Harmony; they'd taken turns staying at each other's places.

But now he needed to focus.

Dunin had called them last night to let them know the FBI had finally made a deal with Rance, and his official statement would be coming in this morning. They all hoped they'd get some answers to Ms. Finkle's murder.

"Moore, Harvey, come in here," the chief bellowed from his office.

They made their way in and sat down across from him.

"Before we get to the statement, there's something you should know. I'm mad as hell the FBI didn't tell us this as soon as they knew."

"Knew what?" Nick was sitting on the edge of his seat.

"They were able to lift some prints from the keys to the Chevelle parked in Mr. Rodney's garage. They belong to Carl Marucam."

Nick jumped up. "No, that's impossible. Carl's in prison. Did he escape?"

"No. Carl's prints were all over the house. An agent went to the prison to find out what was going on. Turns out the man in prison isn't really Carl."

"How the hell is that possible?" Nick yelled.

"When Carl found out he had a warrant out on him for dealing heroin, he paid another man, Jerry Cowan, to turn himself in and claim he was Carl. Cowan agreed, knowing he'd likely sit in prison for two years. The FBI investigated how this had been possible and discovered there were no decent photos of Carl to compare to, and other witnesses testified that Cowan was Carl and had committed the crimes."

"That mugshot we had on our wall wasn't

Carl?" Nick asked.

"No. Both Jerry and Carl had brown hair, blue eyes, and were of a similar build."

The detective paced behind Chase. "Didn't the police pull up Carl's DMV photo?"

"He never had one," Dunin said. "Carl was good about not being seen or wearing disguises. The only photos the state police had were blurry shots of the side of his head."

"Why the hell would this guy do time for Carl?" Chase asked.

"According to Jerry, Carl paid off his mom's mortgage that had been about to go into foreclosure," the chief explained. "We verified it had been paid off by an anonymous source."

Nick leaned on Dunin's desk. "Does this mean that either Rance or Jace was Carl? Or were they working for Carl?"

Dunin held up his hand. "Moore let me finish. Rance Rodney is not Carl, but he also isn't who he says he is."

Chase almost choked on his laugh. "I've been saying that since he came to town."

"And you have been right," someone behind them said.

They all swiveled around to the intruder now standing in the door. Agent Doyle.

"Sorry to interrupt, but there was no one in the lobby. I was in the area and wanted to give you some more information about Ryan Waters."

"Who?" Nick asked.

"Rance Rodney was an alias. His real name is Ryan Waters." She stepped into the room. "He's a known conman with no priors."

Nick flopped down in the chair next to Chase. "No priors?"

"He's managed to keep his hands clean. Until now. According to Ryan's statement, he agreed to come to town to help Jace get some of his inheritance early in exchange for Jace helping him get to know and convince Lauren to let him sell William's cars. You know, the crazy thing is that, up until he was arrested, he really thought Mr. Rodney was Jace's grandfather," the agent said.

"Yeah, he's not too bright," Chase said. "He claimed he came to town to sell cars? Not for the millions Mr. Rodney had?"

"I really don't think he knew. Waters is small time. I think he was easily played by Carl," Doyle said.

"Then Jace is really Carl?" Chase asked.

"Yes. We were able to obtain a photo, and verified it with both Jerry in prison, and our informant."

"Now you have a photo?" Chase asked.

Doyle smiled. "Despite how careful Carl has been over the years, he didn't anticipate that his little girlfriend would secretly take some photos."

"Girlfriend?" Chase asked.

"Yes, a Tabitha Savett. She told us that Carl insisted she not take photos, but according to her, he was 'too sexy not to'. She managed to get a few photos that Carl was unaware of." Doyle frowned. "She'd been enamored by that man, but after she learned the truth, she was happy to share those photos with us."

Doyle continued. "Once Ryan opened up, he *really* opened up. Jace played him, and he's not happy about it. He confessed all he knew. According to him, Jace admitted he drugged Harmony a couple weeks back in order to find out if the police were onto them. He also told us that Jace somehow drugged Harmony when she was in the hospital to keep her asleep. Ryan was very concerned about Harmony's well-being, and he stated he had no idea Jace would go that far."

"To keep her asleep? Why?" Chase said.

"We think he wanted to buy time until they found the keys to the safe deposit boxes. From what we have learned, Jace drugged Tabitha, and then used her to get into the bank and access Rodney's safe deposit boxes."

Nick frowned. "Why would Mr. Rodney keep all his money in safe deposit boxes? I can't wrap my head around that."

"His son finally returned my phone call after I threatened to publicly haul him in for questioning. He told me he thinks it was the dementia. The money had been tied up in investments until about eight months ago. According to the records, Rodney then pulled money out of his investments, and rented safe deposit boxes."

"You had to threaten his son? Doesn't he care about his father?" Nick asked.

"Based on his complaints, I'd say he cares more about his billable hours than anything else," Doyle said.

"Eight months? That would be about a month after Bella Daniel started as his caretaker," Chase said.

"You sure about that?" Dunin asked.

Chase nodded. "I wrote it all down in her missing person report."

"The caretaker is missing?" Doyle asked.

"No, it was a misunderstanding. But the report should still be accessible," he said. "When I was with Mr. Rodney that morning, he told me that 'she said the safe deposit boxes would be safe'. Do you think Bella is the 'she' he was referring to?"

"Where is this Bella Daniel now?" Doyle asked.

"She has an apartment nearby. Maybe she's there?" Chase offered.

Nick shook his head in disbelief. "She was in on this the entire time. How did we miss this?"

Dunin raised his hand. "Slow down. We don't know that for certain. Agent Doyle, did Ryan mention Bella at all?"

"No, he didn't," Doyle said.

"If Carl was in town, why was he going after Mr. Rodney and not Lauren?" Nick was now pacing behind Chase, which was bugging the shit out of him. "As far as he was concerned, he was owed Chanler money. What am I missing?" The detective stopped pacing and glanced from Dunin to Harvey.

"Can you sit down? You're making me nervous," Chase asked.

Nick leaned over the desk. "Chief, she had to be involved. How else would Carl know Donald Rodney had all that money? Or that he had a grandson named Jace? Or that he had just enough dementia, they could literally move in and Donald wouldn't run to the police?"

Shit. Nick was right. Bella Daniel had months to collect information.

Dunin slammed his fist on his desk. "We need to get Bella Daniel in here for questioning."

Chase stood. "I'll go pick her up now."

"I'm coming with you," Doyle said.

She turned back quickly. "Before I forget, there was one thing that stood out about Ryan's statement. Despite throwing Jace, or *Carl*, under the bus for everything he could, Ryan was adamant that Jace swore he didn't hurt Ms. Finkle. He said Jace was in Ms. Finkle's home and saw her walking up the walkway with another man."

"Come on. This is Carl. You don't believe that, do you?" Nick asked.

"Just to be safe, Nick, go back and question her neighbors again," the chief said. "This time ask if they saw her walking with anyone. We need to cover our bases."

"I can't believe Carl Marucam was right under

our noses," Chase said.

"How could you know? You had a photo of Cowan, not him," Doyle said as they took the stairs to Bella's apartment.

After they knocked a third time, and had still gotten no answer, a man walked out of the apartment next door.

"Excuse me. Do you know the woman who lives here?" Doyle asked.

The man shrugged. "Not really, but I do know she doesn't live there anymore."

The hair on the back of Chase's neck perked up. Of course, she left.

"Some guy, I assume her boyfriend, helped her move out."

"When was this?" Doyle asked.

He squinted as he looked up. "Let's see. It had to be a couple of weeks ago."

"And what did her boyfriend look like?" Doyle was ready with her phone to type in the description.

"He had dark hair, and I remember a lot of tattoos. Sleeves down both arms. That surprised me. Didn't strike me as her type. But then, I guess it explains why she didn't want to go out with me."

The man smiled, but when Doyle didn't smile back, he dropped it.

"The guy also had a beard growing in," the neighbor added. "Is there anything else? I need to get to work."

"No. Thank you," Doyle said.

Chase mulled over the description as he watched the neighbor leave. Dark hair and tattoos. Would Carl have been so daring as to show up here after everything that had happened? He'd likely had to return to get the money. It wasn't in the car with Ryan, so Carl must have hidden it.

When Chase had called Bella over to watch Mr. Rodney that day, was the money already hidden at her place?

"That description matches Carl," Chase said. "Except the beard, but I'm sure he can grow one quickly." Why not? Everything else was working in his favor.

"Two weeks? They could be anywhere," Doyle said. She glanced at her watch. "Is there a place we can eat around here? We can talk and see if there's anything else we missed."

Chase took her to the diner, hoping he'd get a chance to see Harmony. He lucked out, and she was working.

He had his Ruben sandwich halfway to his mouth when Doyle jumped up.

"Motherfucker," the agent cursed.

Before Chase could put the sandwich down, she ran out the door.

"Keep this here," he said to Harmony. "I'll be right back."

He ran out the door just in time to watch Agent Doyle tackle a large man from behind onto the sidewalk. She had him down on the ground with his hands behind his back faster than the man knew what hit him.

"Carl Marucam, you are under arrest."

Once the handcuffs were secure, she hauled the large man up, and Chase saw his face.

"Shit," Chase blurted.

Zach stood grinning at Doyle, and the man practically had hearts shooting out of his eyes.

"That's not Carl," Chase said.

Doyle stared at him for a beat then back at Zach. "Dark hair, tattoo sleeves, beard."

"Hi, I'm Zach Brannigan. What's your name?" He was still grinning like a fool.

"Is your wallet in your back pocket?" Chase asked his friend.

Zach nodded.

This was the first time Chase had ever had to grab Zach's ass, but he needed to get that wallet.

Once he had it, he pulled out his license and handed it to Doyle.

She studied the license for a long time before shaking her head. "I'm sorry, Zach. You matched the description for a wanted man."

"I'd love to be *your* wanted man," he purred.

"Really?" Chase said, shaking his head.

"You're a good-looking guy, you shouldn't hide it under all that fuzz," Doyle said as she unlocked his cuffs.

"Is that so?" Zach asked. "When you're done here, you should come into my pub and tell me more about it."

"Your pub?" she asked.

He tossed his thumb over this shoulder. "Brannigan's Pub back there is my place."

Her eyes swept up and down his body, and Chase swore Zach puffed out his chest like some sort of prized rooster.

"Thanks for the offer, but I need to get home and clean my carpets."

Chase couldn't hold back his laugh, which earned him a glare from his friend.

Doyle turned to Chase. "Officer, contact me if you hear from Carl."

"Will do," he said.

Agent Doyle walked away, leaving him and Zach standing on the sidewalk.

"What's her name?"

"Agent Jessie Doyle. She's with the FBI. But don't get excited, she has no reason to come back to Fisher Springs."

Zach crossed his arms and grinned. "I'll give her a reason." Then his grin fell as his gaze caught on someone. "Hey, is that Joey? I haven't seen him in months."

Chase glanced in the direction Zach was looking. It looked like him.

"Joey!" he called.

The man waved, but then turned down the road. It looked like he was heading to the police station.

As much as Chase wanted to talk to him, he knew Joey and his dad were struggling, and needed time to figure it out.

"I have to say, I'm not a fan of his blond hair," Zach commented.

Chase caught one last glimpse before he was out of sight. The man had bleached his brown hair blond, and it was half grown out and looked a bit greasy.

"Looks like he's still using. I hope Dunin can help him," Zach said. "Hey, before I forget, do you have a business card from Agent Doyle?"

Chase laughed. "No, I don't. Nick might, though."

He clapped his friend on the back and made his way back to the diner. Doyle might have abandoned her lunch, but he was still hungry.

Chapter Thirty-Eight

Three months later

"I can't believe you are really getting married today!" Tabitha squealed as she entered the room.

Harmony handed her a glass of champagne.

"I can't either," Lauren said, staring at herself in the mirror.

She was wearing a simple but elegant gown, and the veil in her blond hair made her look almost angelic.

"Are you ready?" Harmony asked. "Chase just sent a text. They're ready to start."

"I am." Lauren stood up.

"Wait." Harmony adjusted the lens on her camera. "I want to get a couple more. The lighting in here is perfect."

After a few shots, they walked into the hall. Harmony made sure to get ahead of them so she could capture it all.

Lauren had wanted Harmony as her maid of honor, but she'd *needed* her as the photographer. And while Harmony couldn't stand with Lauren when she said her vows, she was happy to be the one capturing the most important day of her friend's life.

After the ceremony, Harmony had taken photographs of the wedding party in front of the Chanler Mansion while everyone else mingled in the backyard. As soon as they wrapped up, she walked around to the back and told the guests the couple was ready for them. As people filtered toward the front, Tabitha strolled up.

"It is just gorgeous here," her friend said.

The backyard at the Chanler Mansion was decorated beautifully and was set off with a rose garden behind the altar. Next to the patio, tables beautifully decorated with white table clothes and red rose center pieces were set up for the reception.

"It is," Harmony said as she lifted her camera and took a few more shots.

Her friend stared toward the house. "I wanted to talk to you."

Lowering the camera, she took in her friend.

This year had been rough. Despite everything that had happened with Jace, or Carl, she hadn't been fired. When she gave her statement to the FBI, she managed to leave out the part where she turned off the camera and had sex with him in the bank.

As far as the FBI was concerned, he had used her

and conned her, and the only suspicious time she had been near the bank was the night he'd drugged her and used her to rob the safe deposit boxes. The labs came back confirming she'd been drugged, so the bank hadn't blamed her, and she kept her job.

It also helped that her father was president of the bank. Despite her job being safe, her reputation wasn't. But through it all, Harmony and Lauren had stuck by her.

Kate's reaction was surprising. She'd been jealous of the fact Carl spent time with Tabitha; guess Kate wasn't immune from catching feelings after all.

"Did they ever find Jace?" Tabitha asked with a sniffle.

Harmony turned to see her friend's eyes welled with tears. What was it with her and Kate? Even though they knew Jace was Carl, and he had quite a long criminal record that included suspicion of killing a man, they were both acting like lovesick puppies.

"No, they haven't found *Carl*, nor the money. The FBI believes Bella Daniel hid the money for him, and then they ran off together."

"Bella? The other redhead?"

"That's the one."

Tabitha nodded as her eyes welled up. "Do you think Rance will get out early for good behavior?"

Ryan had been convicted of five counts of bank robbery. He'd denied being there, but the prosecution used the fact his fingerprints were found on all five safe deposit boxes. The jury came back with a verdict in less than two hours, and the judge came down hard at sentencing, tearing into him for taking advantage of an old man with dementia. Ryan was sentenced to twenty-five years in prison.

Part of Harmony felt bad for him. But then the letters started to come to the diner, in which he confessed everything he'd ever done.

Chase had those shut down the moment he found out. She wasn't sure what he did, but Logan confirmed Ryan hadn't sent any more letters to the diner.

Responding to Tabitha, she shook her head. "I hope not. While he might not have been guilty of bank robbery, he stole money from a lot of people."

The memory of his words on that postcard played in her head. She hoped like hell he'd eventually forget about her.

"Why don't you go back out front and find Zach?" she suggested. "He's got the dark, brooding, tattoo thing going on too."

Tabitha shrugged. "Zach's a good-looking guy, but he just doesn't do it for me. I wish I knew why."

*Because he's **actually** a nice guy.*

She couldn't say it, though. Her friend wasn't ready to hear that.

After all the tables were set up for the reception, the rest of the event went by quickly. Chase had been missing for a good part of it, and she wondered if he left.

"They look happy, don't they?" Chase asked, coming up behind her.

"Chase!" She turned and looped her arms around his neck. "I thought you left."

"I did."

"Why didn't you tell me?"

He shook his head. "You were having a good time. I didn't want to ruin that."

"Where did you go?"

"The station. Dunin called. Someone came forward with footage of Ms. Finkle walking with a man. It was taken a day after the last time Tabitha saw her sitting on her porch."

The sadness in his eyes told her it wasn't Carl.

"Who was the man?"

Chase shook his head. "I couldn't believe it. Neither could the chief. But he was there when I got there, and I questioned him." His eyes welled up.

"Chase, who was it?"

"Joey."

"Joey Dunin?"

He nodded.

She was stunned silent. Last she heard, Joey had left town. Once the chief let him go from the force, he was angry and said he wouldn't come back. The poor chief didn't have a choice, but it caused a permanent rift between father and son.

"Just because he was walking with her doesn't mean more happened," she pointed out.

"The King County Sheriff's office brought him in for questioning. Harmony, he admitted he put her body in a lake. Even if the prosecutor believed him that it was an accident, he concealed evidence, and never contacted the authorities. He's going to prison."

"I'm sorry. I know you two were friends. I can't imagine what you or the chief are going through."

"We lost touch a long time ago. I'll be fine. It's the chief... He's broken. First, he lost his wife, and then he couldn't save his son."

She pulled him in and held him while the reception continued behind them.

"Why was he with Ms. Finkle?" she asked.

"He was trying to get money. He was broke and needed a fix. She'd given him money a few months before, so he tried again. She saw through him, though, and said no. He said he got angry and they argued. He followed her up her walkway. Before she got to her door, she slipped on her doormat, which was half off the stoop. He lunged to catch her, but he was too late. She fell and hit her head. He said she died instantly, and he didn't know what to do."

Chase let out a sigh as he watched Nick and Lauren dance. "Harmony, please don't tell Nick or Lauren. Let's let them have their day."

"Of course," she said. "Do you want a drink?"

"Yeah, I do."

As she made her way to the bar, Nick grabbed the microphone from the band's singer, and addressed the crowd.

"Lauren and I want to thank all of you for being here with us tonight. I can't tell you how happy I am that I finally closed this deal."

His eyes twinkled as he stared at Lauren, who was rolling her eyes.

"There was a time when I thought it was over between us," he admitted. "I was miserable and lost without her."

Chase cupped his mouth and shouted, "Yeah, you were."

Nick laughed. "Thank you, Harvey. My best man, everyone."

"Here here!" Zach shouted, holding up his beer.

"Speaking of Harvey, he'll be the next one to get hitched, and I can't wait to be his best man."

"You should be so lucky!" Chase shouted.

All eyes were on them, and Harmony's stomach fluttered at the idea of marrying this man, her best friend. She wanted to spend the rest of her life with Chase.

"What do you think?" he leaned in to ask as she returned with their drinks. "Should we get married?"

She crossed her arms. "That better have not been your proposal, because it needs work."

He tossed his head back and laughed. "No. I will be proposing, but not here, not like this." Setting his drink on the table, he wrapped his arms around her and pulled her close. "And we will need a lot of time to plan your *Ghostbusters*-themed wedding."

She laughed. "Oh my God, how do you remember that?"

He gave her a quick kiss. "You had a binder with all your ideas, and you left it lying around just to piss off your parents."

"They really hated that movie." She shook her head.

"Which makes it a perfect wedding theme. But seriously, there's something else I'd like to work on."

Tipping her head up, she looked into those beautiful brown eyes of his. "What's that?"

"The honeymoon. Want to discuss it in the guest room?"

"Discuss?"

"Mmhmm." His lips were on her neck, moving up to her ear. "It will involve our mouths and tongues."

Now she laughed. "Really? Is that the best you got?"

"No, this is."

His mouth made its way to that sensitive spot just below her ear, and his hand moved down to cup her ass.

"Let's go." She pulled away and started to run. Well, as close to a run as she could get in high heels.

"I love you," Chase said, laughing as he caught her.

"I love you too."

Danielle Pays

Other books by Danielle Pays

The Dare to Risk series
Deceived
Pursued
Played
Consumed
Captivated – A Holiday Novella

The Dare to Surrender series
Chasing Her Trust
Taking Her Chase
Saving Her Target
Trusting Her Hero

Danielle Pays

About the Author

Danielle Pays writes steamy romance novels with a touch of suspense. She enjoys romance as well as mystery and suspense and blends them both using her beloved Pacific Northwest for inspiration with its mix of small towns and cities.

When she's not writing her characters into some kind of trouble, she can be found binging Netflix shows, trying to convince her children to eat her cooking, or drinking wine after battling said children at dinnertime.

Follow her at www.daniellepays.com or on Facebook at https://www.facebook.com/daniellepays/